THE DILETTANTES

THE
DILETTANTES

MICHAEL HINGSTON

A NOVEL

Canada Council
for the Arts

Conseil des Arts
du Canada

Freehand Books gratefully acknowledges the support of the
Canada Council for the Arts for its publishing program. ¶
Freehand Books, an imprint of Broadview Press Inc., acknowledges the financial support for its publishing program provided
by the Government of Canada through the Canada Book Fund.

Freehand Books
515 – 815 1st Street sw   Calgary, Alberta   T2P 1N3
www.freehand-books.com

Book orders: LitDistCo
100 Armstrong Avenue   Georgetown, Ontario   L7G 5S4
Telephone: 1-800-591-6250   Fax: 1-800-591-6251
orders@litdistco.ca
www.litdistco.ca

Library and Archives Canada Cataloguing In Publication
Hingston, Michael, 1985–
     The dilettantes / Michael Hingston.
Also issued in electronic format.
ISBN 978-1-55481-182-3
     I. Title.
PS8615.I55D54 2013   C813'.6   C2013-901667-8

Edited by Barbara Scott
Book design and illustration by Natalie Olsen, Kisscut Design
Author photo by Bridget Gutteridge-Hingston

Printed on FSC recycled paper and bound in Canada

For Kate

TABLE OF CONTENTS

"Sometimes I console myself with the thought that the whole effort is a put-on, which looks, feels, and tastes like a newspaper, but is, in reality, a serialized shaggy-dog story."

LETTER TO THE EDITOR
***THE PEAK*, MARCH 25, 1970**

"Participants from the focus group stated that if they were to describe the personality of The Peak *as a person, [it] would be labelled as geeky, self-centred, opinionated, and a 'hipster on paper.' These are less positive associations."*

**INCREASING READERSHIP OF THE PEAK
BUS 442 FINAL PROJECT,
SIMON FRASER UNIVERSITY, SPRING 2009**

"Aren't they nice, the young? They've stayed up till dawn for two years drinking instant coffee together, and now they're opinionated— they have opinions."

MARTIN AMIS

1

JSUT

The accordion bus wound its way up Burnaby Mountain, approaching the concrete Tetris blocks of Simon Fraser University, and Alex Belmont looked out the window, confused. He didn't know what kind of trees he was looking at.

This irritated him, though at first he wasn't sure why exactly it ought to. What was he meant to know about trees? What was anyone? He squinted and looked again, as if it were simply a matter of reading the bark as it blurred by. Alex had taken this road to school for four years and had never once thought about the trees. He could vividly remember three separate conversations about the vanilla ice cream–flavoured drip coffee they sometimes served in West Mall, but not one complete sentence about what were, now that he took a good look around him, almost literally everywhere. He'd been raised middle class, middlebrow, with a suitcase full of white privilege—why didn't he know this? It seemed unforgivable.

Shade bringers, Newton hecklers, dormant Tolkien warriors. That was all he had. That was *it*.

Alex felt a slow, hot grating on his skin. Then a jab of anger, the kind without corners or handles or targets—though the face of his second-grade teacher came to mind, and she would do just fine. *You made us iron leaves,* Alex thought, *and put them in wax paper between textbook pages. It took* months *to get them flat. Couldn't you have been bothered, somewhere in there, to tell us where they came from?*

Then again, this being Canada, they were probably maple leaves. Hell, these ones here might even be maple tre—Alex tried to stop thinking this thought before it made him feel even dumber, but it was too late. He turned the music on his iPod up a few notches. There were no maple trees in Vancouver.

Did science kids know this kind of thing? He didn't know any, so he couldn't ask them. Probably. Who else? Professors. British people. Birdwatchers in khaki vests. Even little George Washington knew he was vandalizing a cherry tree, and he was all of ten. (Then again, the *cherries* probably gave it away.) *I could assign a feature about it,* Alex thought. *An investigative guide to the things that show up without explaining themselves: trees, flowers, the gravel on all the walking paths.* At least it'd throw a wrench into the perpetual motion machine of Palestine's latest crisis and SFU's lack of school spirit and whatever else got reliably stuck in readers' craws. Convey some actual information for a change.

Yeah, everyone would make fun of it out loud. They'd slap the pages with their fat hands at the bus stop and say, "Fuck's this?" But in private, propped up on their elbows atop narrow residence beds, they'd all be captivated. "No way! Sycamores!"

Alex was pretty sure they weren't sycamores, either.

Somebody behind him belched. The person in the next seat over clapped the belcher on the back with an audible crinkle of snowboard jacket against snowboard jacket. "Booya!" It was 1:20 in the afternoon, a Tuesday, in early September.

Alex gritted his teeth and stared into the wrinkled blue leather of the seat in front of him. Never one to need a reason to despise his fellow students, lately he'd also been struggling with all kinds of new weight on his shoulders: his graduation (pending), his sex life (flatlining), and, most recently, this whole *Metro* situation. Make no mistake: Alex had been foreseeing this particular day for months. He'd be the first to remind you. But nobody had listened to him back then, and he had a pretty good suspicion nobody was going to listen today, either.

Out of the corner of his eye, Alex could just make out the cell phone of the girl sitting next to him, which clicked and lit up as she pounded out a text. The screen read, "i nevr ment 2 hurt u. jsut thought u shld kno that." The girl paused, looking intensely across the aisle and out the opposite window, as if weighing a very import-ant decision. For a second, as he covertly investigated the curve of her chest, Alex wondered how much *she* knew about trees. Then she added "(ˆ_ˆ)" and hit send.

Ugh. Alex slumped back queasily into his seat. *This is how the world ends,* he thought, *not with a bang but an emoticon.*

The bus chugged past the football field and tennis courts, and pulled up to the stop's metal flag. All three sets of doors opened with a mechanical shrug and sigh. Alex got off with fifty or so others and then broke away, cutting up through the enclosed parking lot—know-ledge of this shortcut was one of the few indisputable perks of working at the student newspaper. He walked up the ramp and past the back doors of the *Peak* offices, which were decorated with layers of chalk hieroglyphics from editors of years gone by. To any casual passerby it probably just looked like graffiti. Or maybe some hopelessly muddled art project, the kind some of Alex's friends in the FPA program dab-bled in. Just for fun, he got himself even further riled up by trying to imagine the plaque that might accompany such a bogus installation: lots of lofty talk about "disrupting" ideas that weren't in opposition to begin with. Then he did himself one better, and imagined the grade.

It was masochism, of course. Alex was part of this generation, and knew it, and hated himself and his peers all the more for it. This self-reflexive self-loathing was just another part of their shared identity: to be disgusted by it was only to be more quintessentially *of* it. The whole thing was exhausting to think about, so nobody did.

Theirs was the generation of secondhand irony. They'd inherited it, like an old cardigan, and usually couldn't define or even recognize it in any meaningful way. But they deployed it whenever possible, blithely assuming that things had always been that way. Like that old folk tale—passed down from time immemorial, probably—about the two little fish, swimming along in the ocean, carefree. An elderly fish passes by and says, "Water's nice today, isn't it?" The little fish nod, wait until he's gone, then turn to each other. "What the hell is water?"

Irony let you skip the part where you decided what you believed in. Irony allowed you to look at a painting, or a moustache, or a bombed-out basement, and not give yourself an ulcer trying to scrape together some kind of meaning. Irony was your best defence, and a good offence, too. You threw it up like armour. It wasn't a matter of fitting in; it was a matter of getting through the day.

Inside the high-ceilinged and spiral-staircased Maggie Benston Centre, with a few minutes to kill before the editors' meeting, Alex wandered down past the bookstore. He overheard a cashier idly flirting as her credit card machine hummed in the background. "So," she ventured, "microeconomics, huh?"

"Yeah," the guy replied. "But this is just for breadth credits. What I'm *really* into is macroeconomics."

Alex shuddered. They were both dying for this exchange to be over, he figured. That way they could run into each other two weeks from now at Pub Night, both heroically drunk, reminisce about this two-minute conversation for forty-five, and speculate with a slur and a giggle about the kind of first impression they'd made on each other. Then he'd ironically ask her to dance, she'd ironically buy them more

drinks, and they'd both have sloppy, acrobatic sex on the lawn outside her townhouse.

This was not an atypical train of thought. Alex assumed everybody was spontaneously fucking everybody else, around corners and
under desks, always just out of sight, and that their inane banter was
really the secret password that gained them access to the world's all-
time greatest clique. As codes go, it was actually kind of ingenious.
But Alex just bristled at it, unwilling—unable?—to play along. It wasn't
fair. He was Enigma, he was the Rosetta Stone, and nobody gave a shit.

These two, the cashier and the doofus with the drawstring backpack, weren't particularly good looking. But that didn't matter. Alex
played through the seduction scene a few more times, swapping out
polite rums and Cokes, swapping in cauldrons of Jägermeister, and
shuffling the order in which the cashier stripped coquettishly on the
lawn. Zooming in on the secret places: where orange strap meets
orange cup, her gently freckled thighs.

Alex ducked into the Mini-Mart 101 next door. Less a store than
a room with ambition, the Mini-Mart consisted of one squat aisle
with a strategic island of aspirin and corn nuts in the middle to make
it look like two. You could just barely shimmy past someone if you
held your breath in tandem and neither of you was wider than a sheet
of paper. But that didn't stop the clientele from barging around with
backpacks and poster tubes in tow, turning abruptly and for no reason as if they were alone in an empty warehouse, snagging sleeves
on corners and sending displays whizzing like cardboard discuses
an inch above your head. Recently felled bottles of root beer fizzed
out on the floor next to upended Pop Rocks, creating huge foaming
clouds of stoner science.

After a few minutes of strategic tiptoeing, Alex arrived at the
coolers in the back and picked out a four-dollar imported soda whose
name and ingredients he could not read. He liked the mild thrill that

came with buying drinks like this; it was his way of simulating the way adults gambled. It felt somehow subversive, too, like he was still a kid pissing away his parents' spare coins.

This particular soda was pale blue, with a mascot of a goldfish wearing a ten-gallon hat. It had spurs on its fins.

"Oh! Hello, hi!" said the manager, an effusive, middle-aged Korean woman, as he approached the front counter.

"Hello," Alex said, pinning himself against the wall to let two girls with asymmetrical bangs glide past. As they did, one got a high heel stuck between the floor's wooden planks and bowled headfirst into the pretzels. The other one shrieked, dropping everything she was holding, and immediately sent a text. "How are you?"

"Good! Thank you. Cigarettes today? Calling card?"

"No. Just the soda, thanks."

"You sure?"

"Yes," Alex said. "Thanks, really." The girls, hunched over the floor, took a minute to sort out whose purse was whose.

The manager kept pressing. "New kind of cigarettes," she said, pointing to a nondescript steel cabinet. "Just came in. I have to keep them in here. Locked. You know. Government rules. 'Rich smoky flavour.' Hard to read because of picture of sad children on top. Also because of cabinet."

"You mean the surgeon general's warning," Alex said.

"Oh, a tough cookie. Looking for a deal, hm? I see how it goes." She pointed at the display of calling cards fanned out under the plastic countertop. They glittered with pictures of the world at night, spiderwebs of conversation tying the planet in an ever more tangled knot. "Take two of these instead. No hard feelings, mister."

Alex sighed. "I don't know anyone who lives in another country."

The girls pointed and frowned at a mystery third purse, which didn't belong to either of them and seemed to have materialized out of nowhere. In the back of the store, a flat of Charleston Chews crashed to the floor.

"Eight cents for minute to Senegal," the manager went on. "Turkey, Croatia. Bosnia or Trinidad, *five*. Today only. Big special. But no Tobago. Not included. Herzegovina, forget it."

"Are you serious? I've lived in Vancouver my whole life. I never even had a pen pal. My Asian friends all live *here*. That's how I know them. Who would I want—"

"Did you say Senegal?" The first girl, now sitting calmly on the floor, looked up from counting and sorting their intermingled lip glosses. "Eight cents? Simon C's has them for, like, six. Can you give me a discount?"

The manager thought for a second. "Deal."

"Great. I'll take two."

With an unexpected burst of boldness, Alex turned to her, but found himself still struggling to make eye contact. "Uh, can I ask you something? Who do you know in Senegal?"

The girl shrugged. "My sister. She moved a few years back."

"Are you from Africa?"

"Ha! God, no. I'm from Coquitlam."

As the girl's attention shifted back to the contents of her purse, Alex glanced as far up her pale leg as the stretched fabric of her skirt would allow. He guessed red. Some kind of lace. Probably a thong, too. Alex was part of what he considered to be the truly greatest generation, where girls wore that kind of stuff all the time, and not even to hide the lines, or whatever the original reason was supposed to be. The manager had a clear view, and could have settled the question either way, but she was busy with a calculator, figuring out how much she stood to lose on her deal.

Senegal? he thought with a jealous twinge, back outside the store. *Was everyone so damn* worldly *these days? I mean, really.*

A sister in Africa? Alex cracked the seal on his goldfish soda and recoiled from the smell. Apricots and black licorice. *What are the fucking odds of that?*

The thing nobody told you was that university looked and felt an awful lot like high school, only with the poles reversed. Here the trick was caring too much, or pretending to, or trying to convince yourself that you did. It was a bumper-sticker arms race; it was a prisoner's dilemma, if the prisoner also subscribed to *Adbusters*. So when in doubt, be offended. When in doubt, sign that petition. Go on: talk shit about that TA. It's for her own good, and it would've come out anyway, even if she wasn't standing behind you in that sushi lineup.

The publicity team at SFU (founded 1965, population 26,000) had, of course, done its best to mute these similarities. Post-secondary life was meant to be a bold, clean break from high school, not a poorly disguised continuation of it. So when they toured auditoriums every year to pitch SFU to starry-eyed students and their parents, what the team described was a glorious, relentlessly upward trajectory. They wore suits and carried brochures full of pictures in which under-grads carried no fewer than three books each (official SFU-PR policy) and were always shown laughing ecstatically, giddy at how smart and clever they all were and how teachers were so sober and fair here and how much fun learning was when you weren't ever called a fag. Many of the senior people had put in time on the junk-bond and time-share circuits. They were used to delivering slideshows to packed rooms of the gullible, fingers crossed behind their backs the whole time.

So when the eighteen-year-old bookworms, pre-emptively drunk on the knowledge they were about to soak up, arrived on the hill for their first day, they realized with a slow-burning shock that they hadn't exactly been told the full truth. The biggest betrayal was that they still—*still!*—weren't even in the majority. Everywhere they looked they saw depressingly familiar-looking meatheads, whose marks were just good enough to squeak into general studies and who were still high-fiving anything that moved.

The smart kids, too, were different than advertised: a little less friendly, a little more standoffish. Everyone had a favourite book, but nobody would tell you what it was. So every year the new arrivals figured it was best to just lie low, learn the rules as fast as possible, and fall in line. If you brought up fashion now, it must have a footnote from Michel Foucault on the tag. All uses of the word *Darfur* must be followed by a minute of silence. All chocolate-chip cookie recipes must be postcolonial. *Nerd* was now the highest possible compliment, fetishized beyond belief. The smoothest move an undergrad could make was to sheepishly but loudly admit in tutorial that Heidegger was the only thing on his Amazon Wish List. Then chuckle, look down, and mutter, "I'm such a nerd." Instant swoons.

Discovering even this narrow of a niche was a victory, Alex had to admit, but it still felt awfully hollow. And these kids were his peers—more than that, they were his readership. His target audience. Would they be interested in a two thousand–word feature on trees? Could he be bothered to even try to convince them?

Alex headed back to the office, ready to roll up his sleeves. The *Metro* was coming, and they needed to be prepared. He wouldn't let *The Peak* get caught unaware—especially considering all the advance warning he'd already given everyone. It'd be downright embarrassing. As he walked past the lone remaining pay phone at the bottom of the stairwell, he saw the girl from the Mini-Mart holding the receiver to her ear. Right as he came into earshot, the girl's voice jumped an octave.

"If I'm calling you long distance to explain why I changed our relationship status to 'It's Complicated,' then *wouldn't you say it's complicated?*"

Alex felt strange watching an argument about Facebook politics take place on a rusty old pay phone. Something about it didn't add up. It was like choosing to defend your thesis via smoke signal.

Or writing an email, only to then print it out, stick it in a pigeon's beak, and shoo the poor bird clear across town.

2

UNCONFIRMED SOURCES

On the other side of campus, Tracy Shaw walked toward the Renaissance coffee shop, listening to a girl she'd just met tell her all about her directed studies course and her injury-prone brother and how she'd ended up here, in this suburb, at this school, to study English literature.

"So after the second accident," the girl was saying, "the doctor said, 'You must stay home and rest. Six weeks, minimum. The bones need time to re-attach.'" She winced along with Tracy. "Gross, I know. But my brother doesn't listen. He gets bored and after three days pulls his skateboard out of the closet. I don't know why this occurs to him. He hasn't used the thing in years. Anyway, he jumps on in the driveway and *ten seconds later* is lying on the ground with a broken hip. The board shoots down the road, right into a big intersection."

"Oh my god," Tracy said.

"There's more! Right as he falls, a police car is driving past our house. But they don't stop to help. They just roll down their window, point at the skateboard that's flying into traffic, and one says, very seriously, 'Wear a helmet.' He's wagging his finger." The girl's laughter was as warm and strong as a hair dryer.

It was a crisp fall afternoon. Leaves scuttled along the paths on tiptoe, and the wind came in light on its spiralling route across the

Burrard Inlet. This was real mountain air, the stuff of legend and throat lozenge commercials. Packs of 1st-years sat cross-legged under trees and on benches, their noses held religiously high; a skinny guy with bloodshot eyes stuck his head out of a window in the nearby Academic Quadrangle, breathing greedily. Rumours had swirled for years about SFU's supposedly out-of-control suicide rate, but a day like this downgraded those kinds of whispered statistics to a dark inside joke. It gave the students a subconscious reminder to breathe deep and enjoy themselves now, while time and youth and deferred student loans and temporary feelings of chest-beating immortality were in their favour. Besides, sparkling mountain water was already a finely tuned billion-dollar industry. You had to figure it was only a matter of time until they came with vacuums to bottle the air itself.

This, at least, was a modest version of the motto held up by a student activist group called The Air Up Here, whose bi-monthly demonstration Tracy and the girl walked past on their way to the coffee shop. It looked like a demonstration, anyway. It might have just been four hippy kids playing hackeysack. Sometimes it was hard to tell.

Soon the hill was alive with the sound of djembes.

"The police are maniacs," Tracy said, once they were a safe distance away from the drums. She exhaled sharply and shook her head. "But you know what? I can do you one better. My little brother goes to school in Edmonton, and everyone in residence there plays these huge games of dodgeball. It's just massive: fifty people on each side, industrial-strength boomboxes. So last year he's in the middle of a game, and he winds up and whips the ball as hard as he can. He's a bit of a showboat, so he probably jumped in the air and made a big thing of it. But he throws it so hard that he actually *breaks* his arm. A spiral fracture, all the way from his elbow to his shoulder. Right as he threw it, he says he felt his whole upper arm just kind of sag."

The girl threw her hands over her mouth, delighted. "No!" She was Scandinavian, with elfin features and an accent that, while clearly an insecurity for her, was also unstoppably cute, at least from where Tracy was standing. The girl had the kind of non-threatening exoticism that guys on campus went cartoon-eyed over.

Not that Tracy was competition—she'd been off the market for so long that her interest in what men liked was, at this point, strictly anthropological. "Yes!" she insisted, now warming to the familiar contours of her anecdote. "The best part is that the university hospital is just down the road, and when he went to check in, the doctor was totally unimpressed. My brother says, kind of sheepishly, 'Yeah, it's from a dodgeball.' The doctor just nods, and goes, 'How long have you lived in Lister Hall?'"

"Wow. Just, wow."

Tracy had already let out another spurt of laughter. "He had to get pins, screws, and a whole pile of staples on the outside. His arm is basically an office supplies cupboard now. I keep asking him where they hid the hole punch. And he got all excited while he was in the hospital because they told him it's the same fracture soldiers get from throwing hand grenades. There's just nothing for all that force to go into, I guess, because the thing they're chucking is so light." A new tag to the story floated into her mind without her even searching for it. "He was basically just trying too hard."

The Scandinavian stared into the middle distance, watching the hippies' hackeysack jump and fall (mostly fall). "Then it's decided," she said, nodding with solemnity. "Our brothers must never meet. They'll set both of our houses on fire."

"So what happened to the skateboard?"

"What?"

Tracy felt the familiar tingle in her jaw for a post-class cigarette as they reached the café's awning, but she fought it off. "Your brother's skateboard. You said it went into traffic."

"Oh! It got crushed under a truck, I think. We found a few pieces that night. He made us go out and look for it after sunset. It had his favourite sticker of a skull on the bottom."

"I'm so sorry," Tracy said as she held the door. Inside, the coffee shop was buzzing with activity. "I really feel like a moron—but I've forgotten your name."

"Don't worry about it! It's Anna," said Anna, playfully cocking her head to one side.

Just then Tracy remembered something Dave had once told her, years ago—one of his many cockeyed theories, though this one she was actually a little partial to. It sounded a lot like something her coworkers at *The Peak* might have cooked up, come to think of it.

The idea was that there were exactly three kinds of conversations you had to have with a classmate before you could become friends. First-level conversations were lightning quick, with no question or answer taking longer than five seconds. You usually had this kind of talk inside a classroom before the TA showed up, when the rest of the class looked quiet and distracted, and therefore 100 percent committed to eavesdropping. You spoke quickly because you sensed how many people were listening to your fluffball small talk, and because you didn't want to commit to too much, in case the other person turned out to be a creep, or didn't like novels with ambiguous endings, or all of whose favourite artists—by sheer coincidence—turned out to be fascists. At this point it was still possible to move to a new seat in a different row.

Next was when you could each talk for about fifteen seconds at a time without feeling overly pushy about it. These conversations took place in hallways, or the first time you saw a classmate in a public place, free of the clingy aura of academics. It was common to stall at this level for years.

The third level, however, was critical, and critically short. It lasted for exactly one conversation. Here each response could last a maximum of forty-five seconds—really, as long as you could expect any non–blood relative to listen to you—which was enough time to detail what your term paper was about, or what was *really* wrong with the CBC, or what you and your boyfriend liked to do on long weekends. This conversation had to take place sitting down. By the end you felt nervous and sometimes light-headed at how much personal information you'd let out without thinking, and if both of you were still on board at this point, it was a done deal.

Just then, as they stood in line together, Tracy noticed how Anna's teeth were sticking out in a goofy smile, and how unconcerned she looked about it. In other words, the girl was approaching level three and hitting her stride fast. Unless Tracy hit the brakes now, and hard, she'd have a bona fide new friend in a few short minutes.

But unlike most of the people she worked with at the newspaper, Tracy didn't instinctively hate or fear other students. In fact, she often liked them. After a full year as copy editor—a position that required almost zero contact with contributors, either in person or digitally—she remained largely immune to their acerbic, passive-aggressive ways. In general she preferred talking to writing, which helped her social life, though not her proofreading rigour, and she was the only person on staff who could have entire conversations with other students without bringing up the fact that she was employed by *The Peak*. This was mostly because she couldn't bear those long pauses while they struggled to think of something nice to say.

Tracy leaned over to Anna and said, "This is my favourite coffee shop on campus. I don't know if you've been over here before. It took me almost two years before I even figured out there was an upper bus loop, let alone all this stuff." The complex they were standing in was one of the most recent appendages sewn onto the SFU campus proper, and also boasted a florist, a ghost town of a DVD rental store, sushi and Indian restaurants, an optometrist's office, a pizzeria/donair shop, and the campus's computer store. The whole area, coffee shop excepted, was so clean as to suggest under-use. "It's meant to bring in the people who live in those apartment buildings around the corner. They aren't students or faculty, most of them, but for some reason they live here anyway—even though there's literally nothing to do up here if you don't go to school. Weird, right? Anyway, as you can see, the plan didn't work." Tracy gestured to the over-loaded tables of boys with flipped-up polo collars and girls wearing fuzzy boots whose pom-poms dangled perilously close to the floor. Two of the former perked up when they spotted Anna. "Nothing but rez kids everywhere you turn."

"I wanted to ask you about that," Anna whispered. She held a hand up to her mouth and her eyes darted around, as if she were about to disclose state secrets in the most indiscreet way possible. "Why do they all wear sweatpants? Someone told me that was how to spot the people from residence."

"Oh, everyone does that," Tracy replied. "Sweatpants, flip-flops, golf visors—I've seen yoga pants with a dress shirt. Tucked in. In Vancouver, casual is a right."

Up at the registers, some kind of complication involving a gift card brought the lineup to a standstill. The girls chatted gamely on. They talked about how long the SkyTrain takes between stops. They talked about a popular TV show, wherein a group of attractive plane-crash survivors slowly discover that the island they're stranded on is either science or magic. They talked about how both of their mothers never went anywhere without painted toenails. They talked about their tutorial, for an English class on Shakespeare's later plays. When their own drinks were finally ready, Anna spotted a pair of recently vacated stools and asked Tracy if she wanted to get a seat.

"Can't today, I'm afraid," Tracy said, flashing her own smile. "I've got a meeting. But this was fun. Save me a spot in class next week, okay?" No doubt about it: this girl was sit-down material. She was flattered Anna felt the same way.

Back outside, Tracy lit a cigarette. She wasn't unattractive, and didn't consider herself so, but whenever she talked to a girl like Anna, who actually turned heads, Tracy felt herself standing up straighter to compensate. It was a purely symbolic gesture; Tracy was five foot four, rounding up. And she only ever realized she was doing it afterward, when her lower back began to ache and she felt her spine settle back into its familiar slouch. Oh well. *Better than sticking my tits out,* she thought.

So she was short, with thick-chic glasses and an attractively prominent stomach that she hoped gave off a subtle, second-trimester femininity. Her jeans had double-folded cuffs. She used to wear a blazer with pins all along the lapels, until one day she didn't.

One particular point of pride was that she didn't try to compensate for her figure by making a barrage of hyper-filthy innuendo and constantly reminding everyone that this was a sexual creature. That sex *happened* here, whether you liked it or not. *Those kinds of girls,* she thought grimly, taking a deep puff of smoke, *are the absolute worst.* In photos they always made sure they were squeezing someone's breast (not necessarily their own), and they only seemed to know two facial expressions: tongue sticking out; or chin angled down and mouth slightly open, looking doe-eyed into the camera. Both were meant to remind the viewer of blowjobs. You couldn't reason with these girls.

Tracy was emphatically not one of them. For one thing, she hated wine coolers. She thought they tasted like potpourri.

Pinching the cigarette between her lips, she put on her headphones and cued up Hüsker Dü's *New Day Rising*. The hackeysack circle had now doubled its numbers to eight. All guys. No surprise there. Their clothes were faded, frayed, and contained at least three times as many pockets as Tracy could imagine practical uses for. They never kept the hackeysack in flight for more than a few hits in a row, either, but guffawed and egged each other into trying more and more outlandish moves anyway. Three of them were yelling out quotes from a late-night animated series, all trying to approximate the main character's squeaky, vaguely ethnic voice. If this was a meeting of any campus group, now it was Dreadlock Fans and Owners.

Even optimists like Tracy had little time for the hippies. *You'll never get anything done,* she thought with an arch smile, *not with pants that complicated and slogans that simple.*

Just then one of the guys in the circle looked up and made eye contact with her. His eyes were Alaskan-husky blue, and he wore a long-sleeved waffle shirt with cargo pants that tied around the waist with a thin black cord. The directness of his look froze Tracy's smug train of thought in its place. It also, she realized a second too late, froze her smug expression to her face. *Whoops,* she thought, slipping by. *You're not supposed to let the hippies know you look down on them. Otherwise they'll stop lending you their lighters.*

Tracy walked quickly, smoking and taking long swigs of coffee. First she passed the statue of Terry Fox, fallen cross-country runner and SFU's patron saint, then headed down the steps of the AQ toward the library, where she had to squeeze in some last-minute photocopying before the *Peak* meetings started. She looked at her watch. Five minutes. They actually had an agenda that week—figuring out what to do about the free daily that was soon to be their competition—and Tracy was excited to hear what the others had come up with.

She felt a little guilty she hadn't thought of anything herself. She'd tried, briefly, that morning, while her SkyTrain was stuck between Lake City Way and Production Station for a full twenty minutes in the middle of rush hour. But she'd gotten distracted by the business-looking guy in her train car who'd banged against the window, jabbing at one of the nondescript buildings below. "That's my fucking work!" he announced, letting his finger trail mournfully down the glass. "I just need to get *there*."

At the entrance of the library, Tracy tripped over a bundle of thick industrial cables. *What the—?* she thought, shooting the ground a look while still stumbling into the automated doors. In her ears was a song about a girl who lives on heaven hill. *Nice try, Bob. A little too on the nose, don't you think?* As Tracy righted herself, an arm covered in Gore-Tex shot out and held her back.

"Sorry," said the woman it was attached to. She was wearing a headset and held a clipboard. "We're shooting the monkeys in there."

Tracy yanked her earbuds out. "Again? Come *on*." She stood on tiptoe and peered over the woman's shoulder. Inside the library, sitting on plastic folding chairs in the front foyer, were a half-dozen actors wearing monkey costumes from the neck down, each getting his or her fur touched up. They held their oversized primate heads under their arms like NASA helmets. In the background, a man in a baseball cap waved his arms above his head and pointed at various people holding cameras. Tracy thought he seemed French, somehow.

"I just need in to photocopy two things," she said. "You're between shots now anyway."

"Can't do it," the woman said. She tapped her clipboard with a pen.

"Yes, I understand it's not on your call sheet. Just let me in real quick. Please? You aren't even shooting the reserves, are you?"

The woman's eyes narrowed. "I didn't confirm that. Got it? That's *unconfirmed.*" Her voice turned into a kind of hiss. "I bet you'd just love an exclusive, huh? You know, we come up here to get away from the media blitz, but now everyone's got camera phones and TMZ on speed dial. It's out of control. This is all off the record."

"Listen," Tracy said. "I'm not the press. I just copy edit the stupid student paper. I don't care about any of this. All I want is to photocopy two articles: one that says Shakespeare was a lady, and one that says he was a series of dogs. They're ten steps from the other side of these doors. Then I'll be on my way." Tracy thought for a second, as she finished off her cigarette and squished it against a nearby concrete pillar. "Funny thing about 'off the record,' though."

"Oh no. Oh no." The woman pressed the mute button on her headset, activating a bead of red light next to the microphone. She leaned in a little. "It's different in Canada, isn't it? I *knew* I shouldn't have said anything."

"So let's recap. I'm hearing from a source on location that a crucial scene involving the monkeys is being shot in the computer lab—and possibly the reserves—on the second floor of the W.A.C. Bennett Library. Is that about right?"

"You don't understand. I could get mad fired for this. I've already gotten my official warning—and that rat in Seattle swore on his mother's grave that he was a janitor."

"Possible space theme . . . a dystopian future, maybe?"

"*What?* How did you know that?"

It wasn't much of a guess. Camera crews eager for a Canadian tax break were always floating around the campus, and half of what was filmed at SFU turned the campus into FBI headquarters or the home base for robot dictatorships thanks to Arthur Erickson, whose architectural style was built around concrete and right angles. Tracy was just using her home-field advantage.

"Okay, okay," the woman conceded. "Go on. What'll it cost me?"

"The public has a right to know these things," Tracy said. "Information wants to be free, you know."

"It does? Fuck. Fuck, okay, shit. Listen, if I just let you in right now to photocopy your stuff, will you keep quiet?"

"Hm. That sounds reasonable."

"I'll even throw in a hat. An official one. Only the crew are supposed to have them."

"Deal," Tracy said.

The woman sighed with relief. "Good. Fine. Meet me back here tonight and I'll have it ready. If I'm not here, check inside this plant." Tracy took a step forward, but the woman jutted out her arm again. "You'll have to give me your phone, though. No pictures. I'll give it back on your way out."

Tracy handed it over and brushed past. "There's no camera on it."

"Yeah, that's what the guy in Seattle said," the woman called after her. "And duck down, would you? If the monkeys see a human on set it'll wreck their focus."

3

COMIC SANS

Here's how it happened.

For a few months, there had been distant rumblings around campus that the *Metro,* a free daily that had been blanketing the Greater Vancouver area with celebrity-strewn garbage tumbleweeds for over a year, had plans to expand to Burnaby Mountain. The thing was shockingly well read. Discarded copies pooled by the dozens in back corners of buses and SkyTrains, and even though you were never more than an arm's length away from one, the company employed fleets of retirees and the recently paroled to stand in green aprons in the middle of sidewalks all over the city, bothering people into taking a copy. They repeated the same phrases over and over again. "Free *Metro*." "Paper?" In this respect they had more than a little in common with the panhandlers a couple of feet farther down the block. Each had their slogans. But it was obvious who was flooded with business, and who was literally starved for it.

So far the Burnaby campus had been immune to the daily's charms, for the same reason it would have also shrugged off Noah's flood: it had the higher ground. SFU, Ark-free Since 1965. True, it was nearly impossible to get decent take-out delivered up the mountain, but the upside was that the commute also scared off most unwanted solicitors. As a result, *The Peak,* SFU's official student newspaper, had enjoyed a near-total monopoly. Its only rivals were a sporadically published newsletter by and for business students called *The Buzz!*, and a pamphlet written in Mandarin that, despite impressive distribution numbers, not one person had ever been seen reading.

But now it looked like the *Metro* was making a real play for a presence at SFU. Rick, *The Peak*'s business manager and resident grown-up, heard through one of his channels that the daily would be setting up a booth at Clubs Days, complete with banners and confetti. There'd be an entire squad of fresh-faced excitables wearing headbands and green jumpsuits, ready to chat up passersby and even cartwheel for a paycheque. If things went well there—and really, how could they not?—they'd leave dozens of shiny *Metro* boxes in their wake, scattered down the mountain like breadcrumbs. Apron-clad reverse-panhandlers wouldn't be far behind.

The Peak had two major things to fear from this new competition. One was advertising. Ad dollars were scarce to begin with, and the *Metro* was sure to take a significant chunk of them—and that wasn't even counting the pre-existing clout that came with having successful branches installed in seven other Canadian cities. Let's say a campus business wanted to get the word out about their product, but disagreed with a certain student-run paper's occasional policy of running full-frontal male nudity beside all of the ads. So far they'd had no alternative. But the *Metro* staked its reputation on being wholesome, or at least some hall-of-mirrors facsimile thereof. It had been thoroughly market-tested and focus-grouped in all relevant demographics. It had two pages of soft local news, one page about the rest of the world, and forty about the latest in celebrity diets. It didn't have any penis quotas, anyway, and sometimes that's enough.

The second problem was Sudoku. The *Metro* had it; *The Peak* didn't.

At that week's editors' meeting, this very issue was under discussion.

"We could get it. We could totally get it. I know a guy."

"You don't know anyone."

"Is someone taking minutes? We need to be writing all this down."

"And check this out, right? We'll make it even harder. Bam. Instant victory. Beat them at their own game."

"Bam."

"Oof!"

"You've got it all wrong. People don't want it to be harder. They can barely be fucked as it is. They just want something to stare at on the bus—something to doodle on while they're on the phone. Plus it's already impossible. You ever try it?"

"No. But then again I disagree with the whole idea on principle. Word searches and math have no business in bed together in my personal opinion."

"You mean in a dresser drawer together."

"Just sevens and ones all over the goddamned place."

"See, I can't do anything past intermediate. There's too much to juggle in your head. I get all dizzy."

"Because Sudoku is Japanese."

"Oh, the ones I do are scaled: one to five. My favourite is three. It's okay. Totally doable."

"Do you buy the books? I saw the *New York Times* guy has his own line, but I don't think his heart is really in it."

"Did anyone see that documentary about him?"

"And Japanese people live in small houses."

"Hey! How about a crossword? That would be easier."

"Sure, why not."

"Will Shortz, motherfucker!"

"The first obvious question is what the dimensions should be. With black spaces, or the more economic *Harper's* model. Cryptic or standard. Are themes allowed? What do we think?"

"Come on guys, seriously. This is important. The minutes . . ."

"We should have someone look into potential ink savings re: no blacked-out units. Pull some quick data together. Venn diagrams."

"Hey. Everyone. *Hey:* I really don't care about any of this."

"Me neither."

"I'm okay with that, as long as we don't use any of those answers that keep getting recycled every other day. No *iota,* no *aorta.* Definitely no *eerie.* Or with just one *e.* Like the lake. Shameless vowel-grabs, the lot of them."

"It also works because you could keep a puzzle book in a drawer really easily. That's like its house."

"Do you want to go outside and smoke until this is over?"

"Yes. More than anything."

"Hi all. Sorry I'm late."

"Tracy, over here."

"What'd I miss?"

"Not word fucking one, believe you me."

"Where would we even put a Sudoku? Like what section?"

"I say humour."

"Yep."

"Definitely."

"Touchdown."

"Whoa, whoa. Hold on a minute. All of you can go right to hell. It's the *humour* section—as in jokes only. Don't dump your excess baggage on me just because I'm at the back with the classifieds. No word jumbles, no horoscopes. I'm not the *diversions* editor or whatever the fuck."

"Do you have a better idea?"

"Sure. Yes. Sports. It's a mental workout. Cerebral crunches. Chin-ups for the soul. Give it to Chip."

"Not a hope, chief. I'll stonewall you."

"Or opinions. Give it its own column. Maybe It's Just Me, by Sudoku Puzzle. S. Puzzle for short."

"If I really picture myself smoking hard, my brain will release some sweet, sweet endorphins. I'll clench my fists."

"Would we have to pay this Sudoku guy?"

"Yeah. And who is he, anyway?"

"I should say that he's never actually made one of them before. But he's been meaning to for, like, forever. He's a stand-up dude. A real think tank."

"Are you related to this person?"

"Yes."

"*Jesus.*"

"I bet I could smoke ten cigarettes at once. Someone dog dare me."

"If nobody takes minutes we're never going to remember this for next week. Can someone find the Spider-Man binder? I'll do it. I have a pen."

"Okay, I changed my mind, you guys. We can put Sudokus in the humour section, guys, as long as I get to make them myself. Hand-drawn. Full page. And we'll save time, too, because they'll be unsolvable. Just never print the answers."

"It never . . . none of this is procedural."

"Also they'll be in Comic Sans."

"You use that for everything."

"That's because *it is a perfect font.*"

"Smoke, smoke, smoke, smoking."

"Ugh. It should be illegal to use if you're over eleven years old. You should automatically be registered as a sex offender."

"Rick! Will *The Peak* buy me cigarettes?"

"No."

"Who put this popsicle in the microwave?"

"Don't touch that. I'm using it."

The Peak employed a total of eleven editors and, in a vague homage to the school's heavy-left political origins, had no editor-in-chief. Section editors dictated their own content, and disputes were solved by a show of hands, heroically long-winded emails, and the occasional secret ballot.

So they sat, equals, on itchy couches and around an old wooden coffee table that was spray-painted purple from three redesigns ago, and talked about the larger task at hand. Something had to be done. Decisions had to be made. Action had to be taken. Someone made coffee. That was a start. They all agreed that the *Metro*'s move should be viewed as a direct assault on their autonomy, and that the student government should have already taken swift action to keep the daily at bay. A manifesto was immediately proposed, to unanimous yahs and whistles. Papers were swept off desks. Excessively long pens were drawn. Three people called the state of affairs an abomination. Chip, the perpetually red-in-the-face sports editor, announced he wasn't "going to take this lying down." And stood up.

"We need gumption," he said. "We need hustle. Now's no time to keep our stick on the ice." Chip was round and squat, sporting suspenders and an archaically bushy moustache. He held eye contact with the intensity of someone bound and gagged in a car trunk.

Rachel, the news editor, said, "The thing that gets me is, they can't just come up here and tell SFU students what news is. That's our job." She would know. Rachel had worked there for longer than anyone else could remember, and could cite arcane policies and protocols for which no written record existed. Nobody knew what she studied, but her hair showed constant signs of being chewed on, as if she was forever on the brink of some oral presentation or cumulative exam. "We know this campus. It's our beat. We know what our readers want."

"Totally. And I see where you're going with that, Rachel. For example, I spent all last night Photoshopping pictures of dolphins playing Connect 4. I am willing to donate my work for the cause." This was Keith: humour editor, eater of pizza, and lifelong critic of *The Peak* until he found out he could get weekly free pizza and a warm place on campus to sleep off his drinking in exchange for producing two pages of content every issue.

"Look," Rachel said. "We need to send a message. This kind of behaviour will not stand. Okay? It simply will not."

"I wish we could just tell them to *eff off*," one of the younger editors said from the back.

"Yeah," another agreed. "It's actually sort of mean, if you think about it. Why would they come here just to wreck everything for us on purpose? We're just trying to have fun."

Rachel muttered, *"Some of us* are here for something bigger."

"As if anyone's going to read their stupid paper."

"Eff right off, that's what I say."

"Yesterday their front-page story was Boy Loses Tricycle."

"Ha. Totally."

"Ridiculous, I know."

"Does anyone know if he found it? That story was such a cliffhanger."

Rachel snapped her pencil in half. It was mechanical.

"That's because they're just awful writers," Alex said. "Pure and simple. They wouldn't know an inverted pyramid if they went on vacation to inverted Egypt."

Keith sat up, sensing a riff in the making. "They wouldn't know a lede if . . . they were . . . winning a *race!*" As the words left his mouth, his face screwed up like he'd licked a battery. "Shit. That was awful. I'll get it. It'll come back."

"Plus they only have one writer in the whole place doing news," said Tracy. "Have you looked at their bylines? One guy does all of the city stuff *and* compiles the world section. What a tragedy. Mack Holloway, the loneliest man in newspapers."

"Egypt . . ." mumbled someone from the back. "Oh! An inverted sphinx!"

"Shot in the face by an inverted Napoleon!"

"Yeah," sighed Keith. "That's the same joke a few more times. Fuck, you guys. Step it up already. Anyone else?"

"King Tut."

"He *was* super young."

"Like six or seven, I heard. Baby pharaoh and shit."

"You guys remember when Geraldo Rivera did that TV show where he opened his tomb? I was just watching it on YouTube a few days ago. It was crazy, this super big ratings thing, but then it just turned out to have some broken bottles in it."

"In elementary school I had to do a project on Egypt. I drew the raddest sphinx head for the title page."

"Isis."

"Actually, that's a lie. I totally traced that shit."

"Didn't they have a goddess called Isis? Goddess of . . . grain. Or sleep. Sheep?"

"*Isis!* That's another banned crossword clue."

"Or those snakes that live in baskets."

"*Asp!* Another!"

"Isis is the goddess of desire."

"Really?"

"Yep. 'Isis' is the goddess of *Desire*. No question about it."

"What are you . . . oh. Goddammit. Not this again."

"Hold on: did they find it or not?"

"I think they did."

"Really?"

"Yeah, yeah. There was a thing about it on the news."

"So where . . . ?"

"On a bus someplace. They put out an amber alert, and no problem. Totally found—what was he, Mexican."

"Mexican? What does that even mean?"

"Amber alerts are for missing children."

"Yeah. What are you guys talking about?"

"A tricycle."

"Why would he bring his tricycle on the bus? Someone should abduct that retard again."

"So what do we do?" Alex asked in a near yell. "I mean, literally what do we do next?"

The strategy seemed to work. Several sets of eyes did a slow pan toward his corner of the ratty wool couch.

"We draft it," someone offered. "The manifesto."

"Might I suggest something either dolphin– or Connect 4–related?" Keith asked, tipping an imaginary hat to the group. "I have a picture we could use."

"Okay, first of all, I really don't think we should use the word *manifesto*," Alex said. "Makes us sound like douchebags, don't you think?" He looked around and saw he did not speak for the room. "Fine. Never mind. Does anyone here know how to do this? Has anyone actually done it before? What are we basing it on?"

"Nah, fuck all that," someone said from the back. "It'll come from the heart. You don't need to look up the truth in a *book*. Don't sweat it."

"Right." Alex rubbed his eyes in vigorous circles, pulling toward the inside corners every few seconds. "Okay. Sure. You new guys are great, by the way. Full of moxie." Clapping his hands, he said, "Let's go for it. Who's going to transcribe?" He looked toward one of the youngsters. "You still got that pen handy?"

The girl nodded.

"Excellent."

The rest of the meeting went more smoothly. There was the usual housekeeping to attend to, during which the outrage in the room lowered to a simmer. Those with sections to edit wrote what they had that week onto a blackboard, while the others asked polite, uninterested questions and crossed their fingers that they wouldn't be tapped to pay for dinner that week (reimbursements being a delicate and slow-moving process that few editors could afford to get tangled up in). They made noodles and drank from gigantic aluminum cans of iced tea. Chip compared the bumbling football team to the Maginot Line, and chortled to himself. Page counts were negotiated, accompanied by much scratching of beards and ankles. Suze, the arts editor, threatened to stop giving out advance movie passes unless she started receiving the reviews she was already owed. Next week's open house was discussed. Rachel was firm that ordering sushi was *not how it was done*—two platters of sandwiches and one bullet of Coke, Sprite, and Orange would be fine. What kind of Orange? "Crush. *Obviously.*" They didn't take it to a vote. The manifesto was downgraded to a strongly worded editorial, and then again to an editorial cartoon, writer and artist TBA. The girl Alex had tapped to transcribe it instead took careful notes in the Spider-Man binder. The cover story would be the feature Alex had assigned about home brewing, unless something better came along at the last minute. Keith performed a freestyle rap about his favourite kinds of yogurt. Afterward they all trickled back to their desks and hit refresh on blogs, news tickers, a Word document by accident, and email, email, email, like an itch.

Alex and Tracy waited out the interim until the next meeting in the mini-office traditionally shared by the arts and copy editors. Three of these cubicles lined the back of *Peak* headquarters, each with dividing walls that fell six inches short of the ceiling and a window overlooking the main production room. The fluorescent lights on this side gave everyone who worked under them scalding headaches; Tracy had made a half-effort to cover hers by pinning an abandoned yellow fleece over the fixture.

"Nice job back there," she said.

"On the douchebag manifesto? Yeah, well. Doesn't look like it's even going to happen now, does it?"

"That's what I mean. The best way to make a project go away around here is to start assigning people to it. Looks like congratulations are in order."

Alex let out a short, sandpapery laugh. He leaned against the wall opposite Tracy's desk, which was, in fact, the only one in the office that didn't have a computer attached.

Through the window they saw the front door swing open and shut a few times as people started showing up for the collective meeting. A bunch of discarded CDs, long since passed over for review, had been looped together with string and hung from the door handle, announcing each new visitor with a series of synthetic clacks.

Collective meetings were open to anyone who paid into *The Peak*'s funding, which was basically everybody. Thanks to a neat trick of accounting, this amount got automatically bundled into the university's student fees—most undergrads had no idea they lost seven dollars each semester this way, and the editors were in no rush to point it out to them.

Some obvious first-timers walked around the office in silence, most a little intimidated by the whole subterranean experience, some decidedly underwhelmed by what a dump it was. The more impressionable among them ran their fingers along the chipped table corners in awe and studied the collages of old covers on the walls. A gaudy mix of neon green and blue paint peeked through the gaps of newsprint, the colour of an Easter hangover.

The new kids were waiting for someone to come over and introduce themselves, and officially invite them back to the couches that were distantly visible in the other room. It didn't happen.

Alex asked, "So how are your classes?"

"I have a midterm on Thursday," Tracy said. "Ridiculous, right? We've only had two lectures, one of which consisted of everyone saying what they knew about the Enlightenment coming in. Now it's time for a *test?* Half of it better be on the guy beside me who thought that's when they invented the alphabet."

"An exam in an English class? I thought you guys were allergic to them or something."

"Tell me about it," she said. "This is just a 200-level course, so they have to have at least one exam. Why do you think I'm even taking a course on the stupid Enlightenment? It's a pre-req. I just put off doing it until now."

"I don't know anything about that stuff," Alex admitted. He thought back to his bus ride with a fresh topcoat of frustration. The depths of his ignorance only ran deeper the more he thought about them. His stupidity was large; it contained multitudes.

Alex was briefly cheered up by his own little internal joke—until he remembered he had no idea where it came from. But could he really be held accountable for that? Authorship wasn't exactly in vogue anymore. These kinds of reference points floated out there in the public domain, absorbed into the air's chemical equation. Most of them he'd first encountered as parodies on *The Simpsons* anyway.

"Yeah, me neither," Tracy said. "But so far it's just been history: memorizing which king beheaded which wife or ran away from which duke. I do like Alexander Pope, though. We did 'Rape of the Lock' in high school—everyone managed to nervously giggle their way through. I like imagining this tiny, frail guy running home and making elaborate fun of all the women who rejected him. He's basically a blogger. LiveJournal would've loved him."

"I see a term paper forming: Pope's influence on *Revenge of the Nerds*. 'Wit as muscle.' Some mind/body dichotomy stuff. You could use Descartes, Teddy Roosevelt, Charles Atlas. Or Charles Xavier."

"Mm. Yeah," she said. Tracy was less into these kinds of name-dropping contests than the boys at the paper. It struck her, in fact, as a distinctly masculine pursuit—memorizing stats and figures as if the sum of human culture were nothing more than a set of base-ball cards. She also felt it'd be sexist, somehow, to say this out loud. "What about you?" she added. "Classes okay?"

"Not bad. We've already done *Henry IV* and *V*, and this week is *Julius Caesar*. They're pretty good. I think I'm onboard so far." By this, Alex did not mean he had read the above-mentioned plays. He majored in humanities, which was kind of like English, only you watched more movies and could write your final essay about a picture of a vase. This particular course was called Shakespeare Without Shakespeare, and had only one rule: reading or referring to the Bard's actual plays or poems was strictly forbidden. This point was written at the top of the syllabus in bold italics. Alex had been trying to get in for over a year, on Tracy's urging that recognizing a bad Shake-speare pun was one of the few and lonely solaces of the liberal arts grad. But the course always filled up on the first day of registration.

"Well, stick with it," she said now. "Try not to let all those You-Tube clips get you down. Did I tell you I'm doing a Shakespeare course, too? We should brainstorm together when essay season approaches."

"Actually, I was thinking of maybe sculpting something. My professor would probably like that more—he uses all these weird pottery metaphors. I heard that's what his degree is in."

Tracy got up, shaking her head. "It depresses me more than I can say that I don't know if you're being sarcastic or not." She went over to the stacks of CDs, which lined the arts desk like castle walls, and rummaged for new arrivals. It seemed like all Suze ever got sent was undecipherable punk rock and easy-listening piano ballads from women in their forties. The bulk of it was homemade; Tracy only now noticed how many of the artist photos used the exact same sepia filter.

"Yeah, don't bother. Those are at least six months old," Alex said, over her shoulder. "Keith pawned all the new ones. I saw him slinking away with a bunch of overstuffed plastic bags last week."

Tracy dropped the stack she was holding straight into the trash can. "So what's your plan for getting rid of the *Metro?* We never got into it at editors', as usual."

"What, assuming the douchebag manifesto doesn't bring the administration to its knees?"

"Call me crazy."

"I say ignore it. Ignore it, and it goes away."

"Really?" Tracy asked. "You don't believe that."

"I don't know," he said. "I mean, we've been talking about shit like this for years. Every new batch of editors pulls the same end-of-the-world routine."

"But this seems different. Don't you think? Usually the objects of our paranoia don't have websites and distribution vans."

"They're already set up at all the SkyTrain and bus stations coming up here."

"Exactly. They've got us surrounded."

Through the window, they watched an irate football player bat the door open with one hand and stomp straight back to the couches, where a crowd was slowly congealing; in his other hand he held a *Peak* as if he was choking it. "Either way," Alex said, "I'm out of here come the spring. If the *Metro*'s not on campus by then, all these new fuckers on staff will have run us into the ground anyway."

Tracy smiled, almost to herself. "People say that every year, too."

"It just seems like we don't *do* anything anymore," he said, hearing his tone grow indignant and not doing much to restrain himself. "Last week I was in the back, reading through the archives. Did you know that when 9/11 happened, *The Peak* was all over it? We ran a dozen news pieces the very next issue. The opinions section went nuts. We got hate mail, and all the Jewish groups boycotted us because they thought we didn't come down hard enough on Islam. Maybe we were totally wrong. I don't even know. But at least we had a stance, you know?

"Can you imagine how hard we'd shy away from something like that now?" Alex added. "Sometimes I really wish I could've been part of that era instead—instead of putting out garbage like this home brewing thing."

"Wasn't that your idea?" Tracy asked.

"Only kind of. But—well, maybe it was. Who cares? It's all part of the same slop. I feel like half of what I do now is sit around and make house ads where historical figures act like fratboys."

The noise from the meeting room was returning to a boil. Seats were being taken.

"I think you're just being an old man," Tracy said. "With any luck, this'll all run its course pretty soon."

"Oh yeah?" Alex said. "When Keith walked into the office last week and realized it was the anniversary, do you know what he did? He looked straight at me, giddy as a kindergartner, and said, 'You guys. I'm going to fly two pieces of cake into my mouth to celebrate.'"

"To be fair, that's pretty good."

Alex sighed. "Fuck. I know. That's the whole problem."

A timid knock behind them revealed an unusually nervous kid who appeared to be approximately twelve years old. "Hello," Alex said, eyeing the kid's outfit, which included thick eyeglasses and an alarming amount of official SFU merchandise. *He's no athlete. Too much school spirit? Or just a gift from mom?* "Can we help you?"

"Um, is this where the meeting is? The ad said 1:30."

Tracy and Alex glanced at each other: *a new volunteer.* This kind of thing needed to be handled delicately, since you never knew if they'd turn out to be good news or bad—an editor-in-training or a complete and utter timesuck.

It was Tracy who reacted first. "Absolutely," she said, with just the right amount of maternal warmth. He loosened up before their very eyes. "Come with me—you're right on time."

4

BIG LIPTON

Tracy lived on the top two floors of a character house off Commercial Drive, just past the point where it turned from charming locus for Italian immigrants, bohemian-leaning university students, and rowdy young parents pushing strollers past sunset, to something that resembled the post-apocalyptic: wide, empty streets and an expanse of splintered concrete punctuated by one modest community garden—which was located, for maximum metaphorical impact, in the shadow of a massive SkyTrain support pillar. She'd lived there since her parents' divorce in the mid-nineties, when, after it had all bubbled uglily to the surface, Tracy's newly single mother decided it was high time her thirteen-year-old daughter got to see a world beyond their smarmy, adulterous suburb. Now the deed to the Commercial house was in Tracy's name alone, and she lived there with her long-term boyfriend, Dave.

Indefinite sublet is the phrase her mom used, with a wink.

Most of the time it felt good to not have an asshole landlord to contend with. But as Tracy arrived home late that afternoon, jiggling the door handle and eventually shoulder-checking it open, she thought about how nice it would be to have someone to yell at about all her broken stuff. Cathartic, even.

Cathartic. Her mind drifted for a few blank seconds from Aristotle, to Plato, and then to the Raphael painting of them both, which was also her mental cheat sheet for telling them apart. In the picture, each wore a loose, colourful robe and stood at the top of an ornate staircase. One of them pointed up, signifying the heavens; the other held his hand out straight ahead, signifying the Earth, the here and now, all of the objects and people we're pretty sure we didn't just dream up. Kicking off her sneakers, some other part of Tracy's brain dutifully counted to fifteen as she climbed each squeaky wooden step.

"Dave?" she called, underhanding a purse full of books and cigarettes onto the coffee table. The TV had been left on, and a pear sat kebabed to the kitchen table by the larger of their two functioning knives. A small puddle of juice had spread out from under it and then half-dried in an amorphous, limb-like shape. "Dave? Are you here?"

A muffled yell came from the top of the staircase behind her: "I'm *steeping!*"

After a few seconds Dave came clumping down the attic stairs, bringing what sounded like a flock of medicine balls along with him. A cloud of thin smoke, or maybe thick steam, preceded him as he barreled around the corner into view. His lab coat, stained old-yellow and unbuttoned, flared out behind him. Underneath was a suit vest with a pocket watch chain poking out, and under that a T-shirt showcasing an orca whale mid-breach. He looked like a one-man matryoshka doll.

"I can barely hear you from up there, Trace. Did you yell at the corner?" he asked. "Did you? No. Because you never do." This last bit was muttered; he softly tapped a fist against the top of the doorframe. Dave had a theory that if you spoke directly at the corner of the ceiling where the hallway met the living room, the sound would splinter precisely, then travel like sonar to the rest of the house. He said he did this in the longshot case he started to lose his hearing prematurely, but the truth was that months of listening to nothing but My Bloody Valentine—on knockoff earbud headphones, cranked to their tinniest and most compressed—had already done the kind of aural damage that the recording industry would very much like to draw your attention away from.

Dave had a lot of theories. Tracy wondered if any of them had predicted that she'd come home that day to finally break the fuck up with him.

"Take that lab coat off, you idiot," she said. "We need to talk."

"I told you. I am working. Presently. In my lab."

"Oh, really."

"Yes. Today is chamomile. It's a bit of a madhouse up there at the moment, but some truly interesting specimens are emerging. Data that'll rock Big Lipton to its *foundations*." Dave was a fair-weather hobbyist who liked to skip around from obsession to obsession, and had lately been on a vague environmental kick. He'd hummed and hawed about it for weeks. Baby seals were too clichéd. Whales and the ozone layer were nineties problems; they didn't even make the short-list. He toyed, briefly, with space debris and the huge island of garbage forming in the Pacific. But in the end he settled on the unlikely target of the international tea industry, and had since become very serious about bleach in single-serving bags and something called spoiled fannings.

He sniffed theatrically as he sat down at the table next to the skewered pear. "Anyway, you wouldn't be interested."

Tracy bit her lip. She'd promised herself that she'd do it coolly, not rising to any of the usual bait.

Dave swirled his finger through the puddle of juice and popped it into his mouth. "Anyway, did you check out that link I sent you? The post from 8:29 last night. KISStronaught had his head so far up his ass, he was just asking to be taken down a few pegs. I mean, he had this attitude starting at the very top of the thread—you could see it building steam in little ways, just snowballing over the first few pages." Dave scowled in vivid recollection. "That guy's so smug. I think he's from Wisconsin. Anyway, by the time I got through with him, the post from 2:49 a.m., that was the big one, like five users had PMed me about it. They even came up with a nickname for me: The Mad Dog. Awesome, huh? I put it in my signature."

"No, Dave. I must've missed that one." Tracy was trying hard these days not to smoke within ten minutes of getting home. This was less to prove that she didn't need nicotine than that she didn't need it to deal with Dave.

She hadn't made it once in almost two weeks. "I did read the other things you sent, though," she added. "The—petitions."

"Good, good. Standard rules apply: if you don't sign them, I'm leaving you for someone younger."

And here was the real reason Tracy hadn't yet worked up the nerve to break up with Dave. From very early on in their relationship, they'd adopted a kind of banter based on the mock-premise that the joker was always on the verge of dumping the jokee. It came from an offhand comment made on their very first date, when Dave was so nervous about letting any kind of silence hang between them that he brusquely announced that if she didn't love the tiramisu at the café they were walking to, if it wasn't god-help-him perfect tiramisu, he'd never go out with her again. Tracy was caught off guard, and laughed so hard that she broke out into a coughing fit. The exchange quickly hardened into classic, go-to material as they went exclusive and then moved in together, to the point that their friends began describing other couples making similar comments as "Daventracifying," a nickname that shouldn't have caught on but somehow did.

The problem, of course, came when either or both of them actually were at wits' end, and the other couldn't tell if they were really having what, to all appearances, looked like a fight. Tracy was never 100 percent sure when Dave was genuinely threatening to move out, and Dave never knew for sure if Tracy was serious about catapulting his every last possession onto the train tracks. Should they go into full relationship-save mode, or keep the banter going?

Once Tracy had guessed wrong. It was a few months after Dave had moved in, and she broke down crying after he raised his voice to auctioneer levels and said there was no way he could reasonably be expected to live with someone who didn't appreciate the genius of shoegazer. She'd hugged his knees together, sobbing from a deep and vulnerable place inside her, and said she'd try to listen again, really she would, if it meant that much to him. Then she looked up, nose running, lenses fogged, and all he'd been able to do was meekly back away, embarrassed for both of them but still not sure how to make things right. He spent the next five days puttering around the corners of the house, eating marmalade from the jar and mutely rearranging his record collection. They hadn't mentioned it since.

Tracy looked across the table at Dave, who was picking shards of pear from around the knife and rattling off the subhuman conditions in which chamomile was grown and harvested, taking a long detour into the Nepalese workers' revolution he was helping to indirectly orchestrate with some of his buddies from the forum. Picturing all of the ensuing chaos she was about to set into motion—the crying, the fights, the is-this-really-a-fight fight, the divvying up of the furniture, the changing of passwords and locks—made her feel exhausted. Lately it just made more sense to ignore the problem and focus on the manageable stuff, like what to eat for dinner, or next week's readings. Neither of them was happy, she knew that. Dave's tea crusade kept him upstairs for more and more of the day, and when they were together he seemed to increasingly regard her as an irritant—not to mention an organics naysayer, vampirically trying to suck the passion from his cause. And to think, she'd been the one to first tell him about fair-trade coffee and the arctic seal hunt, all those years and commitments ago. It seemed a parallel universe from here.

On the other hand, for things to get any better—for either one of them—first they'd have to get much, much worse.

"Dave," she started, already feeling an entire night's worth of tears pressing against the dams of her eyelids. "You know I—"

"What?" He looked at her distractedly.

"You know I want only—only the best for y—"

"Come on, Tracy. Speak up already!" Ah, yes. The other side effect of Dave's cavalier music-listening habits was the occasional episode of tinnitus, which drowned out all other sounds completely, the way radio static swarms car speakers when you bump the dial. He tried to cover these attacks, even from Tracy, still, by pretending to be enthralled with some banal object—as he did now, picking up a ladle and studying it intently.

Tracy could already feel the adrenaline slowly subsiding, and something oddly resembling relief taking its place. Sometimes Dave was such a big, commanding personality, she thought. The kind of guy who charmed baristas, professors, and most small animals without even trying. The kind of guy who could instantly transform a dozen strangers into one rapt audience.

But sometimes he was just a sad, overgrown child, plugging his ears and waiting for the world to re-shape itself around his latest harebrained scheme.

She lit a cigarette—0 for 13 and counting—and plopped down in the chair opposite him. *Not today,* she thought. Then, because why not, she repeated it out loud. "Not today." Dave still didn't look up from the ladle. With each pull of her cigarette Tracy took extra relish in the cloud of tar that was no doubt whirlwinding through her lungs; she thought dark, sulking thoughts. Then, since she was apparently stuck with him for a little longer, she decided to announce a few more hidden grievances, the slow-burning kind that inevitably touch nerves and really aren't worth bringing up for the fight they'll set off. The kind of complaints that take years of gathering evidence to see the pattern.

"You never wash between the fork tines," she said, looking straight into the distracted whites of Dave's eyes. His hearing was still pure fuzz. "It grosses me right out. You can't walk down the sidewalk in a straight line. You ball your socks up weird."

Each tick of their kitchen clock pounded in the fall air. The only other sound for several minutes was the persistent glass tinkle of a hobo rummaging for bottles in the dumpster outside.

That evening they crawled into bed together and slept facing opposite walls. Meanwhile, their toothbrushes sat wet and foamy in the bathroom cabinet's stainless steel cup, kissing like vintage film stars.

5

WHAT COLOUR IS A SUNSET?

"Alex! Check this bitch out! It's like Pink Floyd records, right? Only they're painted on the backs of these naked chicks."

"Yeah."

"All in a line, like ten of them. Just hanging out. *Naked.*"

"This is me ignoring you."

"You can totally see their butts."

"I saw it, believe me. You don't have to take it down—"

Tyson went up on tiptoe, all five foot five of him strained toward the top row of display copies, each backed with a thin cardboard sheet and shrink-wrapped to preserve its shape. He shook the one he wanted free from the tiered contraption, brought it down, and held it out at chest height. "Look where their butts smoosh into the edge of the pool. That's the hottest shit in the world, right there. Imagine the guy whose job that is."

"Do you even like Pink Floyd?"

"Imagine what it'd be like to paint butts and tits all day." Tyson flipped the poster (item code: FLOYDPOOL-NUDE) back to face him and held it up appraisingly. He cooed. The poster dwarfed his upper body the same way broadsheet newspapers did old men. "Naked bitches needing planets drawn on them, 24/7, 9–5."

Alex looked back over each shoulder, streams of people swirling past the two of them as they made their way haltingly through the aisles. For two weeks every semester, a visiting poster company turned this corner of the AQ into a winding, synthetic corn maze. It was one of the highest areas of foot traffic on campus; accordingly, over the years it had become a ritual that everyone pay a visit to inspect the wares. "Name me one member of Pink Floyd. Name me one *song*."

"Painting butts, man." Tyson's face peeked out over the top of the poster. "Do you think he's a visual arts guy? Or just some lucky fuckface with a paint roller?"

The company had clearly done its research. Everything they sold was aimed like a homing missile at the modern dorm-room professional. Their periodic table of beers was a consistent big-ticket item; variant posters for suburban boy movies like *Fight Club* and *Reservoir Dogs* sold out early every single year. A young Bob Dylan tuning his bass nestled next to the bartender's guide to cocktails, complete with pictures (item code: BOOZEGUIDE-2). Anything featuring Paris in black and white was a good bet for women and film students. They had WWII-era watercolour propaganda. *Guernica*. Hunter S. Thompson. There was an entire subsection for Dalí at the back, near the windows.

"Tyson, man, focus," Alex said. "I'm coming to you as a friend here."

"Fuck the triangle right off her back, I'm telling you," Tyson mumbled, his eyes glassy. "I got something to put out that handshake guy on fire. Know what I mean? Aw, shit."

"Just answer me this."

"Wrong. The correct answer was My Dick."

"What was the last great thing you read in *The Peak*?"

Tyson's glance lingered on the poster as he considered the question. "Define *great*. Do you mean world-changing? As in, something worth recommending to another human, which you know I'd never do? I'll tell you this: I just read some really great bathroom graffiti. World-class stuff. Not one hour ago. On the hand dryer, where there's that picture of three wavy red lines to simulate hot air? Someone wrote 'bacon dispenser.' Genius. Or, even, what about that video of the guy falling out of the AQ hedge? That thing has, like, ten million hits. I mean, I read *The Peak* every week, but you guys have never come close to shit like that."

"So why do you still pick it up?"

"Because, dude. Because I'll always have a few minutes to kill between classes. Because I like scouting the comics and seeing if any hot girls were interviewed for *Peak* Speak. Because it's there."

"You don't look for breaking news. Or features that are, I don't know, in depth?"

"Fuck no." Tyson dropped the Pink Floyd poster against a bootleg print of Bart Simpson smoking a joint and kept walking. A group of girls gathered a few feet ahead of them. "Be honest with yourself," he said to Alex. "When was the last time *you* looked for any of that shit?"

The girls were looking at a print of Che Guevara's face against a dark blue background. All of them wore cardigans, expensive jeans with coloured stitching on the back pockets, and professionally worn-in caps that were meant to recreate the quaint old-world knitting techniques of their grandmothers. "I think I want this," one of them was saying, "but in green. Do they make it in green?"

One of her friends flipped her bangs out of her eyes and took a big sip of bubble tea. "Green, seriously? That's gnarly."

A third chimed in, "You mean gnarly as in good?"

"God, just drop it already, Melissa," said the bubble-tea girl, flipping her hair again. "I say orange."

"Yeah," the first agreed, "like a burnt, kind of . . . *almond*-y orange. You know? That would just kill it."

Alex took in this conversation as if he was breathing truck exhaust. Tyson followed his friend's line of sight. "Oh, nice. Funny story, actually. Which one do you like?"

"Jesus. None of them," Alex said. "They're trying to figure out which colour goes best with revolution. It's fucking embarrassing. You want to record that kind of bullshit and play it back for them, just so they can hear what the rest of us hear."

Newly engaged, Tyson waved his arms to get Alex's attention back. "See, that's exactly your problem," he said. "You're too worried about the words coming out of their mouths. You've gotta learn to get past that shit. It'll ruin you every time."

The bubble-tea girl looked over at Tyson with an extended, nervous glance, then drew her indecisive friend, who was wondering aloud what shade of orange a sunset is, around the corner toward a tangerine-ish print with "DANCE LIKE NOBODYS WATCHING" written overtop in loopy capitals. (That particular poster [item code: MOTIVATIONAL-DANCE] had been part of a series of blue-chip fixtures in the fridge-magnet and greeting-card industries for nearly a decade; this year marked its maiden voyage into the world of informal home decoration.)

"There are probably thirty girls in this whole school whose personality is a match with yours," Tyson continued. "And guess what? Twenty-nine of them are golems. The other one is already fucking her TA." He nodded at the girls as the last of them trailed out of sight. "Look at them. Probably what, nineteen years old? Psychology majors? They commute from somewhere an hour away, and have recently signed their first Greenpeace petition. Two of them have bumper stickers for the Dave Matthews Band."

Alex's nostrils flared involuntarily. Tyson pointed at them with a triumphant flourish.

"Exactly!" he said. "All of these are real possibilities, right?"

"*Too* real," Alex muttered.

"So just don't think about it, man. Block that shit out. You need to be a zen about sex. A blank slate. I mean, just look at her"—Tyson peeked through a gap in the display and pointed at the bubble-tea girl—"and see what your dick has to say about it. Imagine she's stripping for you, real slow-like: what's coming off first? Decide if you want to see, for instance, her butt smooshed into the edge of a pool. Most of the time you'll get an enthusiastic, jeans-straining yes." In one motion he turned his accusatory finger into a thumbs up, and continued holding it a few inches away from Alex's nose. "It's that simple.

"And besides," Tyson added, "you don't think they do it, too? Trust me: fewer chicks than you think are turned on by magic realism."

"Hey, José Saramago is *not* a magic realist," Alex said, with the pained expression of someone used to making his case to indifferent ears. "There's a difference, okay? He doesn't make people levitate. There aren't any magic potions. What he's actually doing—I think, anyway—is playing with logic, so things that might *seem* magical can happen once you start extrapolating." For the second time that week Alex felt his audience turning on him. "Plus he has a Nobel Prize and lives on top of a volcano. How're you going to tell me that's not awesome?"

Tyson looked at his watch. "It took you twenty seconds to get that out, and now look. They're fucking gone, dude. Presto. See how far that gets you? Now here's a story drawn straight from real life. Pay attention—it's got a moral."

Alex steeled himself. After four years in residence—the average was closer to two—Tyson had fine-tuned a handbook for promiscuity in close quarters that never failed to disgust and captivate. Alex couldn't even imagine having to walk down a rez hallway and see the same girl from the night before, now hungover and inquisitive in a baggy T-shirt and pajama bottoms. How could the two of you have a polite chat about dining hall hash browns when, mere hours earlier, you were licking her naked thighs and memorizing the way she bunched the sheets in her fists for future playback? Every conquest would just be one fewer girl Alex could ever conceivably speak to again, which put him pretty much back where he started: alone and pining.

"Can we get back to my real problem for a minute?" Alex said. "The *Metro* is going to put us out of business if I don't figure this out."

"Oh, Alex," Tyson said. He made the softly nagging *tsk tsk* sound in the most irritating way he knew how. "This *is* your real problem."

They continued their circuit through the poster grounds. All ironic tendencies aside, Alex was comforted by seeing stalwarts like James Dean and those two ladies tongue-kissing still in active rotation. This touring exhibit marked, in its own small way, a kind of mini-canonization of pop-culture ephemera. Sure, posters for new films and buzz bands came and went. But if your face was still recognizable enough for students to shell out six bucks to own a copy ten years after the fact, well, that meant something, didn't it? These minor gods would live on for as long as undergrads had a taste for coarse philosophies about life and death and comedies about unlikely bongs.

But Tyson's X-rated fable couldn't be silenced for long. This one turned out to be the rambling story of last week's Pub Night, where he allegedly convinced a lithe 2nd-year brunette to watch a meteor shower with him from the football field's fifty-yard line. They smuggled out bottles of Alexander Keith's in her purse, and, after fifteen minutes of innocently wondering where all the meteors were and if, just maybe, his astrologist had mixed up her dates again, Tyson made his move. By his count, they had sex four times (field, parking lot, bathroom, bunk), in all kinds of positions that sounded Rorschachian in their convoluted symmetry. He swore that when this girl had an orgasm, her whole body shook like a cell phone on vibrate.

Alex was never sure how much of this stuff was made up. It made him wonder what percentage of all the world's sex anecdotes were real—fifty percent? Forty? One detail he knew for sure was a lie: Tyson swore that after two of the four sessions he came all over the girl's tits. Impossible. No matter how good an idea it might seem in the heat of the moment, Alex knew nobody would take a stripe to the chest, mop themselves off with a Kleenex, then agree to act as bullseye again a few hours later. There was no way.

Tyson also threw around variations of the phrase "she loved it," but Alex wrote that off as par for the course for someone raised on pornography—the kind of person who mistakes a simple sexual courtesy for some throbbing, primal need.

"Anyway," Tyson said, drawing the story to its roundabout conclusion, "the point is that I wore my trick underwear that night. And pay attention here, because underwear is one of those things that you barely notice on the way off, but becomes hugely fucking important the next morning. So when this girl wakes up and looks over, the first thing she sees is my back—facing the wall is also crucial—and 'I LOVE TO FART' written in huge chunky letters across my ass." He spread his arms in victory. "Don't you get it? I'm in the clear for*ever*. Who would ever want to admit—"

"Point of information," Alex said.

"Ugh. What?"

"Where do you even find shit like that? Don't tell me custom order."

Tyson shrugged. "Vegas. Or those prize machines at Safeway, next to the gumballs."

The aisles around them were getting more and more crowded, so they decided their pilgrimage was just about complete. Tyson took a picture of the Pink Floyd poster with his phone, and on an urgent whim that he later couldn't identify, Alex bought a print of Norman Rockwell's *Gossip* (item code: ROCKWLEL-GOSSIP). Something about the closeness of the pairs of faces drew him to it—the way they all reveled in their small, shining moments as gatekeepers of knowledge, even though it was obvious the phrase they kept repeating had long been garbled beyond the point of utility.

On their way out, Alex and Tyson came face to face with the bubble-tea girl and her brunette friend. The friend had settled on a glossy portrait of NDP leader Jack Layton, his shiny head and arctic-white moustache framed by a starburst of the party's official shade of orange.

Alex wondered where the other girls in the entourage had disappeared to, and he couldn't suppress a quick smile as he pictured them dropping off like a space shuttle's booster rockets, spent and not missed.

Tyson and the bubble-tea girl made eye contact almost involuntarily. "Hi there," he said, grinning. "How're things? Cool. This is Alex. Have you guys met?"

"Hey," Alex said, lifting his poster bag in lieu of waving.

"Hi. I'm Christine." She smiled, and took another sip, which made a scraping sound as the tea ran out. "This is Maggie." Alex involuntarily imagined the two of them sitting naked on the lip of some exclusive hotel's pool. It really was uncanny—they both had legs that curved like highways.

Tyson gestured to Maggie. "What did you go with?"

"Oh, the NDP guy," she said. "You know, he's always serious, and he does karate chops when he talks. I've been looking for this shade of orange all week."

Maybe Tyson is right, Alex thought. *Maybe I should just go for it. I know I can be charming—if only I had some kind of in.*

As if on cue, Tyson turned to Alex. "Awesome. My buddy here got this one of all these people whispering."

"Oh," Maggie said, "do you like Rockwell?"

"Yeah, definitely," Alex said. "Totally." He was about to go on, but got hung up on one small point: why *had* he bought the print? The real answer was too long and complicated to say out loud. He hadn't even really processed it yet. And would anyone else understand? They'd probably just give one of those awful clipped, condescending laughs. No, small talk demanded something concise. Something witty. Equally concise and witty—and also self-deprecating. So he'd need one perfect sentence, split 33-33-33. How was he going to manage that?

Wait, how long had he been *thinking?* Say something!

"I like the, uh, colours," he said finally. "The . . . shadows. Plus the whole thing is like a grid? You know? It reminds me of math, or something."

Maggie nodded slowly, but spared him the eviscerating chuckle. "Right," she said. Tyson jumped in again, jabbing a thumb toward Alex and making some kind of throwaway joke to keep the conversation going. Alex's head was throbbing so hard he didn't hear a word of it.

He tried to draft a joke of his own that would win the girls back—something that would cast him as the affectionate goofball he knew he was, deep down—but gave up. It was all too much, too depressing. Any illusion that flirting was actually going on had already disappeared. He couldn't tell which of the girls Tyson was pursuing, and he didn't care. He didn't want a part in any of it. It was all so creepy and *obvious.*

Still. That Maggie was really something. Her eyes the same green as a Disney lagoon.

Just as Alex made his move to leave, Tyson smacked himself in the forehead, as if he'd just remembered something. "How rude of me," he said, clapping Christine on the shoulder, who winced. "Alex, this is the girl I was telling you about.

"You remember," he added, smiling brightly. "From the Pub? The meteor shower." Tyson leaned in a little toward her. "I fired my astrologer, by the way. Turns out those guys mostly do horoscopes."

SIMON FRASER STUDENT SOCIETY
CLUBS DAYS SIGN-UP SHEET—FINAL

- ☐ All the World's a Stage, Indeed!
- ☐ Altered Reality Club
- ☐ Anime Club
- ☐ Arab Students' Association
- ☐ Ballroom Dance Club
- ☐ Beard and M(o)ustache Fellowship
- ☐ Beer O'Clock
- ☐ Bhakti Yoga Club
- ☐ Breakfast for Dinner
- ☐ Breakfast for Dinner for Breakfast
- ☐ Burnaby Mountain Toastmasters
- ☐ B.C. Young Liberals
- ☐ Campus Crusade for Christ
- ☐ Canadianized Asian Club
- ☐ Cheerleading Club
- ☐ Cigarettes for Dinner
- ☐ CJSF 90.1 FM
- ☐ Debate Club (This Semester's Topic: the Death Penalty)
- ☐ Does Anyone Out There Remember Snap Bracelets?
- ☐ Dreadlock Fans and Owners
- ☐ Fair Vote SFU
- ☐ Falun Gong Club
- ☐ Filipino Student Association
- ☐ Finish Your Drink, There Are Thirsty Kids in Africa
- ☐ For Fuck's Sake They're Just Eggs—Eat Them Whenever You Want
- ☐ Free the Children
- ☐ General Purpose Club
- ☐ High Altitude Poetry
- ☐ Hiking Club (Formerly the Outdoor Club)
- ☐ Hindu Student Association
- ☐ Home Brew League
- ☐ "I Actually Don't Own a TV, So..."
- ☐ iAid
- ☐ iAIDS
- ☐ iBoner
- ☐ I'm OCD for 'Twilight'!
- ☐ International Club
- ☐ Jazz Band SFU
- ☐ 3K! (Korean Kampus for Khrist)
- ☐ Laura Lost Her Phone

- ☐ Legalize It—You Know What I'm Talkin' Bout
- ☐ Marxist Club
- ☐ Marxist/Leninist Club
- ☐ Marxist Mad Lib Club ("Workers Have Nothing to Lose But Their ___")
- ☐ MAWO-SFU
- ☐ The Metro Newspaper
- ☐ Muslim Students Association
- ☐ 'Mystery Men' Is an Underrated Film
- ☐ Nathan Sucks: The Club
- ☐ The New Outdoor Club
- ☐ Origami Club
- ☐ The Outdoors Club (Not Affiliated in Any Way with the New Outdoor Club)
- ☐ OXFAM-SFU
- ☐ The Peak Student Newspaper
- ☐ Petition for the Inclusion of Calamari on the Pub Menu
- ☐ Pirate Club
- ☐ Pork Chops for Dinner
- ☐ Psychogeographers
- ☐ Raisins, Stay the Eff Out of My Cookies
- ☐ The Real Orange County
- ☐ Reverse Psychology Students Union
- ☐ SFU Hillel
- ☐ SFU Pipe Band
- ☐ Shredderz (Ski and Snowboard Club)
- ☐ Simon Fraser Student Society
- ☐ STFU, Pipe Band
- ☐ Student-Palestine Solidarity Committee
- ☐ Students for a Brick-Based Renovation Coalition
- ☐ Tappa Tappa Kegga, SFU Chapter
- ☐ Thai Student Association
- ☐ UNICEF-SFU
- ☐ Unusual and Obsolete Audio/Video Club
- ☐ UVoice Bilingual Magazine
- ☐ Vegetarian Club
- ☐ Viewfinder Digital Photography
- ☐ When I Was Little I Thought Chocolate Milk Came from Brown Cows
- ☐ Will Whatever I Write Here Really Be My Club's Name Hello Send Click
- ☐ Zombie Militia

6

THOSE SQUIGGLES ARE WHAT WE CALL PUNCTUATION

The morning that opened Clubs Days was a standard Vancouver grey, with a sheet of speckled clouds that covered the city like a wetsuit. Rain was implied and assumed. This was layered sweater weather—the beginning of scarf season.

At 10:00 a.m. sharp, Chip showed up to take the first shift manning *The Peak*'s table. Foot traffic was still light this early in the morning, so, armed with pushpins and a roll of duct tape, he took his time laying out a collection of old covers, a dozen or so copies of the current issue, and two blank sheets of paper for any potential new sign-ups. Chip got right down onto his haunches to make sure the latter were exactly parallel. The standalone corkboard behind the table remained empty, because the editors still hadn't gotten around to making or ordering a proper sign. Satisfied with his efforts, Chip smoothed the edges of his moustache, adjusted his suspenders, and surveyed the territory around him.

Clubs Days took place every autumn in the vast open-air expanse of Convocation Mall, with SFU's many student-run organizations arranged in a grid for maximum interaction potential. And once the students got buoyed by the presence of their fellow club members, it actually, miraculously, seemed to kind of work. The boost to the general on-campus mood was undeniable, at least for these few days—a small glowing pulse in the heart of a concrete robot. Obviously the members themselves were the most easily swayed, hugging and cackling and generally carrying on like it was ComicCon all over again, but the mood was so earnest, and so rare, that even the most solipsistic passersby were drawn into the public fray. People who usually pretended they didn't speak English found themselves giving out their email addresses for future updates; many a hot dog was eaten with a prefatory shrug and a "What the heck?"

(This was the mood, by the way, that the administration spent the rest of the year desperately trying to replicate, as everyone returned to their well-defined little routines and a stony silence blanketed the school once more. The advertising campaign had yet to be devised that could rebrand the school as anything but a commuter campus—the term was watermarked into every square foot. SFU: Closed Weekends Since 1965.)

As people wandered past his booth, Chip could make out only brief snippets of their conversations.

"I think about the death penalty every day, so—"

"—lobsters wearing lobster bibs—"

"—told that guy to go fuck himself right off."

Each one drew the same jolly chuckle from him. Chip couldn't get enough of the swarm of crowds like this—it was why he volunteered for the early slot every year—and manning a booth at Clubs Days also gave him the opportunity to indulge his inner salesman. This despite *The Peak*'s ever-fluctuating reputation on campus, as well as its lack of interest in improving said reputation, which didn't make them the easiest sell to the student populace. Chip wasn't the least bit fazed. In another lifetime, he'd have spent his entire working life wandering door to door, cutting tin cans in half with specialty knives and gobbling up slices of homemade pie. But you can't choose your generation.

"You there," he called to one passing duo. "Could I interest you in joining your venerable student newspaper?"

"—it all depends on how you define *think*. Ontologically speaking."

"Excuse me," he called to another group, "what would you say if I told you—"

"—already Talk Like a Pirate Day? Oh no! I left my hat at home."

One guy wearing headphones eventually stopped long enough to glance at the spread of old covers on the tabletop.

"Welcome!" Chip said, thrashing his hand from side to side in a violent-looking wave. "On behalf of *The Peak,* I'd like to wish you a hello and good morning."

The guy lifted one headphone up and said, "What the fuck is *The Peak?*" Before Chip had a chance to respond, the headphone snapped back down and he was gone. Chip checked to see that the sign-up sheets were still parallel.

On the whole, the morning was slow. Live music wasn't set to start until the afternoon, and most of the booths offering free food were still trying to assemble their grills. By the time Alex showed up, in a sour mood, after lunch, Chip had amassed just seven signatures on the first sheet of paper—and "buttz," "FREE PANCAKES" (twice), and "FREE PARIS HILTON" were not considered valid answers to the question "What Section Are You Interested In Contributing To?" On the other sheet, Chip had drawn an elaborate but wildly out of scale re-enactment of Lawrence of Arabia's railway raids.

"Good afternoon!" he said to Alex.

"Yeah, we'll see."

Alex settled into the other chair and looked at the table next door. It sat ominously empty, with nothing but a placeholder "METRO NEWS" sign on top. Alex placed a bottle of glowing pomegranate soda in front of him, then settled into chewing his lip, arms wrapped around his stomach in an awkward self-hug.

The student society made a point of putting similar groups in clusters, which sounded like a good idea until you spent two minutes in the middle of a shouting match between the B.C. Young Liberals and the various Marxist clubs that lobbed verbal grenade-insults like "Alienation!" and "Carbon tax!" at each other. They also argued over who should be allowed to wear red. And that was nothing compared to the fistfights that broke out between The New Outdoor Club and its bitter offshoot, The Outdoors Club (Not Affiliated in Any Way with the New Outdoor Club). *The Peak* was usually sandwiched between a prim girl with unbearably good posture from *UVoice* and the goofballs at High Altitude Poetry, but this semester *UVoice* had been moved two rows back, nearer to the Canadianized Asian Club and 3K! (Korean Kampus for Khrist).

Replacing her, allegedly, was the *Metro*.

Except so far they hadn't shown.

For the past few days there'd been whispers around the *Peak* offices about a fleet of trucks about to start smuggling green metal newspaper boxes up Burnaby Mountain in the dead of night. Or a viral text message campaign that was on the verge of launching. Even a confetti cannon, flown in specially for the occasion. But now? Nothing.

Alex's inner skeptic took little solace in these wild-eyed theories. On the other hand, surely even a junk paper like the *Metro* would have the wherewithal to show up on time to its own unveiling. Lord knew those distribution ghouls rose with the sun. So yeah, maybe the whole thing was a false alarm after all—another of those overly camouflaged performance art pieces by some amateur culture-jammer. Or maybe Keith set it all up, just to be a dick.

A freckled kid walked past *The Peak*'s table, wearing a flannel shirt and jeans so tight that he moved like an action figure. He winked at Alex as he went by, and gave him a thumbs up that he tried to disguise by cupping his other hand around it like a parenthesis. Poking out of the giant camping bag on his back was the unmistakable head of a boom mic, which he'd awkwardly tried to conceal with the help of an ill-fitting floral lampshade.

"Look at that fucking guy," Alex muttered, as the kid tottered away into the crowd. "That's the worst disguise I've ever seen."

Chip looked up from his drawing. "Who?"

"Him." Alex motioned again. "I forget his name. With the microphone on his bag."

"I don't see any microphone. Where is he? Behind the chap with the lamp?"

"Oh, come on, what is his *name?*" Alex irritably drummed his fingers on the table.

Clubs Days was a cornerstone of *The Peak*'s news beat, always reliable for a photo essay and soft cover story, but Rachel considered it far beneath her talents. So it always fell onto the associate news editor's plate instead. Technically the two positions were supposed to work in tandem, but Rachel always cleared up that misunderstanding right away; news, so long as she was running it, would be a meritocracy. And she was the best. (She was also the sole judge.) This guy with the lampshade-microphone was the latest model in the associate news factory line, and just a few weeks into his first semester on the job.

Currently the associate news rookie was wearing his Average Student disguise, which he probably hoped would lead to getting real, hard quotes without the biases that come with tedious red tape like full disclosure.

Alex watched him approach the High Altitude Poetry table, where three thinly bearded guys sat at typewriters. They took suggestions from the crowd and each wrote one line, in character, before passing it on down the line; this year featured a scruffy Beat poet, a Gold Rush–era prospector, and a talking inukshuk.

"So, fellow students," the associate news editor announced, lowering his reedy voice a full octave, "how's the turnout this year? Looks to me like it's been fairly average thus far." He pressed his way right up to the front, the lampshade rocking dangerously back and forth above. "And you, poets? Any thoughts regarding the state of poetry in the world today? How's the decline? Steep as ever, am I right?" He broke out a rehearsed laugh, all shoulders and teeth.

Meanwhile, a girl in a polka-dot blouse was eyeing *The Peak*'s table from across the aisle. She slowly approached, eyes glued to the sign-up sheets.

"Hello there!" Chip bellowed.

No stranger to the protocol of Clubs Days, the girl didn't meet his gaze right away. "So this is the newspaper, right?" She ran a finger along a turned-up corner of the latest issue.

"Right you are, m'lady. Right you are." Chip rested his hands on top of his stomach. His stare was as direct and unnerving as ever, though she didn't know that yet. "Are you a reader? Dare I say, a *fan?*"

She shrugged. "Sure. I mean, I read it every week."

"Every week! Ho! Did you hear that? Looks like we've got a *fan* on our hands." Chip slapped Alex on the forearm, but he was busy watching the rookie news editor try to drum up a quote from the talking inukshuk. "Well," Chip continued, "feel free to peruse our catalogue, as it were. One thing's for sure: the price is right. Though if you really are a fan, as you claim to be, you'll no doubt have seen these particular editions already."

Getting people to sign up for *The Peak*'s mailing list was an intricate courting process. Maybe it was easier for other groups because their demographics were so clearly defined. Religious and ethnic clubs all knew exactly what questions to ask potential members, and their ranks remained as healthy as ever. You stuck to your bases, and you didn't campaign where you weren't wanted. Does

Anyone Out There Remember Snap Bracelets? didn't waste time chatting up those who did not remember snap bracelets.

But what could *The Peak* say to win anyone over? Pardon me, but do you have a strong opinion re: democratic checks and balances? How about the news as written by twenty-year-olds, at a school that doesn't offer a single journalism course?

Okay, how about irony? How about *lots* of it?

Chip said, "Our latest edition is, naturally, the one on top of our little display here."

"Yep."

"You are currently looking at a copy of it."

The girl sighed. "Got it."

Chip picked up his own copy and opened it to the table of contents. "A fine issue, if I do say so myself. Featured this week are"—his eyes flitting down the page—"a news story regarding ongoing delays to the construction at the upper bus loop, a feature on popular myths about triceratops, a movie review for some festival . . . something, and the debut column from a Mr. S. Puzzle." He looked at Alex. "Is that last one right?"

"Mmhm," the girl said, doing her best to sound distracted. "Just trying to read this."

Alex was still scowling at the undercover rookie, so Chip turned back to her and drummed on the table for a few seconds. He whistled something to himself. Then he asked, "What story are you reading right now?"

"Nothing," she snapped. "I'm having a little trouble focusing, y'know?"

"Of course, of course. My apologies. Browse away."

Another few seconds passed. The rookie could now be heard trying to covertly interview a group of students at the Muslim Students Association table.

"I'm Chip, by the way. Sports editor comma the. Present and accounted for. Chip."

"Oh, never mind," the girl said, as if she'd tried to do someone a favour but just couldn't see it through. She finally looked up, and when she saw the intensity of Chip's eye contact she actually stumbled backward before fleeing the scene.

"I'm always in need of volunteers," Chip called after her. "Do you want to cover the football game tomorrow?" She picked up the pace. "Five hundred words! I can get you in for free! And this here is Alex! He does *features!*" Finally, he gave in. "Shoot. Off the post and wide. Thought I had a sale there."

"So what you're saying," the rookie was repeating in the distance, "is that you're here to promote the interests of Muslim students on campus." He gingerly slid a pencil out from his sleeve.

Someone rushed over to *The Peak*'s table, checking and rechecking the time on his cell phone and asking if he was too late for the free pancakes.

Overhead the clouds held their threat, but after an uncertain few hours, it was starting to look more and more like a bluff.

Alex became vaguely aware that Chip was trying to get his attention again.

"What is it?" he asked.

"I say, isn't the *Metro* meant to be at that table, portside?"

"Indeed they are," Alex replied. Chip seemed to be eyeing it with even more intensity than usual, and Alex was about to turn around to see for himself when he stopped in disbelief. *Did he just say* portside? In the year they'd worked together, Alex was still no closer to figuring out what made Chip tick. He was a type, no doubt about it, but not one of the usual ones—no Cardigan-Wearing White Kid Who Only Listens To Booty Rap, or Activist Who Wants To Keep Reminding You How Shitty George W. Bush Is, or Belligerent Vegan. Chip's particular quirks were as follows: speaking in a jumble of war and sports jargon, and dressing like a younger version of Rich Uncle Pennybags. Today his shirt was already ringed with sweat, despite the temperature, and his hair and the swoops of his moustache were more slicked than usual. Could a person be so completely out of touch? Not anti-fashionable so much as a-fashionable. Chip would get a free ride through university, Alex figured, where eccentricities like these were encouraged, incubated, even subsidized. But if he wasn't a millionaire within a couple years of graduation, some street toughs would pummel him to bits, looking for where he stashed his time machine.

"I say," he said softly, still looking in the *Metro*'s direction, "I don't like the looks of it."

Alex found this concern reassuring. He still wasn't sure anyone else on staff had given serious thought to what the *Metro*'s presence on campus would mean. The lost revenue, not to mention the lost readers, who were fickle and easily courted to start with. Alex had been around long enough to remember, not so many years ago, when *The Peak* really was broke, in fact near total collapse—though that time, like every other time, the damage had been largely self-inflicted. Last time it had taken Rick, at the time a savvy business grad student, nearly an entire year to shake them alert.

Just then two guys came up and slammed their fists on the table. Chip's pen skittered onto the floor.

"Why didn't you print my article?" one asked in a low growl.

"You'll have to be more specific," Alex said. "What section was this for?"

"Opinions. Last week."

"Well, the opinions editor isn't here right now, so I couldn't really—"

"It was about the bus," he said. "Ten things that piss me off about people on the bus. Number one: take off your fucking backpacks."

Alex already knew the story, if not this guy's version of it. At least once a year someone wrote one of these straight-shooting litanies of complaints. They almost always began, "OK," and petered off somewhere around item seven. Engaging with these kinds of dilettantes was Alex's biggest source of dread around Clubs Days, where he always felt like an open target. Having a difficult-to-find underground office had its perks.

"Again, I can't speak for the editor," he said, "but from what I heard you had some problems with our edits—specifically, the fact that we would be making some."

The guy and his friend banged their fists again in response. It was meant to be done in tandem, but the friend was a half-second too late. They exchanged a quick look. "I wrote what I wrote," the first guy said, "and that's it. You put in anything else, one new word or squiggle, it ain't mine anymore."

Those squiggles are what we in the industry call punctuation, Alex thought. Then he thought, *Don't say* industry. "Well, we do have rules concerning those squiggles."

"That's his style," the friend said, backing him up like a jittery hype man. "It's his voice. Tryin' to make everyone fit into the same *box,* man."

"You don't believe in commas?"

"Commas ain't me," the guy said. "It's bourgeois. 'Pause here,' or whatever. Don't tell me where I'm supposed to pause, okay? Do not do it."

They high-fived.

Alex sighed. These guys were so blatantly testing out their newly sprouted Marxist ideas, seeing how all that ideology squared with the world beyond their classroom. Clubs Days was, if nothing else, a particularly fertile petri dish. "I'd also recommend that in the future you not send in the piece as a PDF," he added.

"Number two: people on cell phones can go eat shit."

"You're really going to have to take this up with the editor."

"Not good enough," the guy said, shaking his head like a wet dog. "Promise me."

"Promise you what?"

"That it'll run next week."

"Like I said—"

"On the cover."

Jesus. "Are you serious?"

"You owe me. It's my right."

"Wow."

"To be heard. Freedom of expression. All that."

"Yeah," said the friend, his eyes bugging out a little. "That's democracy, bro. Ever heard of it?"

"I thought you guys said you were Marxists."

Both of them flinched. "We're *Leninists.*"

Alex unfolded his hands and threw off his slouch. "Let me get this straight. You think it's your constitutional right to have your every half-baked thought on the cover of a newspaper? You think that qualifies as a public service? Remind me again, what was the one near the end—about the elderly?"

"Old people smell weird. Number eight."

"Ah yes." On days like this, graduation couldn't come soon enough.

"Okay," the guy said, "listen up." He hesitated, then leaned in conspiratorially. "Honestly? You seem like an alright guy. I got no beef with you. You're part of a capitalist machine, and your little newsletter here is a bag of hairy balls, but whatever. Just give me one of these pancakes I'm hearing so much about and you and me will be cool."

Alex did a full circle sweep of the Clubs Days grounds. "Who the fuck keeps saying that? We don't have any pancakes."

It was then that Alex realized the *Metro*'s table was no longer empty. A large green balloon now sat on top of it, being slowly inflated by an automatic air pump. It looked vaguely human, but so far only the torso had taken shape. On the floor in front of it were four stacks of that day's *Metro,* evenly spaced and all exactly square to one another. They'd appeared so swiftly and precisely it was as if they'd been air-dropped by a fleet of drone pamphleteers.

Alex walked over to the table and knelt down by the stacks. "My god," he said, putting a hand out. "They're still warm."

A piece of paper was affixed to the front of the table. Most of it was taken up by the *Metro* logo, a 3D rendering of a globe in forest green. Underneath that, though, was a timer. *Oh, shit,* Alex thought. It wasn't paper at all, but an ultra-thin LCD monitor. The timer was counting down to a date just under a week away. Next Monday morning. Their launch.

"Chip," Alex yelled, jumping back to his feet.

The sports editor sauntered over. "Yes?"

"What do you mean, 'yes'?" Alex said. "It's *this*. They're here."

"That's an affirmative."

"I can't believe this is really happening. They're really here. This is a thing now."

"Indeed. I must say," Chip added, "you seemed awfully calm about it before."

"What?"

"When I told you earlier. You hardly blinked."

"You—are you serious? How long have you known this was here?"

"Mmm. Maybe five minutes? It was back at the table. You were watching that lad with the lampshade. But I understand: cool under fire. Not letting them see you sweat. A noble quality, really."

Alex stood up and took another quick survey. He was looking for aprons, newspaper boxes, anything in that telltale shade of green—

even the monotone catchphrase: "Free *Metro.*" There were too many people around to get any clear sightlines. A general smell of popcorn and sickly sweet carnival snacks filled his nostrils. Too much noise in general. Too much motion. Between the speakers being set up on the mainstage and the crashes of amateur outdoorsmen brawling and flipping tables over in the row behind him, he couldn't focus on anything.

The talking inukshuk said, "Inukshuk."

Chip was still talking, but Alex steamrolled over him. "Did you see someone setting this up?"

The sports editor chuckled. When his stomach shook you could hear the sound of coins rattling from some unknown pocket. "I dare say, this kind of thing doesn't set up of its own volition, now does it?"

"So you did see someone."

"Affirmative."

"Where did they go?"

Then he saw it. A 1st-year approaching from the Rotunda held a copy out in front of her, its pages open and flapping in the breeze as she read. Then, across the mall, two girls with ponytails were smoking and doing the Sudoku. *That fucking Sudoku,* Alex thought. All of a sudden, rolled-up copies started poking out of back pockets all over the place, each with a green globe blazing menacingly from the top of the cover, perched there like the eye of Sauron.

Alex saw green spots everywhere. It swept over him like a sickness. He had to sit down.

Taking cover underneath his own table, Alex propped up his knees and rested his face between them. His stomach muttered expletives; his head swam. *No. This isn't my problem,* he kept telling himself. *I won't even be here in six months. This is happening to someone else. Not me.*

The next bits happened in a greasy blur. A big portable stove being wheeled over and propped into place. A string of track jackets being unzipped all at once. Chip briefly crouching by his side, one arm pulling Alex into the slickness of his damp armpit, singing a verse of "For He's a Jolly Good Fellow." The clang of a hundred cast-iron frying pans. A lost, stuttering voice asking if anyone remembered him from last week's meeting. Sizzling dough. Syrup.

Alex did his best not to projectile vomit his glow-in-the-dark pop into his own lap. He got uneasily back to his feet, and came face to face with someone dressed in jeans and a pristine *Metro*-green windbreaker. The man looked barely older than Alex, and grinned with teeth that were just off-white enough to assure you they were natural. He pulled a megaphone up to his mouth and flicked it on.

Almost immediately his speech attracted a crowd of people five rows deep. Alex watched in horror as the stacks of free copies were hoisted onto the table by volunteers in head-to-toe forest green, disappearing in minutes flat. The crowd also took in the gleaming, whirring contraption that was spitting pancake batter onto frying pans a few dozen servings at a time. The sizzle alone functioned like a tractor beam.

With a final hiss of air, the balloon snapped to full attention, revealing itself as a bulbous replica of Rodin's *Thinker*—only with a *Metro* showily inserted into its left hand.

Breathing shallowly to keep his nausea at bay, Alex shoved his way through the pancake free-for-all that ran directly in front of *The Peak*'s table. Chip and now Tracy were sitting there, quietly taking in the whole thing; next to them gaped the awkward guy in SFU gear from last week's collective meeting. He was back to officially sign up for something, but now the pen was frozen in his hand. Behind his glasses he looked just about ready to cry. Alex knew the feeling.

7

THE WORST THING EVER

Alex stood on a concrete pathway near the SFU residence buildings, shivering through the fog. Classes had just let out, and students streamed past in both directions. *Look at me,* he thought, fiddling with his notebook. *Out in the field. Just like a real reporter.* Ten minutes later, when the crowd had thinned to a stream and then a trickle, he panicked and finally worked up the nerve to flag down a student and explain what he was working on.

"Oh yeah, I know that guy," she said, pointing drowsily over her shoulder. Alex found her strangely unimpressed by his press credentials. "I think he's from Shell. Their front door's busted, so if you pull super hard it'll probably just snap open. You didn't hear it from me."

"Tracy!" Keith yelled out. "Help me."

The copy editor stuck her head through the window separating the two rooms. "What?"

"I'm making a list. I need you."

Tracy walked around to his side, her energy already flagging, and pressed her teeth into one of the caramels she kept stashed in her desk. "What is it?"

"Since that guy said my section was the worst thing ever last week, I'm making a list in response called The Worst Thing Ever."

"And you want to know if it's libelous."

"No. I need your help making it. You're the only funny chick in this office." Keith said this last part unnecessarily loud, spinning around as he did so to face the room. There were a few half-hearted boos; a shoe bounced off the back of his chair, launched from parts unknown. Nobody looked up from their computers, so he spun back. Tracy noticed he was wearing the film crew hat she'd been given as payola—even though she'd never actually given it to him, only left it unguarded on a table for a couple of hours. "Why do you always think it's libel?" he added.

"Because literally every time it is libel. Though this sounds pretty okay."

"The subtitle is Fuck You Adrian Jones."

"Of course it is."

"Can subtitles have subtitles?"

"No."

"Oh."

By every available metric, Clubs Days had been a resounding success. It was the talk of the campus, insofar as anything that actually happened on campus could be considered the talk of the campus—and the most buzzed-about part was the triumphant unveiling of the *Metro*. A couple of irate phone calls from Rachel to the administration confirmed that the daily's permit to distribute on campus had finally been approved, effective the following Monday. Only then did the first real wave of chilly comprehension hit the editors: several of their fears were about to materialize. Mainly unemployment. A wave of malaise swept over the office, followed by the darkly comic installation of a big calendar in the production room with the days leading up to the launch Xed out with Sharpie, one by one. It became known as Bizarro Christmas, the day when a magical stranger would show up and take all of their toys away from them.

Worse still from a PR perspective was that the defining image of the week's activities—the year before, for instance, being the spectacle of the vice-president of Viewfinder Digital Photography accidentally setting his track pants on fire—was Chip, whose indignation had been eventually trumped by his hunger, and who had devoured an entire stack of pancakes, each emblazoned with a 3D globe grill mark. When a photographer in a green jacket asked him to pose for a picture, Chip gave the camera a big, dumb thumbs-up.

The image ran on the cover of thousands of *Metro*s across Greater Vancouver the next day. And in an unmistakable act of turf-war provocation, the caption underneath identified Chip as sports editor of "student newsletter *The Peek*."

When she first saw it, Tracy ripped the cover off and stuck it to the office wall for motivation, right next to the calendar. Several rusty darts held the page crookedly in place.

"What do you have so far?" Tracy asked.

"It starts out normal," Keith said, pointing at the screen. "Hitler. Stalin. Super Cancer. Stalin with a Hitler Moustache."

"Nice."

"Hitler if He Could Shoot Cancer Out of His Fingers. Cake that Is Part Chocolate, Part Poo. A Machine that Scalps Orphans. Stalin Sitting on Hitler's Shoulders, Wearing a Big Overcoat that Makes Them Look Like One Really Tall Person." He looked up at her. "That's it so far."

Tracy was silent for a few seconds, processing. "Pretty good," she decided, turning to leave. "But it already seems kind of long, no?"

Keith's voice shot up again. "I know, I know. But, hey—how's the descent into weirdness? I feel like it's maybe too fast." Tracy turned on her heels and slowly came back. This constant need for attention and approval was a tiny bit endearing, she had to admit. Keith and Tracy's office relationship had begun as a standard copy/humour editor dynamic—a continuous battle of envelope pushing and pulling, with the occasional veto mixed in—but had, somewhere along the way, slowly morphed into actual brainstorming sessions. Once she'd gained his trust, Tracy realized that Keith's boundaries were all or nothing, pretty well across the board: you were either his enemy, or his very best friend. Something was the best thing ever, or it was the worst thing ever. How she'd managed to make the jump, she still had no idea.

"Okay," she said. "So the joke is that people in arguments always jump to Hitler comparisons?"

Steve spoke up from the cluster of computers behind Keith. "I like to call it the law of the internet," the opinions editor said. "Give any online discussion long enough and people will start calling each other fascists."

Tracy chewed her caramel with care, making a *thhuck* sound on every upstroke. A group of editors at the next table were busy teaching themselves to build a house of cards with the help of a Russian YouTube tutorial. The production editor was trying in vain to remember the name of a brand of discontinued chewing gum she'd liked as a kid. This theory of Steve's had a name, Tracy thought. Godwin's Law. She knew this, and Steve knew this, and Steve knew that she knew this. But she didn't correct him out loud, because what would be the point? The whole office already knew Steve was a plagiarist. His letters page was a mosaic of repurposed letters from old issues of *Time, Chatelaine,* and *Owl*—anything you could find lying around a dentist's office, Tracy thought. All of his contributors' names were made up, too.

She kept her back turned to Steve, and instead leaned in to give Keith's computer her renewed attention. "We could do a reversal," she said. "After the moustache one, could it go Hitler with a Stalin Arm?"

"Hm. Maybe."

"For symmetry." She paused. "Or maybe Two Stalin Arms. I don't know. Is that funnier?"

Keith's face grew solemn as he mulled this new possibility. Eventually he shook his head. "But then he'd just look like a T-rex."

"You sure you aren't with security? Because I have, like, *a hundred* bongs on me right now."

"Just let me in, please," Alex said, his neck craned up at Shell's second-floor balconies, waving his newly purchased notepad like a white flag. "The door won't open."

"No lie: this bottle of Snapple I'm holding? Bong. This bunch of grapes? *Tiny bongs.*"

Alex looked around for someone else to help, but the courtyard was empty. Students were either inside or gone home for the weekend. The weak sun was wandering low on the horizon. Fuck. Had he left it too late? Alex glanced up irritably and muttered, "That bottle is half full."

The guy scratched his chin, bleary-eyed. "You're tellin' me." He took a long drink and slapped his knee. "Oh man. Do you remember Fruitopia?"

"Or maybe another mundane one in the middle," Tracy said. "Bad Christopher Walken Impressions. A Vinegar iv Drip. Ten Thousand Spoons When All You Need Is a Knife."

"Fuck off," said Keith. "You will not stand there and try to feed me Alanis Morissette references. Got it? Not in this post-9/11 world."

"Yeah, yeah."

"Post-Obama world."

The editors had agreed at that week's meeting that they had to fight back immediately, but it was now approaching dinner time on production night and only Alex had come forward with anything resembling a plan. Even he'd admitted to Tracy that it was a long shot.

At the beginning of the semester, a YouTube clip had started circulating that showed a guy stumbling through a garden at night. He looks around, in that exaggerated way attempted only by drunks trying to appear sober, then climbs up some kind of tall, leafy tree. The camera awkwardly climbs with him. Near the top there's a brief pause as he takes in the view, then an ominous crack, and then the guy tumbles wildly back to the ground, pinballing off branches and foliage like a pre-industrial Charlie Chaplin. Just as he hits the ground, flopping to a halt somewhere out of the frame, you hear him groan, "Agh, my nards." The camera pans back, revealing what is now clearly the rectangular hedge, landscaped hill, and general quasi-symbolic clutter of Simon Fraser's own AQ Garden. End of video.

The theory went that this garden, one of the centrepieces of the campus, had been designed to represent all of Canada in miniature—but, apparently, only after having its parts shaken up and redistributed like flakes in a snowglobe. The artificial hill in one corner stood for the Rocky Mountains. The scummy pond, split in two by a jagged concrete walkway, was both the Pacific and Atlantic Oceans, which made the little rock island on one side Newfoundland. Any vaguely flat section could be considered the prairies. In another corner, facing the Rockies, sat the skeletal outline of a tall, blue metal pyramid that was quarantined by a thick hedge; this, everyone agreed, was Quebec. The statue of Terry Fox stood for the person of Terry Fox, standing as he did at the eastern edge of the whole thing, just about to launch into his heroic cross-country run—though to believe this part of the theory you'd have to ignore the fact that both his starting and finishing point were inconveniently located in the same place.

As for the rest of the gardens—the reflective egg statue, the little valley-ish thing beside the Rockies—well, even the theory's staunchest defenders had to admit it was gibberish. But the garden was distinctive nonetheless, cluttered and ornate like a billionaire's yard sale. Anyone who'd ever been to SFU recognized it in the video right away.

For some reason, the hedge video tickled the internet in just the right way and went viral, linked to by blogs and predatory infotainment sites the world over. There were now parodies of it, as well as video responses, at least two unauthorized T-shirts, backlash, backlash to the backlash, and a contest sponsored by some middle-tier late-night talk-show host. When Alex pitched his idea to the other editors, the video had thirteen million views and counting.

His plan was to take on the guise of an old-fashioned, beat-walking journalist, the kind Alex revered from *The Peak*'s glory days, and track down the makers of this video. Thereby giving the final chapter of his university career at least the beginnings of a sense of purpose, and at the same time maybe helping save this newspaper he felt such a weird kinship with. As he wandered the Shell halls, trying doors at random and scouting for anyone resembling an authority figure or security guard, he felt privately gassed-up and energized by the whole thing. His fear of talking to strangers was no match for the prospect that he might come back with a real story—one that an average student might actually be interested in reading. For the first time he'd be able to use the word *scoop* unironically.

And he knew he didn't have long. The video had been posted three weeks ago—a digital ice age. A more typical lifespan for one of these things was roughly an afternoon, after which it would quietly disappear back into the ether of zeros and ones. All kinds of mini-genres for these videos had crystallized—the cute overload, the epic fail (Macbeth's vaulting ambition for the twenty-first century)—and already, fresh territory was scarce. People had *standards* all of a sudden. Now they demanded topicality, substance, and production value for their three minutes of leisure time. Even if Alex broke the story wide open, there was a very real chance that nobody would give a shit about it come Monday, *Metro* or no.

"Will Darfur make an appearance?" Tracy asked. The university government—the Simon Fraser Student Society—had recently launched a massive and omnipresent Save the Children of Sudan fundraising effort; as such, it was frequently on the editors' minds when they needed a boundary of good taste to cross. "I feel like Darfur should make an appearance."

"Definitely," Keith said. "Just Darfur would be funny."

"What about Darfur Shoplifting from an Organic Market?"

"Red Skull, Newly Elected President of Darfur."

"You mean the comic book villain?"

"I guess so," said Keith. "Or whoever. Someone really bad."

"Darfur's National Anthem, as Played by Chad Kroeger."

"Mm."

"As Sung by Bobcat Goldthwait."

"Hnm." Keith thought for another second. "Darfur Beating the Harlem Globetrotters."

Tracy nodded. "With a No-Look Shot from Half Court?"

"At the Buzzer."

"On Make-a-Wish Night."

"While Your Face Is on the Jumbotron, Crying."

"Because You Had Twenty Bucks on the Globetrotters."

"Plus You Have AIDS."

She laughed in spite of herself. "Classy."

"This is stupid," Keith said.

"Yeah, kind of."

The Peak's production-room phone rang, and Keith made a quick dive for it, knocking over the latest iteration of the house of cards and making the group of junior editors throw up their hands in quick but muted frustration. The production editor, who sat right next to the phone, got there first. It was Alex, she announced, and relayed a few details. "Says he's on the right floor—uh-huh. Okay. And he's getting close. Yeah. Is that it?" She hung up the phone uninterestedly and went back to crafting the perfect status update. Tracy thought back to the *Metro*'s unveiling at Clubs Days, and the look on Alex's face from behind the pancake lineup. She'd felt upset, sure, but nothing compared to him. He was livid. She didn't think he'd sat still for more than a few seconds since then. Meanwhile, it was all she could do just to corral this room long enough to get a newspaper made before the sun came back up.

"You hear that?" she said to the editors, pulling Keith off the floor and back to his chair. "Looks like our big exclusive is coming through after all."

"No way," said Steve. "He'll never find anyone. It's too late. And besides, the whole idea is boring anyway." The others mumbled something without looking away from their computers. Possibly in consent, possibly protest; Tracy couldn't tell. Music blaring out of three different sets of speakers fought for everyone's attention: the sugary rush of The New Pornographers from one corner, dissonant Swedish jazz from another, while a bunch of rappers inside Keith's laptop warned that they were not to be fucked with. Meanwhile the affable but soft-spoken photo editor was experimenting with different-sized flashes, giving everyone fuzzy purple dots on the inside of their eyelids.

"You don't know that," Tracy said to Steve. "At least he's doing something. The rest of us are just sitting here, hoping it all goes away on its own. The truth is we're all fucked come Monday."

Back in his seat, Keith wriggled out of Tracy's grip on his shirt. "I hate to say it, but Steve's right about this one," he said, and stood up to address the room. "If I could have everyone's attention." A few people turned to look at him. Mostly, the bustle of production day wore on. The printer buzzed and spat out pages-in-progress. Through the news cubicle's window, Rachel could be heard doing a phone interview. Rick was in his back-corner office, working with the door closed and locked. The house of cards went up; the house of cards fell down.

"Hey! Buttflaps!" Keith flipped his chair over, making a dull plastic thud on the carpet. Its wheels spun in the air aimlessly. "Who here thinks Alex is going to get this hedge story thing?"

The production editor kept her eyes fixed on her screen. "He better," she sighed. "Otherwise we've got no cover."

"Thanks, *mom*," Keith said. "God. Anyone else?" The associate news rookie scurried past him, grabbing a stack of long sheets from the printer and power-walking them back to Rachel's desk. A pop song about pharaohs and chess pieces kicked in. The rappers reminded everyone that fucking with them was still unadvisable. "No? Anybody?" Keith sat down, overjoyed with himself. "In your *face*."

"They're ignoring you, dummy," said Tracy on her way back to her own desk, where a fresh stack of copy awaited her. "You know, finishing their sections? So we can get out of here at a reasonable hour?"

"You should do a story about my dick! Ha!"

Alex inhaled calmly, methodically. He needed to keep an open mind. He had to remember not to hate the reader. "Thanks. We'll consider it. Again: do you know where—"

Another guy in a polo shirt appeared in the next door over. "You from the newspaper? I got an idea. Why don't you do a story about my *dick?*"

"Your friend just said that."

"Oh." He looked genuinely sad.

The process at *The Peak* worked like this. A new issue came out every Monday morning that classes were in session. Assuming, that was, that the delivery person got them out on time. So let's say Monday afternoon. For the satellite campuses, sometime Tuesday would've been nice. The new issue then circulated for a few days. Mid-week was the editors' meeting, where the next issue was planned, content for each section shared, and any floating in-house content assigned. All of this got written onto the back room's blackboard with bright cigars of sidewalk chalk. For some editors—opinions, humour—these meetings were basically just a paycheque hurdle, since they never received any content at all until at least Thursday night.

Friday was production day. And a day it was. In other words, forget about scheduling classes then, even in the morning, before anyone else bothered to show up to the office. It was the principle that counted, and in this, the editors' usually haphazard loyalty was unshakeable.

Production day had its own internal protocol. When an editor decided to run a particular story, he or she gave it a quick once-over before adding it to the stack on Tracy's desk. Eventually it would come back, red-penned and full of lovingly sarcastic marginalia, and from there the corrected file was imported into the layout program. Many an hour could be spent on the next step, wherein the story was cut up, formatted, and laid out on the digitized page. The section editor then stole photos from the internet, inserted captions and text boxes as necessary, and fine-tuned everything at a meticulous and frequently glacial pace. When things weren't going an editor's way, doing layout felt like trying to build a sandcastle with both hands asleep. (More than once Tracy had spun in circles in her chair while waiting for new pages to edit, complaining to Suze, "Isn't technology supposed to make this go *faster?*") Once everything was lined up, the page got printed at full size and sent off to the copy and production editors for approval. It'd come back with new sets of red and purple corrections, respectively, and the whole process got repeated for final.

All it took was someone like Keith to throw the whole operation into disrepair. To call his sleeping schedule erratic would be putting it lightly. In fact, Keith claimed to have never known eight unbroken hours of sleep since elementary school, when one night he discovered a marathon of *Dr. Quinn, Medicine Woman* on late-night CBS. It was an awakening, subtle and inscrutable, his version of the Virgin winking back at him from a tortilla. Many hours later, as the first rays of sunlight hit his living-room curtains, he stood up like it was any old morning and sauntered off to school. In recent years Keith had taken to all-night raves, and took sprawling, coma-level naps to make up the difference. Production unofficially started at noon, but he never arrived at the office until an hour or two before dinner.

"Don't worry," he yelled to the retreating Tracy. "My section is going to be awesome."

"Really." Her voice was muted through the wall. "What else is in it?"

"It's simple. I'm going to—"

The front doors flew open as a middle-aged man in tasteful brown slacks and a lot of frown lines on his forehead stormed in and looked around. "Who's in charge here?" he bellowed, and held up a page from the most recent issue. "I paid good money for this ad, and I do *not* think it is appropriate for this picture of a—this—well, this *penis* to be sitting there next to it. I think a full refund is in order, not to mention some sort of printed correction."

Keith turned his head only slightly toward him. "Shut the fuck *up,* dude," he said. "Whoever you are, nobody likes you."

The man in tasteful slacks looked stunned for a second. "I am the owner of Tom's World of Flowers, young man," he said. "That's who I am. Now: where is the fellow I spoke to on the phone when I bought the ad? Your business manager?"

Keith now turned to him fully, and crossed his arms. "You're looking at him."

"Excuse me?"

"I'm the business manager. And according to my calculations, you are a date rapist."

"What? Who do you think—"

Keith cut him off again. "Listen, you want to be useful around here? Help me think of funny things that rhyme with Vagisil, or else *fuck off* and get me a ginger ale."

"Never heard of him. You sure you got the name right?"

"I told you. I don't know his name."

"Actually I think you're in the wrong building altogether."

"Shit." Alex looked around frantically. Time was running out. "Really?"

"Look, I'll level with you. I don't 'go' to this school." She did air quotes and then kept walking.

The rest of the editors whooped and clapped. Keith started a chant of *Va-gi-sil* and beckoned with both hands for the others to join in. The tasteful-slacks man turned purple, unable to get another word out. Back at her desk behind the window, Tracy slouched down in her chair. *Not the time, guys,* she thought. The man took one last look around the office, in search of any flickering signs of support. Not finding any, he turned to leave.

"Guys! What on earth is going on out here?" Rick had emerged from the cocoon of his office and stood at the edge of the production room in disbelief.

"Va-gi-sil! Va-gi-sil!" The chant now joyously filled the office. Keith waved his pencil around like a conductor. Even Rachel joined in, rhythmically tapping her still-live phone against the window from the other side of the glass.

Rick stormed down to the doorway and offered his hand to the tasteful-slacks man. "I'm so sorry about this," he whispered. "They're good kids, really. They just sometimes forget that their computers are connected to a printing press, and these little inside jokes eventually make it out to the rest of the world."

"In all my years," he spluttered. "This kind of thing is extremely unprofessional."

"Absolutely. You're 100 percent right about that. Please, let's sit down and talk for a minute. I'm sure we can find a solution." Rick clutched his stomach with his other hand and winced. Then he righted himself, and led the tasteful-slacks man through the chaos of the production room back to his office. "Isn't it time for dinner or something?" he hissed to the editors over his shoulder. "Just get the hell out of here so the grown-ups can talk."

"Oh, thank god," Alex said as another door, on another storey, slid coolly open. He wiped his brow even though he was not technically sweating. He had to admit that his resolve had been wavering a little there, but now it was doubly, triply reinforced. "You're real. Tracking you down has been—"

"No worries. Come on in, man. What do you want to know?"

For dinner the editors went upstairs to the Highland Pub. What the *Peak* office lacked in horizontal real estate—its two neighbours being a parking garage and the meeting room for droning Christian sing-alongs—it made up for in verticality. Up one flight of stairs was a coffee shop owned by the student society, and also the last remaining place you could still get London Fogs for a reasonable price. Up one more was the Pub.

The editors pushed three tables together in the middle of the main floor and grabbed a stack of menus off the bar counter. The Pub was constitutionally incapable of turning a profit, and therefore chronically understaffed. You got used to doing things for yourself.

One large conversation about Rick's outburst in the office splintered immediately into five smaller, unrelated tangents. A Canucks game shone out from the various televisions. Keith ordered five beers before sitting down.

The guy grinned, his teeth gleaming white. His chin was a right angle. A row of bobble heads nodded along from his desk, next to a tastefully overflowing laundry hamper. The whole scene looked like an Axe Body Spray commercial.

"What do you mean," Alex said, his own imperfect jaw clenching, "you want to get paid?"

Two of the younger female editors vigorously compared sex lives, using cutlery as props, while Chip did several back-to-back spit takes from two seats over. Tracy was trying to convince Rachel that *The Little Mermaid* was actually a feminist cartoon. The web editor

97

shared a plate of yam fries with the associate news rookie and listed his twelve favourite web comics, in ascending order. Keith asked whoever wandered past their table what *they* thought was the funniest thing about Darfur. The photo editor stuck his earbuds in. Suze and Steve playfully argued over which animal Rex Murphy most closely resembled: raccoon or platypus. (Everyone else assumed the two of them were covertly sleeping with one another—no platonic banter was that cute.)

"She loses her voice. The female lead is literally and metaphorically mute, and this is how she wins the man. You call that progress?"

"Go back and watch it again. Ursula is a *commentary* on the patriarchy—she even says, 'The men up there don't like a lot of blabber.' She's calling attention to it. My god, it's obvious."

"Number four is Penny Arcade. It's weird how they draw themselves so thin and cool-looking, but I still like it."

"I say raccoon. Final answer."

"Yeah, you would say that."

"Then my legs were kind of—well, I can't do it *here*."

"I think you're giving the talking cash registers at Disney way too much credit. That they're capable of making 'commentary' about anything."

"Hey buddy—yeah, you. Know any good Darfur jokes?"

"Platypus all the way, lady. It's the nose."

"Number three? Maybe Achewood. Obvious."

"You've got to take charge. At a certain point I had to tell him, 'It's not a rabbit's foot, babe. You don't just rub it for good luck.'"

"*Pffffff!* A thousand apologies."

"What about their government? Don't they have, like, a funny government? Get back here."

It was warm, and comfortable, and the Canucks won in overtime, and even Tracy didn't think about the *Metro* the entire time.

Alex imagined the paper with his story in it being fought over at newsstands. He imagined the online version shooting up the Reddit homepage. Very cautiously, he reached for his wallet, then stopped. "Wait. No. Even if I had fifty dollars, I couldn't—" He flung his notebook onto the ground and stood up. "We're done here."

Back in the office, their stomachs full of veggie burgers and red-and-black-flecked bar fries, the editors settled back down for the final stretch. Rick's office was empty and dark. If anyone slacked too hard now, Tracy, who, along with the production editor, had to stay until the very last section's very last page was finalized, was happy to poke and prod them into action. All of the critical times had been pinned to Tracy's corkboard, next to her improvised style guide, for easy reference.

12:21 a.m.—last SkyTrain.

12:35 a.m.—last bus.

2:19 a.m.—last night bus.

After that, options were slim. You could either sleep on the couches, where you'd be greeted several times in the night by members of the graveyard janitorial staff, or else brave the unlit forest paths and try to stumble down the mountain, where bears were still routinely spotted, into the outer fringes of Burnaby. SFU: Petitioning for a Zipline Since 1965.

The editors had just sat down at their computers when a small voice piped up from the doorway. Tracy recognized him as the same nervous, bespectacled kid who'd hung around *The Peak*'s Clubs Days table for most of the afternoon, not saying much, but nodding at everything anyone else said. Tonight he must've spotted the editors up in the Pub and trailed them back to the office.

"Are you," he said to Keith, "uh, are you still doing that list?" Spinning around to face him, Keith stared without blinking. "I heard you talking about it," he added. "Before. The one about Darfur." He nervously rubbed his hands against his crisp, SFU-brand sweatshirt.

Keith kept staring. Eventually he wiped the stray pesto sauce off of his hands and folded his arms. "What's your name, awkward guy?"

"Claude," he said. "I'm just visiting. I don't work here. Obviously." He did a kind of half wave, half flinch, as if he were expecting some combination of pie-in-face and football-in-groin. "I was just thinking, you know, that the Darfur thing seems a little, I don't know, too soon?"

"Interesting. And what do you study, Claude?"

"S-science. Earth science."

"Listen. There might be a billion ways to climb a mountain or whatever, but there's only one rule in comedy: if you think it's too soon, then it's probably already huge in Dubai."

"What?"

"Our website gets a lot of traffic from the United Arab Emirates. I think I've got my finger on the pulse of something huge. Did you come here to get free dinner?"

"No, I—"

"Because we already ate, asshole. Have you ever read *A Thousand Plateaus?*"

"No, I—"

"Correct. Nobody has. Now, what do you think is the worst thing ever?"

Claude blushed. He had no idea if he was expected to be funny here or not. Panicking, he decided against it. "I don't know—Twitter."

"*Yes.* That's going in." Keith started typing with floppy fingers, all too aware that Tracy would have to clean up his mess later.

She peered down from behind his chair. "What if the scalped orphans were also in wheelchairs?"

"No. God no. Maybe—*maybe*—they could be dyslexic. Or hungry."

"Two Paper Cuts in Five Minutes?"

"Better." More floppy typing.

"What about Scurvy?" asked Claude, barely holding back a nervous giggle.

Keith stood up, clapped both of his hands on Claude's shoulders, and looked him right in the eyes. "That's fucking terrible," he said, enunciating each word.

Claude's expression wobbled. "Oh. Well, how about—The Black Plague?"

"Jesus," muttered Keith, plonking back down in his chair. "Did you grow up inside a goddamn Monty Python sketch?"

Tracy stepped between them. "Hey, forget it," she said, giving Claude an encouraging pat on the arm. "Really. Keith is an asshole. It's just hazing. He doesn't mean any of it."

Keith got a faraway look in his eyes. "Shut up for a second, both of you. I've got it: Getting an Abortion in Darfur." He threw both hands in the air. "It's *perfect.*"

A wave of disapproval came in from around the room, equal parts muttering and groans. Keith had hit his target. He looked so proud.

"I'm sure our lawyer will love it," Tracy said, patting her pockets for more caramels.

But Keith was already halfway underneath his desk. "See you guys next week." He tucked his sweater under his head as a makeshift pillow and was out cold within seconds.

A few minutes later the door swung open, and in came Alex, his head held low. He was carrying a shiny plastic bottle in the shape of a trophy. But this trophy was see-through, and full of a cloudy purple liquid. He held it to his chest like a comfort blanket.

"So?" Tracy asked, trying to act casual. "Did you find the guy?"

Alex barely broke his stride. "Technically," he said. "You could say that. Did anyone save me some yam fries?"

He sequestered himself in the archive room and used its decade-old computer to pull a feature from the Canadian University Press newswire more or less at random. With no scoop, with no story at all, he had to start his entire section over from scratch, and pronto. Luckily, the newswire had access to nearly every student newspaper in the country, and as such was full of add-water journalism. He chose a story on the rapidly changing economy of Liberia—or was it the ecology of Libya?—that had obviously begun life as a term paper. Alex dumped the text into InDesign. Then he added a few pull quotes, picked an appropriately abrasive title font, and boom: he was already halfway there.

Frankly, the whole thing was impenetrable. But then nobody read features anyway. Alex'd be the first one to tell you.

He emerged just after eleven and started gathering up his stuff. His lips were stained purple; the trophy bottle lay sideways and vanquished on the ground behind him. On his way out he stopped by the copy desk, where Tracy sat hunched over in her chair, working her way through sheets of paper with "2nd" written loopily in the top corner.

She looked up. "You done already?"

"That's it, that's all."

"Even your part of page 2?"

"Yeah," Alex said, his eyes aching in mysterious ways. "I just stole the wire synopsis. Turns out I had it backwards: it was about liberty in Ecuador. Who knew? I'm having trouble remembering if I even read the thing." He looked around. "Where is everyone, anyway?"

"Dunno. Keith's napping. Suze gave that Claude kid a CD review to work on—you should've seen the look on his face. Then she took off with Steve somewhere." She let this last bit hang in the air.

"Oh, I see," Alex said, pausing for dramatic effect. "They're off *sexing* each other."

Tracy sighed. "Nicely played. And hey, about the video thing—I'm sorry it fell through."

"Yeah, thanks. It's not a big deal." Alex was still irritated, though, as if he had a splinter in one palm and fingernails too long to get a good grip on it. "You know the weirdest part? The guy actually would've done it. But he wanted me to pay him."

"Wow," Tracy said. "Really?"

"So I just walked out. I mean, I *had* to walk out. That's breaking some kind of major rule. Isn't it?"

"Honestly? I have no idea."

"Me neither. I've actually been kicking myself ever since it happened." He paused again. "But I think I was right. Fuck. I think."

"Either way," Tracy said gently, "maybe next time involve the rest of us, okay? You ran off before we could even send someone along to get a photo of the guy."

"Yeah. You're probably right. But it's going to take the *Metro* a few weeks to make a dent up here anyway, right? We've still got time. I just got a little fired up."

Tracy's eyes brightened. "Hey, how's Secondhand Shakespeare going? My class read a great play this week. Remember those? Plays?"

"I don't want to talk about it."

"Ha! Spill it, loser."

"Yesterday," he said grimly, "we sat through an hour-long presentation of pop songs where Shakespeare is one of the many things that aren't relevant to the singers' lives. Algebra was another big one. After it was over, someone asked what it is we really *mean* when we say 'Shakespeare.' It seriously may have derailed us for the rest of the semester." Alex adjusted his slipping backpack. "Okay. Night. Hope you don't end up on the couches."

Tracy smiled all the way now. "Dave's coming to get me," she said. "Did I tell you? I've been avoiding his phone calls lately—for a bunch of complicated, dumb reasons. I won't bore you with the details. But things are starting to look up, I think. I found a note on our kitchen table this morning about a dinner reservation at that sushi place over at Lonsdale Quay. I'm supposed to think he left it there by mistake. And then he offered to come pick me up tonight. How cute."

"Hey, cool. Have fun." With that, Alex was out the back door, his footsteps echoing in solitude back up the parkade ramp.

Hours later, after Tracy had yelled at him to wake up and finish his Darfur list already, Keith shot up and hit his head on the under-side of his desk, making everything on top shuffle a couple of inches to the right.

He looked around for the long-departed Claude. "Hey, where'd Chuck Norris go?" he asked, blinking and rubbing his eyes. "That guy was alright."

Style Guide

As a general rule, *The Peak* uses Canadian English and follows the conventions of Canadian University Press style. Yet for reasons that are no longer clear to anyone, we also use British spellings whenever applicable (e.g., foetus, utilise, spare tyre). Since Canadian English is really just a passive-aggressive hybrid of British and American anyway, it's unclear how much "Canadianness" remains in our rather lopsided interpretation. But there you have it.

In addition to the above-noted rules, the following words and phrases are permanently banned from appearing in *The Peak* in any capacity unless being used ironically, in which case single quotation marks must be clearly deployed (e.g., "Bartholomew sure did 'rock the party'").

NOTE: This is the only instance that single quotation marks are used. If someone is being quoted, or you mean to say so-called, use double; if someone is being ironic, use single.

This is v. important.

- dollars to doughnuts
- liveblog
- ninjas (generally)
- 'nuff said
- pirates (generally)
- 'za (as in pizza)

If you have questions, or are unsure whether your phrase is on the blacklist—which is subject to rash and immediate change—just ask me (Tracy), or leave a note on my desk.

If I'm not available, assume that it is blacklisted until notified otherwise.

8

A TALE OF TUTORIALS

The crowd in the hallway outside AQ 5009 started buzzing when two girls, an apple-cheeked nineteen-year-old and a grizzled 5th-year double major, broke several weeks of silence to acknowledge that they shared another tutorial that semester, too. After a few minutes of pleasantries, the teenager's real friend in the class showed up with a plastic bag brimming with sour keys and gummy fried eggs. The candies were quickly distributed three ways. Then the friend turned and offered one to the 2nd-year in the spotless Oxford button-up who, up until then, had been leaning quietly against the heating vents. Before long there were nine of them, all laughing and doing impressions of their professor's vocal tics and hand gestures, the chatter becoming steadily louder until someone from inside the classroom came over to the door and closed it with a huff.

It was 11:23 a.m., Monday morning, Bizarro Christmas.

Alex, meanwhile, had gotten to school several hours earlier. He needed to see the *Metro* boxes—so inviting, so full, and so infuriatingly well distributed—for himself. To confirm it. The whole situation tugged annoyingly at his sleeve, rendering him unable to focus on anything else. He'd spent the entire weekend half-awake and restless.

The copy he carried with him up the AQ stairwell came from one of the twenty-one boxes he'd counted scattered around campus, but as he flipped the pages, Alex was surprised to feel almost nothing. It wasn't so scary when you were actually looking at it. Really, the *Metro* was the same pile of horseshit it had always been—today's front-page story was about some local dogs that resembled famous Hollywood dogs—only now it had migrated up one measly hill. The ink still smeared on a finger's first contact, and the faded dishwater-grey pages still made it look like hamster-cage carpet in the making.

This was supposed to be his downfall? *This?* He wanted to laugh.

Alex came around the corner of the AQ and saw the backs of his classmates filing into the emptying room. With them went their communal air of secrets and sugar crystals, leaving what felt like a vacuum chill in its wake. Sometimes he felt his entire university career was nothing but looped footage of him walking into a room two minutes too late.

The tables inside were arranged in a loose rectangle, and, seating patterns having been pretty much established since week two, Alex took his usual place beside the apple-cheeked girl and a few empty seats to the left of Oxford shirt.

Two *Metro*s were lying on his table. Two *Metro*s, and none of his paper. This was easy enough to rationalize: the *Peak*s probably hadn't even been put out yet. He could picture them in big cubic bundles on the loading docks right now, bound and gagged with neon zap straps. As he shrugged his jacket off, Alex noticed everyone around him sucking on sour keys. He gave them all an instinctive frown, then settled into doodling on the back of that week's lecture notes.

Tutorials at SFU were designed to supplement the lectures, which usually took place in huge, multi-hundred-person-capacity halls where raising your hand to ask a question was tantamount to academic suicide. It was hard enough sounding eloquent when surrounded by legions of your snickering peers, without having to keep up the illusion that you were having a normal conversation across an echo chamber the size of a football field. In fact, SFU's lectures were still cozier than those of its older brother, the gargantuan University of British Columbia. But dialogue had been a cornerstone of the upstart school's constitution, and as a result, these seventeen-person discussion blocks, led by underpaid graduate students, were here to stay. SFU: Sibling Rivalry Since 1965.

Alex's TA stumbled into the room, juggling a stack of shifting looseleaf papers, several manila folders wedged under one armpit, a bulletproof travel mug, and an ancient lime-green Discman connected by a long, knotted cord to a set of beefy headphones that threatened to devour his neck. His name was Eli, and his thesis had something to do with *King Lear* and plate spinning. He had long ringlets of blond hair that fell just below his nose, and thick jowls, though he was not especially chubby anywhere else. Today he wore one of his many striped shirts, unbuttoned over an off-white T-shirt, with the sleeves rolled sloppily to his elbows. In the divide between TAs who stuck to recapping and clarifying material from the lecture, and those who tried to spruce things up by inserting their own bright ideas into the curriculum, Eli fell, enthusiastically, into the latter category.

On the desk in front of him, he smushed his papers together so that they leaned tenuously against one another for support. "Well," he began, "how did everyone enjoy Thursday's lecture?"

A few murmurs and nods of approval.

"Good, good. Personally, I thought Professor Devereaux made some very salient points about iconography in our post-Industrial age—the fish tank in Luhrmann's *Romeo + Juliet* [1996] as 'postmodern' Christian bumper sticker was, I thought, rather brilliant." He leaned forward, as if giving his students an illicit heads-up. "I've seen excerpts from his new book," he added softly, "where this kind of approach fully reveals itself. It is a real . . . *delight*."

Satisfied, Eli resumed full volume. "Are there any questions about what we covered last week?" It clearly bothered him when there were, but the apple-cheeked girl raised her hand anyway.

"Yes," he exhaled. "Eleanor."

"Hi. Professor Devereaux mentioned there's been a recent movement to compile all of Shakespeare's references to products and, like, material goods—to create a profile of what he was maybe like as a consumer?"

Eli waved his hand dismissively. "You're referring to the Hawk v. Handsaw Coalition. Some interesting work there, but frankly, most of them are loonies." He chuckled as if this were beyond obvious. "Either way, they're of no relevance to this course."

"But don't you think," she pressed, "all the same, that it might be of some interest to know what Shakespeare would've thought about all this stuff we're looking at?"

"Right," said the double major from the other side of the room. "What if Will's favourite colour were blue, and we spend all our time wondering about a pair of red sweat socks with his name on them? That's got to count for something."

The syllabus for HUM 335: Shakespeare Without Shakespeare was jam-packed. Even though anything penned by the Bard himself was strictly off limits, the reading list was loaded with all kinds of hand-me-down resources: diary entries from contemporaneous Globe audience members, apocryphal biographies, Japanese manga (where every character for some reason wore a gleaming spacesuit), films written by or starring Kenneth Branagh, quotes from early *Simpsons* episodes, street graffiti, fortune cookie scrolls, films enjoyed by Kenneth Branagh, and the latest ad campaign for a brand of skateboard shoes that the class was only allowed to refer to as Those Scottish Sneakers.

Eli slowly shook his head. "A classic error," he said. "It's what we call the intentional fallacy. You see, we can never say for sure what

Shakespeare *meant* to express in his work. We have the end products, yes. But these are necessarily fallible. Incomplete. They are merely rough drafts that cannot lose their watermark. To equate that with a writer's supreme vision is akin to—well, saying my mother's famous coffee cake recipe is the same thing as the cloud of black smoke that pours out of my sister's oven every Christmas." He looked out the window, pondering. "So would the Bard have been a Coke or Pepsi man? We'll never truly know."

Alex muttered to himself, "I don't think that's quite what the New Critics had in mind."

"Are there any other comments on this?" Eli knew that the best way to deflect an unwanted question was to open it up to the room; in that sense, it was a page right out of *The Peak* editors' playbook. "Okay. On to new business." Eli took a big sip of coffee and began burrowing through his stacks of paper, finally coming up with the desired sheet.

"As you all know," he said, "your first essays are due in a few weeks. You should all still have the topics I distributed last class, but if not, that's okay: there's now an Exciting Alternative." You could actually hear the capital letters in Eli's speech, in the same way he implied sneaky scare quotes around grad-student-quicksand terms like *postmodern,* or *text.*

Alex had already grown to hate these flights of fancy. Was it too much to just write his two essays, earn his 10 percent participation grade, and move on? Was nothing allowed to be just boring anymore? Did university have to be *wacky,* too?

Eli cocked his head, looking first bemused, and then increasingly unsettled. He'd expected more of a reaction. Several seconds passed.

Oxford shirt eventually gave in. "But what *is* the alternative?" he asked in a flat deadpan.

"Ah, so glad you asked, Jeremy! After consulting with Professor Devereaux, I am thrilled to announce that, should any of you choose to do so, you may officially forgo all of the assignments listed on the syllabus." He paused again, evidently expecting gasps of disbelief. But Alex's generation lived in decidedly more jaded times than whatever was running through Eli's head. "Just—just ditch the whole lot," the TA added.

Only one student, a 2nd-year in a black turtleneck who always sat at the TA's immediate right, was still furiously taking notes.

"Okay . . ." Alex said.

"What's the catch?" asked Eleanor.

Eli's jowls seemed to frown with him. "Geez, you guys. No love for the art of suspense, huh? You just want answers, answers, answers. 'Will this be on the test?'"

"Actually," the double major said, "we're trying to figure out if there's even going to *be* a test."

Eli held his hands out in surrender. "Fine. Wonder no longer. No need for a drumroll or anything." There wasn't one. "If you decide to take on this alternate curriculum, the only thing you must produce by the end of the semester is: your very own Shakespeare adaptation."

Jeremy coughed into his sleeve. The turtlenecked girl's pen scratchings only barely filled the silence.

"Now, don't worry," Eli continued. "It doesn't have to retain all of the nuances of the source material—in fact here I suggest you follow Professor Devereaux's ethos, and consult it as sparingly as possible— and it doesn't have to be fancy. If you want to make a film, it doesn't have to be feature-length. Your *Richard III*–inspired hot air balloon doesn't have to meet Transport Canada regulations."

Slowly, the implications of this new project began to dawn on the class. Restrictions, possibilities, and especially loopholes. And since the social barrier had already been weakened by their shared pre-class snack, actual discussions started to break out, to Eli's shock and joy. Cheap sugar lasered through the students' veins. They took turns pulling apart their TA's idea and reassembling it, looking for weaknesses like a raptor at an electric fence.

Eleanor raised her voice to interrupt. "Are you sure Professor Devereaux approved this?"

The rest of the class froze.

"Absolutely," Eli snapped back—though his cheeks twitched a little as he said it. "So as I was saying, your adaptation doesn't have to be perfect. But it must be artful. And it must capture the spirit of the Bard's ideas, in whatever style, length, and medium you choose."

Alex, who had been privately mulling the project over, thought back to what he'd half-joked to Tracy earlier. Maybe he *should* sculpt something. When else would he get the chance to do something so perverse for a pretty much guaranteed A?

The conversations grew steadily louder and more expansive. Alex wasn't included in any of them, but his mind was racing with too many possibilities to be envious. Falstaff pop art. *Titus Andronicus* brand meat pies. A re-worked clip from *Aladdin* with Shakespearean verse dubbed overtop of the cranky parrot. It became a kind of Mad Lib, an undergrad's drinking game: see how badly you can desecrate a legend. (Tyson had a similar trick he played with Beach Boys songs, where he'd quietly sing to himself his own ultra-graphic reinterpretations.)

Alex felt up to the challenge. His lungs swelled with adrenaline, just like they had at the outset of his viral video stakeout. After all, he'd always considered himself an artist. Time to prove it.

He started scribbling down notes of his own.

At the front, Eli took in the room with a huge smile. The number-one topic of conversation in TA offices across the department was not which pedagogical—nobody was so crass as to say *teaching*—style worked best. No, it was how to make the students do anything. Literally, any thing. Speak, sneeze, whatever.

"Everyone," he said, "settle down." His voice wavered with emotion. "Is it fair to assume that some of you would be Interested in doing this?"

Seventeen hands shot straight up.

After tutorial let out, and Eli had re-gathered his mountain of paper and tottered off to his office, flush with pride, the same bunch of students who'd bonded in the hallway waited behind in the classroom, still buzzing with sour keys and their gossip-worthy new assignment. It was now after noon; a plan to "continue this discussion" at the Pub was quickly taken up.

Eleanor nudged Alex, who was sweeping a series of pens back into his bag. He looked up and saw her cheeks flaring a light Braeburn red. "Do you want to come?" she asked, before quickly adding, "We're going to the Pub. Didn't know if you heard."

"Oh," Alex replied. "Yeah. It's nice of you to ask, but I have to meet a professor. Office hours."

What? Why am I saying this?

She shrugged. "Okay," she said. "See you next week."

Alex couldn't believe it. He realized, watching Eleanor's ass sashay out the door, that his automatic response was to say no to things—even to things that would almost definitely not be torturous. It was out of his control. *No. Nah. I would, but.* Who builds a brain with such shoddy reflexes?

The classroom wasn't booked for next period, so Alex took his time getting ready to go. It was a nice ass, he thought. A bit too big, but she used it well. He imagined her demurely sitting on the edge of a private swimming pool, a curvy Pink Floyd model awaiting her spray paint artist. The image came to him almost too easily.

Alex went to close his binder, and saw that his absent-minded doodling during class had transformed into something far more elaborate. He'd accidentally drawn a crude blueprint of SFU itself, with lazy but unmistakable circles written all over it: in front of the library, in Maggie Benston and West Mall, at the bus loops, and dotted throughout the AQ hallways. The locations of the *Metro* boxes.

So much for not letting it get to him. A line from the ether of his subconscious leapt to the fore: *The lady doth protest too much.*

Alex crumpled the page up and pitched it into a nearby garbage can. *No kidding,* he thought.

9

NO SOAP RADIO

Tracy looked up from her chair at Cornerstone, saw Anna coming her way with a cheery wave of her coffee cup, and panicked. She wiped her nose and tried to look away, but not fast enough. It wasn't until Anna got a few steps closer that she made out Tracy's red eyes, and the way her hands were balled inside the sleeves of her sweatshirt, the fabric stretched taut up each arm. Anna's cheeriness gave way to a look of concern. She rushed to Tracy's side, and went in for a hug just as Tracy fell toward her, sending a dry, unsatisfying, bottom-scraping sob into the edge of her armpit.

"We broke up," she managed to get out. "He left. It's done."

"Start from the beginning," Anna said, lowering herself into the next seat over. "Everything makes sense when you start at the beginning."

Privately, Tracy remembered Dave's rules about campus friendship. They were both sitting. Hell, they just embraced. It was official.

"The beginning," she repeated, for the moment feeling a little calmer. Her breathing came in practised intervals, and she was wringing a slippery bag of Kleenex between her fists. "See, I find that's when everything looks worse—when you can see it all cleanly laid out, but still nobody reacts in time. It's like watching a bird fly into a window in slow motion."

She didn't want to say the other part out loud, the part that was gnawing at her the hardest and also the one she couldn't begin to explain. Namely: why was she the one who felt like her bones were being snapped, one by one, from her toes on up, when for weeks she'd been on the brink of doing the exact same thing? She felt almost jealous. Attic-dwelling Dave had finally stepped up to the plate.

She ought to be relieved. So why did she have to be the one who felt like garbage? He was the one who'd been so horrible. Well, so had she. But so had *he*.

They sat in a back corner of the café, near the windows. An artificial fire blazed nearby behind glass, while a muted TV dangled from the ceiling, its closed-captioning lagging a few hopeless seconds behind the action.

"The beginning," Tracy said again. "Okay. Basically we met at the very start of 1st-year, and we've been dating ever since, minus maybe the first ten minutes or so after we met. It happened really quickly."

Anna sipped her coffee. "Where did you meet?"

"Rez, actually. In the Land of Endless Sweatpants. We lived on the same floor. There was this party—what they officially call a 'community-building exercise'—where we played this drinking game called Edward Fortyhands. Do you know it?"

Anna shook her head.

"Probably for the best. It's also sometimes called 80 Oz. to Freedom, after that horrible Sublime song. All you do is duct-tape a huge bottle of beer to each of your hands, and then you can't take them off until they're both empty." She gave a watery smile. "Like most things in residence, it's about getting way, way drunker than you want to.

"Actually, in its own weird way, it *is* a community builder, since you're all in it together, doing this ridiculous thing as a group. I mean, it's, like, two litres of alcohol. The only thing anyone can talk about the whole night is how crazy it is that they're even having a conversation with these huge beer mitts on.

"But the problem is that if you get there late, after everyone else has started, it's impossible to catch up. The train has left the station. And that's exactly what happened with us: Dave and I both showed up to meet friends, and we each got there late enough to see everyone giggling and, you know, belly-bouncing without us."

"I'm sorry," Anna said, "I don't mean to interrupt, but I'm having trouble picturing this game. How do they open the bottles with no hands?"

"Ha!" Tracy laughed, and immediately regretted it. Her head was a delicate potion of fluids, and any slight jolt could set the whole thing off foaming again. "Teeth, mostly," she said. "Or feet. Sometimes you'll find a busted-up countertop the morning after."

"Weird. Okay. So tell me about Dave."

Hearing his name spoken so matter-of-factly was another strange sensation. The contents of her head started to slosh from side to side, and she drank more of her own coffee to try to even herself out. "Well," she said woozily, "the first thing you should know is that he didn't always look this way."

Anna took another polite sip. "I never had the pleasure."

"Right." Of course she'd never met him. How could she have? Tracy and Dave had just been together for so long that she felt as if some ghostly projection of him followed her wherever she went, broadcasting her taste in men and companionship to everyone around her. Was that what people meant when they called their partner a ball and chain? Hers wasn't a literal weight, though that might have actually been preferable: at least chains broke when you dropped something heavy enough on them.

"He was wearing this green cardigan," she continued, now nearly whispering. "Buttoned all the way up. With a T-shirt that said

'LOCAL SPORTS TEAM.' He was easily the best-dressed person there. I remember laughing at how depressing that was—the first of my many lofty hopes for university falling flat. But he thought it was because of some joke he'd made. In retrospect, I think that must've softened him up." Tracy stared out the window at the rain tapping against the pavement. "Neither of us had much to say, until I mentioned I was reading Baudrillard for the first time. I might have used the phrase *changed my life*. Or *blew my mind*. Maybe both. Dear god."

"Let me guess: *Simulacra and Simulation?*"

"Not sure. It was that ten-page excerpt everyone reads. Something about copies and originals, truth and Disneyland. Undergrad catnip. Anyway, Dave perked right up. It turned out he'd devoured that essay as a fourteen-year-old—you have to understand, he never got out much. We started talking about how university itself is a perfect example of simulacrum: how everyone grows up seeing people on TV playing characters in university, and how that completely shapes the way they think you're supposed to act once you get there. But that's what *everyone* does. So there's no such thing as an authentic university life, because blah blah blah. You can imagine how clever we thought we were." Tracy drained the last of her latte. "Then I slept with him. Do you want another one of these?"

"I'm okay," Anna said. "Wait. What? You what?"

"Hold on." Tracy stood up and patted at her pockets. "Be right back."

A few minutes later she returned, bearing a steaming crimson mug. "Sorry about that," she said. "The barista insisted on showing off the new pattern he'd learned in my foam." She tilted the cup toward Anna, who, still confused, straightened up to take a look. "Don't strain yourself: it's a leaf. What a shocker. When you've got a jug of hot milk for a paintbrush, your options are limited. Leaves, and hearts—and those are just slightly less busted leaves. Jesus, those people. It's not a *skill*."

"You seem in better spirits," Anna said.

Tracy considered this carefully. "No, I wouldn't say that. Where were we again?"

"You were at the part where you slept with a guy you'd just said hello to."

"Ah. Right." Tracy felt herself warming up to a story that had long been workshopped into perfection. "Dave got this devious look on his face. He asked me if I wanted to live out another part of our pre-ordained 'authentic' university experience. 'Have you ever seen *Undeclared?*'"

"No. What is that?"

"That's what he asked me," Tracy said.

"Oh."

"So in the pilot, the two main characters sleep together at their first college party, just to see what it's like. They figure randomly having sex is something you're supposed to do there—just another habit you pick up. But then it gets awkward again, and the rest of the show is about them maybe getting back together."

Anna bit her lip, fumbling for the right tone. "Let me get this straight. You had sex with Dave because of a TV show?"

"Yeah."

"Because of an episode that was *itself* about simulacrum."

Tracy shrugged. "Yeah, basically."

"Is that ironic?"

"Probably."

"And this sex on the show, it essentially wrecked the people's chance at having a normal relationship, yes?"

"What can I say—Dave was a charming fellow. Probably still is, in his way." This last sentence trailed off.

"Okay. I think I understand. And," Anna leaned in conspiratorially, "the sex was—?"

"Well, a bit rushed, as you can imagine," Tracy said. "We went to the communal bathroom on the next floor, and while we were doing it I think we were both trying to remember what it looked like on the show. But it was good. Surprisingly good, actually. No psychological damage on either side. Though I never did anything like that again, for obvious reasons.

"And, of course," she added, "I found out later he was on mushrooms the whole time."

"This is a very strange way to meet someone," Anna said.

The ballad of Tracy and Dave went on for another half-hour, with Tracy's every effort to omit or abridge thwarted by Anna's anxiously raised eyebrows—the look of a child who can tell her parent is skipping ahead in a bedtime story. Anna was an excellent listener. She never checked her watch or looked out the window, except out of courtesy during the most intimate sections. Her body appeared slightly magnetized forward in her seat. Tracy noted that her new friend would probably make a pretty good copy editor: she took the text on its own terms, and patiently followed it wherever it led.

After that first time sleeping with Dave, things did indeed get awkward between them, just as the prophet Judd Apatow had foreseen. For the next few weeks when they saw each other at school, neither was sure of the proper etiquette for their situation. A kiss on the cheek seemed ridiculous, but so did not touching at all. They settled on a goofy salute, until Tracy declared the whole thing too bizarre, and insisted they start from scratch and take each other on a real first date. At the end of the night, Tracy kissed Dave once on the lips and went back to her room alone. She shut her door and beamed.

Once they were back on the usual relationship trajectory, Tracy and Dave got along swimmingly. When they announced they were moving in together, it wasn't much of a shock to their friends and family; in fact, half of them could've sworn it'd already happened months earlier. The sex cooled off rather quickly—especially given its initial prominence—but they settled into a routine of late-night studying and complementary hobbyhorses. She put the bug in his ear about farmers' markets and podcasts. He got her to listen to Hüsker Dü, and told her old-timey anti-jokes like The Aristocrats and No Soap Radio. They met somewhere in the middle.

"And then I got pregnant." Tracy had seen this part of the story coming, but couldn't stop herself. Now it would all have to come out. "Right away, Dave wanted to terminate it. I wasn't so sure. But what choice did I have, really? It's not like he had any room to back-track if I *did* decide to keep it. As soon as I walked out of that filthy clinic—alone, by the way—that was the exact second I knew it was over between us."

"Oh, Tracy."

"And he never figured out how to talk about it. Not to apologize, either. Nothing. I just remember that first night, I couldn't stop cry-ing. And when Dave came home, all he said was, 'There's a population problem anyway.'" Tracy's voice was steadily rising. "A population problem! Can you believe that?"

"*No*," Anna said, shaking with anger. "No. That son of a bitch."

Even Dave seemed to recognize this was the beginning of the end. Only once did he try to lighten the mood, Tracy remembered, with predictably ghastly results. It was months later, and this un-resolved grief still hovered over the day-to-day of their relationship. For whatever reason, that afternoon they'd both seemed in better spirits, and Dave was trying to meekly test the waters.

When Tracy quoted the critical word back to Anna, she could see the girl's inner editor creep forward once more. Anna was putting a big, fat mental question mark beside *abo-bo* the same way Tracy had; it seemed to spontaneously grow one of Microsoft Word's dis-approving red squiggles under its feet. Now they both felt queasy.

Saying the word out loud had soured the air around them. Even the ambient noise of the café turned oppressive.

A holy rage flooded Tracy with adrenaline. Sirens were going off inside her stomach and head, but she didn't care. Between harried breaths, she told Anna about Dave's tea crusade, which he took up shortly afterward, and which kept him in a room by himself for more and more of the day. This part of their relationship was too recent and raw to have been incorporated into her well-worn anecdote, and she struggled with where to go from here. One conversation came to mind, and she latched onto it: the first time he told her the story of No Soap Radio.

"So a guy and a girl are having a shower together," she said to Anna. "He reaches for the bar of soap, but it slips out of the dish and onto the floor. As he bends over to get it, she holds her hands out in refusal, saying, 'No soap radio!'"

Dave had laughed so hard, Tracy went on, talking faster and faster, pushing out entire paragraphs in the space of a single breath. He'd actually pounded a fist against their kitchen table, which at the time she thought was an obvious affectation but was now coming to accept, in retrospect, as genuine. Simulacrum incarnate.

All of a sudden her brain and gut threw a joint revolt. Both started to gurgle violently. Her vision got even fuzzier. Tracy lunged toward the closest trash can just in time, and emptied the contents of her stomach directly into it.

She'd wanted to laugh along with him, but couldn't. It didn't make any sense. All she could come up with was to awkwardly smile and say, "So all that build up is for nothing? What's the point?"

"What do you mean?" he asked. "The joke is that there is no joke."

Tracy's stomach squeezed itself into a knot; her lower back cramped, and even her toes clenched violently. But in between heaves she felt Anna's thin, cool fingers holding her hair back for her. After a few seconds, Tracy's heartbeat started to calm down. The coffee shop's air conditioning was like a cool breeze.

But with Dave, she'd just lit a cigarette, and felt her expression subtly change. "It just seems like a waste of time," she'd said, speaking huskily through a beam of smoke.

'Back to School' for Troubled Holtz

By MACK HOLLOWAY
for Metro Vancouver

CAMPUS BUZZ The actor who once impaled a corrupt university professor on a harpoon wrapped in barbed wire is set to return to the classroom this spring—only this time the cameras won't be rolling.

Former teen heartthrob Duncan Holtz, now 27, announced his re-enrollment at Simon Fraser University at a press conference Wednesday afternoon.

He said education has always been an important part of his life.

"People see me, and they think I'm just a pretty face attached to an even prettier body, with the whole world at his fingertips [...] I'm so much more than that," Holtz explained. "I'm excited to go back and finish what I started, back before fame and fortune came a-calling."

Holtz briefly attended SFU in 2001, studying "broadly" until a surprise casting in TV's *Felicity* sent him south of the border. At that time he was widely considered one of Hollywood's fastest-rising stars, going on to star in the popular *Maximum Death* franchise, among other films, but he has since run into trouble with both the press and his fans.

His latest film, an experimental work entitled *Volcano Dreams*, drew the longest consecutive boo in Sundance history upon its premiere in January.

Asked if he plans on getting involved with any groups on campus, Holtz laughed and said he would keep his options open.

"Is there a beer-drinking club?" he asked with a chuckle. "Who knows? Maybe I'll run for student body president or something."

10

STET / SIC

By mid-October, Alex's official count had already needed several updates. The *Metro* pillboxes were spreading like dandelion spores, pollinating every corner of SFU with bits of freewheeling fluff: from twenty-one boxes that first morning to twenty-five, then to twenty-eight. By the time there were thirty, he'd stopped counting altogether. In every cluster of newspaper boxes, *The Peak* found itself surrounded by green. The *Metro*'s front-page tagline, asking readers to "pass on" their copies once finished with them, led to brittle, crusted stacks piling up on tutorial desks and in departmental hallways. The takeover was quiet, but most definitely hostile.

And as rumours begat newer and more elaborate rumours, word around *The Peak* was that the *Metro*'s distribution army was also about to storm Burnaby Mountain. So far the editors had only had to contend with the paper itself; the prospect of actual flesh-and-blood employees walking around was too scary even to entertain.

"Swear to God? I saw one of them. Okay? I *saw them*. I was in the AQ, and I caught this glimpse just before it disappeared around the corner: a green toque."

"I saw one in my lecture last week! He was huge. I don't know how he even fit into those little desks."

"What—you mean like taking notes and everything?"

"Guys. I need you to focus up here."

"Gave me the absolute jeepy-creepies."

"They're coming after us. They're *targeting* us."

"Yup."

"Oh, for sure."

"And why would they do that?"

"Jesus, Rick, haven't you even seen *The Wire?*"

"Oh my god."

"Best show ever."

"*Ever.*"

"It's all about snuffing out the competition."

"Shoot 'em dead, hide the bodies, take over their corners."

"*Blam, blam, blam.*"

"And duh—that's us!"

"That's you, maybe. I'm Omar: renegade with a heart of gold. Where's my shotgun at?"

"No, I'm Omar."

"As if. You're D'Angelo."

"Shut up. *You're* D'Angelo."

"Ha, ha."

"At least I live through the first season. Not like Wallace over here."

"Who's he, again?"

"'Omar comin'!'"

"No, you're doing it wrong. It's '*O*-mar comin'!' Emphasize the first part."

"'*O*-mar coming!'"

"Don't pronounce the *g*, idiot."

"'*O*-mar comin'!'"

"'*O*-mar comin'!'"

"'*Shee-it.*' Remember that guy?"

"This sounds an awful lot like a conspiracy theory. Why on earth would they be out to get you personally?"

"Look, all I'm saying is that every time I press the Coke button on our vending machine, a Sprite comes out instead. Are you hearing me, Rick? *Green* Sprite. A refreshing lemon-*lime* soda."

"Not saying, just saying."

"*I* heard they're owned by a shadowy Asian conglomerate. The CEO is this former underground samurai who was exiled from his clan because he loved murdering too much."

"Well, that's why you have to always keep your clan in the front."

"And let your feet stomp."

"Sounds like someone should've protected his neck."

"Point of order: is it true that cash rules everything around me?"

Four people yelled in unison: "C.R.E.A.M.!"

"This is not why I asked to come to this meeting. Did anyone here read my email?"

"I did."

"Thank you. So you, at least, understand that we are already quickly losing ground."

"Sure, but, I mean, how many copies do they even put out on campus each day? Five hundred?"

"No way. More like five thousand."

"What is this, Mathoholics Anonymous? If you guys are going to sit around and do calculus all day, I'm leaving."

"Totally. Let's leave this boring shit to the business students."

"Or economics, maybe?"

"Yeah. Maybe."

"Does anyone know which of them handles this kind of thing?"

The photo editor tentatively raised his hand, but nobody noticed.

"Dummies. SFU doesn't have economics courses. Everyone knows that."

"What? My friend *majored* in economics here."

"Tell him to reread his transcript. He's been fleeced."

"Okay, then I'll summarize the email," Rick shouted, banging his fist against the coffee table until there was quiet. "I've called an emergency meeting with the board tomorrow night. Ad revenue is down significantly—no thanks to that stunt you guys pulled on the flower shop owner. So is our pick-up rate. Right now we're still waiting on some solid numbers to come in, but as soon as we know what's going on, we'll figure out what the best plan is going forward." The noise picked up again in complaint. "In the meantime, if you could try to keep things a little more—how can I put this—reader-friendly, it would make my job a lot easier." Rick ripped open a package of chewable antacids, popped three into his mouth, and shut his office door behind him to a chorus of boos.

Rachel called them all back to order, and on to new business. The annual spoof issue was due out at the end of November, and the staff usually spent months half-seriously bouncing ideas off one another before frantically making a decision with days to spare; the frantic time was now fast approaching. Notes from the previous meeting read, in their entirety: "Discussion about spoof descended into making fun of dead astronauts."

Meanwhile, Tracy had all but checked out as copy editor. She'd unloaded the bulk of her editing onto some poor work-study student, and filed the rest from home. There had been no calls, no emails, nothing in the way of explanation—though this would've been a formality anyway. Everyone knew why. And since they had no vocabulary in their sardonic rapport for an actual personal crisis, all the other editors could offer her were meek smiles and vague motions of sympathy whenever she came by, which was usually just to pick up a paycheque. She hadn't technically resigned, and nobody wanted to be the one to force her hand. Only Alex seemed to notice the spike in typos in her absence.

On top of this was the whole Duncan Holtz thing, which nobody quite knew what to do with. Rachel was adamant that this was not news. "Let the *Metro* handle the celebrity gossip," she said. Without a new movie to peg it to, Suze didn't see how it qualified as arts coverage, either. Besides, everyone was already used to film stars loitering around campus. Would it be any different if one of them was also enrolled in a course or two?

When Keith found out about the celebrity's impending arrival, he squealed with delight and declared that *Fang City,* the late-nineties supernatural melodrama Holtz starred in for the CBC, was his favourite show of all time. In Tracy's absence, Alex had taken over dutifully updating the "Keith's Of-All-Time List" pinned to her corkboard, which by then was a veritable graveyard of contradictions and half-remembered names.

He also wrote an uncharacteristically aggressive Editor's Voice, after a poll for one issue's *Peak* Speak asked "Has the *Metro*'s arrival on campus changed the way you consume print media?" and resulted in the equivalent of a blank stare. Alex couldn't take it anymore. Did SFU students really, he wrote, not understand what it meant to support a paper like the *Metro?* Did they not realize that this capitalism of convenience could have a disastrous financial backlash for a certain losing party?

It drew exactly zero response, in print or online. Furious, Alex went onto WebMD and decided he was getting an ulcer. He washed down this diagnosis with a litre of mint cherry ginger ale.

For his free-form Shakespeare project, Alex eventually decided to write a straitlaced adaptation of the early comedy *Measure for Measure.* Sculpting something wound up being too embarrassing to consider in any but the most abstract terms; like most of his generation, Alex aspired to prickly eccentricity but lived, behind closed doors, in the soft and the unthreatening. Nearly every meal he'd ever eaten could be described as comfort food.

The genre he kept returning to was the Hollywood blockbuster, in all its terse, flexing, machismo-oozing glory. Secretly he'd fantasized about becoming a writer for as long as he could remember. He never imagined himself actually sitting down to work, though—only giving thoughtful, post-Pulitzer interviews to Charlie Rose during which he expounded his many searing opinions about life and art. Truth be told, Alex had never needed an excuse to keep putting off his dreams a few months at a time, like a snooze button. Arm's length was still a bit too close for comfort.

He settled on a screenplay.

Sitting in various coffee shops around Vancouver in one marathon evening, Alex struggled to piece it all together. His plan was to satirize, to subtly skewer Hollywood rather than coarsely pummel it to bits—satire being irony's nobler and better-dressed sibling. It was something to shoot for, anyway.

Alex's odyssey began at a tiny, triangular café located at the spot where Main hit Kingsway in a sharp diagonal. He ordered a large house blend to stay and propped his laptop open in the corner. "Do you have wi-fi?" he asked. They did not. He opened a new Word document. He called it OUTLINE.doc. He wrote three bullet points and spent ten minutes adjusting the formatting and font. He tried to guess the passwords of the locked wireless signals his computer picked up from surrounding apartments. He watched two guys with intricately greased-back hair smoke cigarettes outside.

Ninety minutes later he was at an all-night coffee shop way up Main, where he ordered a scone. The cashier asked him if he wanted it warmed up, then tried to high-five him. Alex saw an obnoxious girl from the previous semester's Classical Mythology tutorial and stridently avoided eye contact. At his table, he read the local alt-weekly, which had begun life, decades earlier, as a self-proclaimed pinko rag staffed by a bunch of *Peak* alumni. He thought about writing one of those theatrically hostile letters to the editor that could win you two free CDs from the bestseller list. He reread two acts of the play. He thought about which CDs he'd ask for if he got published. He wondered if Tracy was okay. He realized his table didn't have an outlet for his laptop to plug into. His battery died.

A long walk and a quick trip on the B-Line later, Alex strolled into the JJ Bean on Commercial Drive. He ordered a raspberry oatmeal muffin and an Earl Grey tea—"Could you add a shot of raspberry to that, too? Just to see"—and sat at the big ring-shaped table in the middle of the shop. He plugged in his computer and re-opened OUTLINE.doc. He made another new document: DRAFT.doc. He flicked between the two documents, taking pleasure in the butterfly-tilde shortcut Steve had taught him just the week before. He reread the rest of the play. He wrote a rough prologue, then deleted it with another flick of his wrist. He tried to download a pirated version of Final Draft. He googled "Final Draft" to make sure he was thinking of the right thing.

At a minimalist café a few blocks further down Commercial, full of people who looked like they'd rather be smoking, Alex ordered a cappuccino. He sat down in a perfectly round chair at a perfectly square table, took a sip of his drink, then spat it back, disgusted, into the mug. Why the fuck did he keep coming here?

He headed back up to Commercial and Broadway, side-stepped the circles of teenage hoodlums in front of the A&W, and took the SkyTrain downtown. Green pillboxes at every turn. He thought about ways to fight back. Tactics both high- and low-road. Varying degrees of smear campaign. Two crumpled *Metro*s sat on the seat next to him. Alex walked in the door of a coffee shop near SFU's

Harbour Centre satellite campus. He pawed at his stomach and decided he should eat something more substantial first. Down a block, he came to the site of another familiar turf war: the Battle of Dollar Pizza.

One of Vancouver's unofficial claims to fame was its business model of selling slices of pizza—at all hours of the night—for a buck apiece. Though *business model* might be stretching the truth a little; it was generally accepted that these grubby shops were either fronts for clandestine drug empires, or relied on teams of homeless people to supply them with wheels of stolen cheese, or both. Sitting side by side on the corner of Pender and Seymour, in the heart of the downtown core, were two of the most visible players: 2001 Flavours and FM Classic. Everyone had their preference, and the allegiances ran deep.

Alex was a lifelong 2001 Flavours man. He ordered three slices and a can of pop, gave the cashier a five-dollar bill, and got change back. *Maybe co-existing isn't so bad,* he thought, looking at the lineups spilling onto the sidewalk at each place. *But then we'd all have to become cocaine dealers on the side, too.*

He wiped the last remnants of grease onto his pants and walked back, satisfied, to the coffee shop near Harbour Centre. Alex sat down next to an outlet and plugged in. He asked if they had wi-fi; an owl-shaped Italian man at the next table over said yes, they did. He logged in, re-cracked the spine on his copy of the play, and re-opened DRAFT.doc, keeping his half-drunk can of pop displayed prominently on the table. If anyone asked, he bought it here.

He cracked his knuckles one by one, then started writing.

This habit, of working on essays while nomadically jumping from shop to shop, beverage to beverage, was a fairly recent development. For all of 1st-year, Alex had had a set routine, carried over from high school, which involved barricading himself in his bedroom two days before the assignment was due and listening to Philip Glass soundtracks on repeat until dawn. He wrote furiously—at least seven hundred words every hour, punctuated by an actual egg timer—with no revisions. All edits were to wait until that final next day, after a buffer of twelve hours' sleep. This was before coffee, too; in the heat of those early writing spurts Alex drank gallons of green tea, out of what had once been a plastic flower vase.

Once Alex ran into Dave at a party and brought up this phase of his life, as well as his pet theory that it was the low-caffeine teas that truly wired you awake. Dave had gotten a very serious look on his face, clasped Alex by both shoulders, and promised to look into it right away.

In 2nd-year, however, Alex's methods stopped working. His parents had grown concerned about the toll these on-again, off-again study habits were taking on their only son—all because one time, in his nocturnal wisdom, he'd blockaded his bedroom door with a sofa and then, on his way out the next morning, accidentally stepped in some soup left for him on the floor in the hallway, and shattered the bowl. Then, to his growing horror, Alex found his trusty study aids failing him for no apparent reason: green tea started to taste flat and metallic, and the neighbours' dog somehow ate his Philip Glass mix CD. He was suddenly rudderless, and his grades and self-esteem started to waver accordingly.

It was around this time that he got hired at *The Peak* after a few semesters of volunteering, and on his first production night, a knowing senior editor had wordlessly slid him a steaming plastic cup from Higher Grounds. At first the coffee kept Alex alert but jittery, and he'd had to keep moving as a survival tactic, just to focus on the screen in front of him. Now his restlessness was a ritual that verged on superstition, unconnected to the caffeine but just as essential to his success.

Alex looked up from his work-induced trance to see a mop sliding across the floor and the café's stone-faced cashier pointing to an imaginary wristwatch. He checked the time on his laptop. Nearly an hour had passed—an hour in which he'd had a rare stint of pure productivity. No emails, no flashing updates to his RSS feeds. A glorious, all-too-brief period spent off the grid. Ignoring the cashier, he wrote a self-congratulatory Facebook status update to this effect. When nobody liked it in the first five minutes, and with the mop jabbing at his feet, he deleted it and left.

Trying to keep the productive streak alive, and with the time now fast approaching midnight, Alex took the SkyTrain back to Main Street before hopping on another bus, just as the rain started splattering like paintballs. A few minutes later he ducked back into the twenty-four-hour shop, which was now readying itself for the graveyard shift. It was busier than before—mostly UBC students, Alex decided, with an instinctive sneer—and he looked around for a place to sit.

Before he could move he saw Claude, who was standing by himself in the lineup. A stack of newspapers was pinned unsteadily under his arm; on closer inspection Alex saw that they were all *Peak*s—at least a semester's worth.

"Hey," Claude said. He was still oppressively nervous, even now that they were outside the office. "Alex. It's me—Claude. How are you?"

Alex took his best shot at a jovial smile. "Hello, Claude. I'm good." He pointed to the newspapers. "What've you got there?"

Claude's face bloomed a dark red, and he grew even twitchier. "Oh, these. I don't know if Suze told you, but I'm, um, working on a story? A CD review." Alex nodded tentatively. "So I wanted to go through the old issues. You know, to see how you guys do them. I just don't want to get it wrong—it's my first article, after all."

Impressive, Alex thought. Rare was the volunteer these days who didn't kick down the front door, looking not so much to learn as to brazenly vomit up all the things they thought they already knew. "Hey, that's great," he said. "I'm sure you'll knock it out of the park." As Claude's eyes widened to process the compliment, Alex was already gesturing toward the mass of people beyond. "But I've got to finish off this essay, so—"

"Oh, totally. Totally. Sorry to have rambled on like this. My bad."

Just relax, dude, Alex wanted to tell him. *Nobody at our paper is worth tripping over yourself like this, I promise you.*

He didn't get more than few steps away before seeing that the girl from his old tutorial was still there, and now joined by a group of her friends. Alex froze in place, but it was too late: she'd spotted him, and was in fact calling his name and waving. He took a quick look over his shoulder—even Claude would be more fun to sit with than these people—but the kid had vanished. Sighing in defeat, Alex shuffled over to her table, where some kind of card game was under way. There was a stack of dog-eared textbooks to the side, their yellow secondhand labels from the SFU Bookstore half-heartedly picked at.

She said, "Sup?"

"Hey," Alex said, nodding like an idiot to the rest of the table. "What are you guys up to?"

The girl—Alex struggled to remember her name, which he'd barely registered the first time around—stared down at the cards on the table. She was deathly pale, so white it was almost a medical concern: the kind of girl who'd describe herself to strangers as "kinda bipolar?"

"Well, we *were* playing Asshole, up to a few minutes ago." She looked to the guy next to her, who took over the explanation, his shoulders still lightly bouncing. "Then we started pitching reality shows to each other." The whole table burst out laughing, clearly not for the first time.

Great, Alex thought. *A goddamn snake pit.* Suddenly he remembered a similar conversation he'd been lured into before their shared tutorial, where he'd been forced to consider which was his favourite *Ace Ventura* movie for an agonizing fifteen minutes. *Just what I need right now.*

But he had no choice. Alex reluctantly pulled out a chair and sat down, keeping his feet tensed and ready to jump up again as soon as he could move somewhere else—anywhere else—and get back to work.

"So you wanna play?" the girl asked, her eyes shining mischievously.

Even worse, Alex thought. *She thinks we're actually friends, torn apart by cruel circumstance and conflicting class schedules. She doesn't remember that I* hate *her.*

"Sure."

"Awesome. It's like this," said her friend, the one who seemed to have thought the whole thing up. "You know how there's all these shows now where they, like, *transform* someone from one thing to another? Like a makeover show, or where people switch jobs with each other?"

Alex nodded again, though he was distracted by the sheer number of wristbands the guy had on. They were stacked up well past each wrist, like a game of leather Jenga.

"But now," he went on, "it's like they just greenlight these shows based on the words in the title sounding alike. So we're pitching our own shows. Show him, Paul."

A lean guy with long sideburns and a horizontally striped sweater said, *"From Crook to Cook.* A story of second chances and following your dreams."

Alex felt a smile cross his face without his consent. *Yeah, it's kind of funny,* he thought. *But don't encourage these assholes.*

Now the girl chimed in. *"From Busy to Busty.* Re-prioritize your life with a set of double-Ds."

Ugh, Alex thought. *That sucked.* Just like that, he felt comfortable again—it was the familiarity of condescension, of having his low expectations met. This was a role he knew he could play.

The faces around the table froze, and Alex realized he'd grunted his disapproval out loud. The girl was frowning with embarrassment. There was a long pause.

But then the group's fourth, a chubby dude in an artificially vintage Nintendo T-shirt, piped up: "More like *From Busey to Busty.* Check this out. Can extreme plastic surgery bring this man's career back from the dead? It'll take thirteen pulse-pounding episodes to find out the answer: no."

Uh-oh. Alex found himself actively holding back real laughter. A wave of warmth hit him, as if he had on one too many layers, which he did not.

"There you go," said Paul. "What've you got, Alex?"

"Um . . . *From CEO to C-3PO.*"

The others looked around the table, as if they weren't sure who should break the news. Eventually the girl chuckled politely. "Not bad," she said. "Though it doesn't really make sense, if you think about it. Don't worry. It takes a while to figure out. You'll get better."

Now Alex's own brow furrowed in humiliation. *It was* supposed *to not make sense,* he growled to himself, snapping back once again. *I was making a comment on the* idea *of—rather than taking the easy route and simply adding to the—*

Oh, who was he kidding? Alex had to face it: he was simply not willing to actually try, even at a game as dumb as this one. Because trying might lead to failure. This strategy might get him somewhere back at *The Peak,* where the entire culture, which he'd helped build, centred on condescending to an imaginary reader. But now? Now he was just ruining other people's fun. He was spewing venom in every direction, for no reason at all, and the worst part was that they all knew it.

There was no denying it: the only real asshole at the table was him.

Alex decided to make amends, and quickly. "Wait. I've got another one." *Just go. Do it. Nobody's watching you.* He said, "*From Barista to Barrister.* A parable for our upwardly mobile times."

This time the entire table erupted. "Now that's awesome!" cried Paul, slapping Alex on the shoulder, to his secret delight. "Keep it going."

"*From Minor to Miner,*" someone said.

"Gold. Literal gold."

"That'd have to be a period piece. 'Charles Dickens presents.' For some reason you can't throw toddlers into a pit of coal the way you used to."

"*From Junky to Hunky.* For when heroin chic is the new heroin."

"*From Etymologist to Entomologist.*"

"*From Racist to Bassist.*"

"*From Banker to Wanker . . . ?*"

"What's the difference, am I right?" They all laughed again.

After a minute of silence, everyone deep in thought, Alex said, "I've got it: *From D.A. to DJ.*"

"Swish," said Paul. "That's some secret identity shit right there."

"You want the trance? You can't handle the trance!"

Out of the corner of his eye Alex saw a table open up, but for the next little while he pretended he didn't.

"So what's your deal, man?" asked Paul. It was now well past midnight, well past Alex's self-imposed break from work, and the café's once-rowdy crowd was now thinning out, separating the amateur crammers from those trying to make a career of it. Paul had discarded his striped sweater, revealing an identically striped V-neck shirt underneath. The girl (Victoria, it turned out) and her other friend (Eddie, or maybe Teddy) were making towers out of individual peanut butter and jam packages. Nintendo guy had been in the bathroom for going on a half-hour.

Before he could answer, Victoria looked up. "He works at the newspaper!" she exclaimed.

"No kidding—*The Peak?*" Paul asked. "What do you do there?"

"I'm the features editor, actually," Alex said, sitting up straighter in his chair. Finally, someone who appreciated the work he was doing. It didn't happen nearly as often as he'd like.

He was much more familiar with the reaction he was getting from the rest of the table. Vacant blinking, even a yawn from (T)Edd(y)ie. Alex knew why: they didn't read his section. Worse, they didn't even know how to pretend they did. He could practically hear their excuses. *Two thousand words on why comic books aren't just for kids anymore? An exchange student's garbled memories of life back home? Who has time for that?*

"Cool, man," Paul said finally. "I used to read your guys' paper all the time."

Used to! Trying to salvage something, Alex asked, "Why did you stop? If you don't mind my asking."

Paul thought for a minute, looking sternly toward the front of the store. "The comics were too weird. Like, that week everything was all hand-drawn? It looked like a drunk guy did it in twenty minutes." *Twenty-five,* Alex thought, remembering Keith lying under his desk with a Sharpie in each hand. "Anyway, I mostly just read the *Metro* now."

This is how it begins, Alex thought. *Our slow descent into noth-ingness. We are officially circling the drain.*

"But don't you think," he said out loud, "it's important to have a place for new writers to gain experience, and develop their voices? Isn't that valuable? *The Peak* is a training ground, too, you know."

Victoria wrinkled her nose as her tower of jam toppled over. "Yeah, but why would I want to watch as some stupid poli-sci major learns how to write in complete sentences about stuff nobody cares about? I mean, hello?"

This stung, but deeper down, Alex felt as if he'd stumbled onto a major insight. Who *was* their paper intended for? Readers or writ-ers? It was a question he'd never considered before.

(T)Edd(y)ie looked up sleepily from his peanut butter contrap-tion. "I heard you guys are going to have to shut down."

"Who told you that?"

"I dunno," he said, shrugging. "It's just what people are saying."

"Who? What people?"

(T)Edd(y)ie looked at Alex blankly for a second, then went back to work. "I don't know."

Alex leaned forward, suddenly riled up. This was exactly the kind of shit that was going to sink them—when the students, the people who *ought to know better,* turned their backs on *The Peak.* Loose lips, sunk ships, et cetera. Spineless. Pathetic. "Just give me a name," he said. "Who is saying all this crap about us? Why would you even say that to me right now? Do you think that's what I want to hear?"

Victoria laughed nervously. "O-kay," she said. "I think we all need another cup of tea or something."

As Paul and (T)Edd(y)ie wandered off to the front counter together, Alex began drastically re-assessing the hangoutability of these people: from giving them the benefit of the doubt to taking it the fuck back. He started finding faults everywhere he looked. The matching stripes on Paul's clothes now looked far too manicured, too precious. (T)Edd(y)ie's T-shirt—which read "I Have a Black Belt in Keeping it Real"—now landed well on the wrong side of clever. Maybe Alex's first impression, hasty as it had been, was right on the money. Fuck these people.

And Victoria—well, Alex considered her with fresh eyes. They were alone at the table together. *Could I?* he thought. *Is it possible?* (Tyson briefly appeared in his thoughts like a Jedi counsel, chanting, "Cock, cock, cock.") Victoria was shrill, yes. But not without a certain kind of litheness that in someone with a better personality might be called *grace*. Her eyes were sharply green, her face round and inviting. She was wearing a lacy tank top with no bra underneath. Her breasts were small and well-shaped enough that he guessed she didn't need to wear one very often. All in all, she passed the swimming pool test with flying colours.

And she *had* invited him over here in the first place. That had to count for something.

"So, Victoria," he said to her, "I was wondering, are you, at all— do you have a boyfriend?"

Just as the words left his mouth, Paul and (T)Edd(y)ie arrived back at the table, teapot in hand. *Oh no.*

"Oh my god, are you *hitting on me* right now?" Victoria said. Her jaw actually fell open an inch or two. "That is so adorable!"

"What's adorable?" asked Paul, sitting down between the two of them.

"Alex just asked me if I had a boyfriend!" she said.

"No way!" Paul said. "Alex, you dog!"

No, no, no, he thought, face mashed hard into the palms of his hands. *What am I doing here? I have an entire screenplay to write, for fuck's sake.*

Across the table, he heard (T)Edd(y)ie, who evidently hadn't been paying attention, ask everyone what it was they were all laughing about. And Nintendo guy could be heard finally emerging from the bathroom—*he'd* need filling in, too.

Pull the ripcord. Get me out of here.

The next day, Alex dropped by the *Peak* offices to print out his Shakespeare project on his way to Eli's office. It was finished, it was ironic, and Alex hated it. His dream of artfully skewering Hollywood had withered and died on the vine, right next to all of his other fancy writerly ideas. What he was about to turn in had eventually been fired off in an hour and a half. It was no better than an overlong *Mad Magazine* parody. *Blechsure for Blechsure.*

Alex half-nodded to Steve, who was perched at one of the main computers, scanning his email for anything he could turn into content for the coming issue. It was, he claimed, the usual wasteland. Then Steve started chuckling to himself.

"What's so funny?" Alex asked.

"This guy thinks the SFU motto is *French*," Steve said, gesturing. "He wrote a letter about doing your homework or whatever, and he says at the end that *nous sommes prêts* is fucking French." He laughed again, louder. "I'm keeping it! I'm using it!"

After a pause, Alex said, "It is French."

"What?"

"It *is* French. It means *we are ready.*"

"I know what it means," Steve said. "But is . . . are you sure?"

"Yes. What language did you think it was in?"

"Man, I don't know. Latin?"

Alex made a scoffing noise.

"What? Come on. You've got to admit it sounds a little Latin-y."

Getting up from his own computer, Alex thought, *Everyone knows you make it all up, man. You don't have to keep talking up your imaginary writers.*

He stood beside the printer as it spat out his pages. The editors all made liberal use of it for anything they needed a hard copy of, school-related or otherwise. They justified the extra cost to the newspaper by reminding themselves of how underpaid they were, given the hours and workload, and the fact that paper literally grew on trees.

A counter-argument could be made, however, that since their paycheques came from student fees, and given the quality of the product, as well as their readers' middling satisfaction with it, that, really, they were making *too much* money.

Alex hoped the board would not come to the latter conclusion. But since all financial matters were in its hands, he just crossed his fingers that the math would continue to work out in his favour. His only job was to take care of the paper itself. And the readers. And also the writers. But how? Was it even possible to do all three at once? He mulled this over while pirating twenty-five pages plus the cost of ink.

"So I looked it up," Steve said, looking over. "You're right: French."

"I know. That's why I laughed at you."

"It's too bad, though. If the guy was wrong—"

"But he's not. Right? You get that?" *And "the guy" is you. We all know it. Why Suze would want to sleep with a moron like you is a mystery.*

"Fuck. Yes. I'm saying if he *was* wrong, and if I ran the letter anyway, we could put one of those brackety note things after the mistake. You know, where it's like we're saying, 'Look how this writer fucked up. We're not going to fix it, even though we totally could.' I forget what those're called."

"You mean a *sic?*"

"Yeah! But inside those, um, square brackets. What are those ones called?"

"Brackets."

"No, the square ones."

"Those are brackets. You're thinking of parentheses."

"Oh."

"There are also braces, which look like old-timey parentheses. Nobody uses them anymore."

"Yeah, um. Anyway. *Sic*s are hilarious."

Privately, Alex agreed with him. The *sic* was indeed the truest, most merciless arrow in an editor's quiver. If an exclamation mark was like laughing at your own joke, a *sic* was laughing at a joke someone else didn't even know they were making. Like a whisper at an art gallery, it quietly announces, *Psst—this is all bullshit.*

He and Tracy had joked about it a bunch of times. Before she disappeared, that is.

Instead, Alex said, "You ever hear of a *stet?* I like those, too."

"Yeah, Tracy writes that on my stuff sometimes. Usually next to a big scribble. Isn't that the same thing as *sic?*"

"Kind of," Alex said. "*Sic* means the writer fucked up. *Stet* means the editor fucked up. Both are from the Latin—unlike the SFU motto. Out of curiosity, who wrote that letter of yours?"

Steve clicked around—a little overdramatically, Alex thought. "Trent Sip," he said finally. "Trent 'Whalebone' Sip."

Liar. Liar. Liar. "He included a nickname?" Alex said. "That's weird."

"I guess. I've seen weirder."

This kind of shit doesn't help the paper. It doesn't help readers. And it definitely doesn't help writers. Why have we put up with it for so long? "And what's your full name again? You have a middle name, right?"

"Yeah. Earl. What does that have to do with anything?"

"Steve Earl Botwin," Alex repeated. "So formally, I guess it'd be Stephen, right? Stephen Earl Botwin." He repeated it aloud a few more times. "Quite a name, that is. It's—elastic."

Steve kept clicking around. "You're one to talk, Castlevania."

They both stood for a second in the haze of the computer screen. Steve squirmed a little in his seat. Alex let his thoughts drift to the pile of *Top Gun*–inspired gibberish he was about to hand in for a grade, and then to Tracy. Someone should really check in on her.

"Did you hear about this board meeting?" Steve asked.

Alex snapped back with a twinge. "Yeah," he said. The email had been sent at 2:00 a.m. that morning—meaning that Rick had been up at least that long, dealing with the *The Peak*'s various money hemorrhages.

The meeting was scheduled for that evening. At 6:00 p.m. sharp, after the other students had retreated to their cozy homes and left the SFU campus grey and desolate, its right angles soaked in streaks of rainwater, the *Peak* board would decide the fate of its ungrateful children—who would, in turn, paw their stubbly chins and kick rocks no matter what.

SFU: Sent to Bed Without Dinner Since 1965.

11

THE BOARD MEETING

It was even worse than they thought.

According to Rick, *The Peak* was running out of gas. If the newspaper were one of those old coal-powered trains, now would be the time to start throwing luggage and furniture into the furnace, all in the name of maintaining a little forward momentum.

And yet it wasn't that the *Metro* had put a huge dent in *The Peak*'s pick-up rate after all. Apparently students weren't omnivores so much as scavengers, willing to ingest whatever print media was closest at hand. Usually that did mean the daily, with its ever-present green pillboxes. But not always.

No, the real problem had deeper roots. And it wasn't complicated: advertisers, most of them on-campus businesses, hated *The Peak*. They'd hated it for years, it turned out—its delusions of grandeur, not to mention its patronizing anti-capitalist pose—but until now they'd never had an alternative. As soon as the slightest wedge of competition forced itself in, virtually all of them jumped ship.

Monopolies, said the member representing alumni, tend to work like that.

As Rick explained to the others, his voice scary-calm, a metal ruler serving as his makeshift pointer, what had to happen next was the equivalent of emergency surgery. There were tough decisions to be made at every level of the entire operation. Should they drop their page counts? Cut wages, or entire sections? Switch to online-only? Nothing was off the table at this point. And while Rick appreciated that each member had the right to disagree with his assessment, the fact was—now swatting the ruler against his palm with a cleaver's *thwack*—that unless something drastic was done right away, pretty soon there wouldn't *be* a rest-of-the-board to have these disagreements with.

The temperature in the room seemed to drop ten degrees on the spot. Everyone felt mildewy and uncomfortable in their seats. Rachel and Suze, the two staff representatives, felt so unprepared for this news that they couldn't muster a single argument in their defence between them. Even the usual row of pizzas sat untouched for most of the meeting, until one judicious board member pointed out that if they were thrown away, the list of unnecessary expenses would only grow a little longer. The slices were folded up in jagged pieces of paper towel and stuffed into pockets and handbags to be eaten, maybe a little guiltily, later on.

12

COLLECTED POEMS

One day not long before the Christmas break, Alex worked up the nerve to call Tracy. He'd heard reports around the office that Dave had whimperingly fled the scene for good—retreating to his parents' house with a hastily packed suitcase and an armful of lab beakers and desert-island records.

After a rambling explanation of how he found her number in the staff directory, Alex asked Tracy how she was doing. All he heard back through the line was a raspy chuckle. She was taunting him, he thought, daring him to give up on this half-hearted charity project. He should just quit. Yet despite his brain's red alert, he plowed ahead and insisted they go book shopping for the upcoming semester together. Alex made a point of suggesting Bibliophile, which was Tracy's favourite used bookstore, as well as only a short walk from her house.

He got there early, battling with an unruly scarf. Taking in the Commercial Drive foot traffic, Alex had no idea if he should mention the cause of Tracy's withdrawal from collegiate society. Maybe that was the tactfulness she needed right now. Or maybe she'd have no time for any pretences at all, and so he should rip the bandage clean off—refer to Dave directly, and by name—right away. Both options made a lot of sense and at the same time none at all. He stood in front of the store for a few minutes, scratching his neck through the wool of the scarf, wondering if even waiting outside for her was an overly polite gesture. She might think it weird, or even sexist in its latent need to protect. Too many possibilities. He went in, the overhead bell chiming as he kicked his shoes clean on a worn-down doormat. Only then did he become truly aware of how nervous he was, how much he really did want to help, and how labyrinth-lost he was trying to navigate all the attendant subtleties of heartbreak. He thought back to their last real conversation, and the poor deluded look on Tracy's face when she still thought Dave was just taking her out for a romantic dinner. *God,* Alex thought, *what am I doing here?*

Bibliophile was one of Alex's favourite bookstores, too. The tall shelves, jutting in and out like edges on a huge puzzle piece, made for plenty of quiet corners in which to browse without having to worry about anyone eavesdropping on your taste. It was a humbly made-up store, clean and welcoming. A sign in the window said they only bought "gently used" books, and you could tell they meant it. Classical music from CBC Radio 2 provided a soundtrack that was both key to the experience and easy to tune out. The store charged a little more, but that extra dollar functioned like insurance: here you were guaranteed not to find dried blood, or a pubic hair, inside anything you bought.

They also had a full shelf called Anchors and Cannons, devoted to seafaring fiction, which brought Alex endless delight, even if he'd never so much as cracked open any of the books that got shelved there.

He was only just taking stock of the new-arrival wall, marveling at the fleet of current event/political tomes that, only months old, were already rubbing up against their expiry dates, when the bell went off again and in walked Tracy. She looked as though she'd been fighting off cabin fever, or maybe just been kept awake for several consecutive weeks.

"What the fuck, Belmont?" she said, shoving him roughly and sending him back on his heels. "You don't even wait outside for a lady anymore?"

Shit. He should have waited. He knew it. "Sorry, yeah. Sorry. I was going to, but—"

She waved him off and unbuttoned her jacket. "I'm just kidding."

"Oh. Well, good." Apparently Tracy had emerged from her break-up with an even dryer sense of humour than she'd gone in with. This invitation was way too premature—they were just colleagues, and here he was, trying to push a friendship on her that she obviously didn't have time for. She was as unequipped for human interaction as he was. They stood there for a second in conversational stalemate. Radio 2 droned on in the background like a posh fruit fly. "So should we . . ." Alex began, with no clue how he was going to end the sentence.

"Start crossing some of these books off our lists? Thought you'd never ask." Tracy smiled demurely, sealing off the Question of Dave for the time being. "You did make a list, didn't you?"

Alex drew a jet-black Moleskine notebook from his inner jacket pocket. "I did, actually."

"Excellent." She moved swiftly past him and waded into the stacks beyond.

Half wanting to give her some space, and half falling into his own bookstore trance, Alex let her go. Instead he moved along his familiar trajectory, alphabetically through the fiction section. Running his hand along the distinctive ridges and textures of the spines, he felt his head automatically cock to one side. He imagined his own paltry collection at home swelling and multiplying. Piles and piles of paperbacks. Swallowing his desk, lining his walls, surrounding his bed like castle walls. Never mind his poverty. This was an irresistible daydream, and one in which he wanted to bask for a little while longer.

Eventually he made his way to his touchstones: Bellow, Mura-kami, Roth, Saramago. Alex liked to check in with these guys (and they *were* all guys) as if they were old friends. It came from a basic curiosity about the economics of used bookstores—whether having these books in stock suggested a spike in his pals' popularity, or a drop. Was giving them a spot on the shelf the stores' way of respond-ing to demand? Or were they desperate to unload some dead weight?

Picking up a bright orange copy of *Portnoy's Complaint,* Alex fanned the pages with one thumb. To him, there was no better proof of a life fulfilled than seeing your name on a cover. No matter how slim or underappreciated the rest of the book was, this was a concrete marker of one's legacy—even the bare fact of one's existence. Books outlived everybody. Plus they were a renewable resource, able to be re-opened and re-experienced at the drop of a hat. Whatever mea-gre amounts of love or hate Alex gave to this world would fade, and soon. Maybe they were gone already. But a book could be his way of making a permanent mark on the world. It could be his cannon, he thought, thinking back once again to the niche sections behind him. His anchor, too.

He wandered down to the P/Q junction to check in on another of his standbys. Alex hadn't read most of this guy's books (in fact, this was true of every author on his mental checklist); he admired their dense, world-building, tail-swallowing qualities, but even then mostly in theory. No, the kinship he felt for Pynchon owed more to the man's reputation as a recluse, which let thousands of kids just like Alex fill in the gaps, each according to his own particular moral pal-ette, the same way sons did absentee fathers. Combing the shelves at Bibliophile this time, he was met with a dead end. Nothing. His gaze shot right into the threadbare Qs before he even quite realized it.

But as he reversed course a name caught his eye, one he'd only ever noticed glancingly, subconsciously. It was the one that almost always closed out the P section if there weren't any of Pynchon's paranoia-soaked doorstops kicking around: Barbara Pym.

He pulled out the paperback, which was primly designed but with pages yellowed from age, and scoured the back cover for clues. Who was this woman? Alex had no idea. Yet he'd probably cursed under his breath a dozen times upon seeing one of her books sitting there in lieu of his beloved Thomas P. Probably the only reason his brain had registered her name at all was because of the slight Marvel Comics connection. *Hank Pym, founding member of the Avengers and the world's first wife-beating superhero.*

Maybe this female Pym was an amazing talent, Alex thought. Maybe she was lucid and hilarious, with big ideas and juicy dialogue, ahead of her time and now criminally forgotten. She could've been essential reading fifty years ago, for all he knew. Maybe she'd even had a book banned—for speaking *too much* truth, too clearly. She could well turn out to be Alex's all-time favourite writer. And this whole time all he'd associated her with was a feeling of mild disappointment at not finding that copy of *V.* that he wouldn't have bought anyway.

But there was an unpleasant subtext to the Pym/Pynchon arrangement. Even if Alex were to somehow distil all of his ideas onto the page, inflating his anecdotes to the right levels and avoiding all of the embarrassing snares that first-time novelists so often get tangled up in, nobody in their right mind would ever buy his book. He was wrecked right out of the gate.

It was his last name: Belmont. His (as yet unwritten) book would inevitably be shelved immediately next to those of Saul Bellow. What self-respecting reader would look at the two of them, and then go with the untested, overwrought young punk? It was enough to make him close his laptop on the spot. Plus, anything he wrote would inevitably be compared to the Nobel laureate anyway, since Alex, like his idol, had a habit of trying to capture the entire universe in every sentence. He didn't need to give critics such a readymade way to phrase the insult.

Besides, what could he do to give his book even the hint of a fighting chance? Think of a hilarious title? Kidnap Chip Kidd and make him design a cover that could outshine the majesty of the all-black Penguin Classics? Should he switch to non-fiction, or sci-fi, just to get a fair shake in a different part of the store?

Alex remembered reading an essay that pointed out how sad it was that an innocent woman's one-line obituary will read, "She was Timothy McVeigh's mother."

Well, he thought, *for every titan of literature, there are two lesser writers who will forever be remembered as their bookends.*

He took the Pym novel with him and started consulting the real list in his notebook. A few minutes later he emerged with two of the six titles he'd written down—not a bad showing. Alex then went to find Tracy, who was wandering, in her own trance, along the opposite wall.

"Ready, then?" he asked, glancing at the stack of identically designed paperbacks—seven or eight at least—in her arms.

"Ondaatje," she said, as if the man's name were a curse word.

"Ah. Say no more."

"Next semester is my CanLit pre-req. I put up a good fight, too, but I couldn't escape it—or him. So I'm just going to buy up his whole damn catalogue and call it a day."

Alex offered his condolences. "It happens to the best of us," he said. For a moment he felt like they were a pair of grizzled World War II veterans comparing shrapnel wounds. "What about Atwood? Did you ever have to do her?"

"*Handmaid's Tale,*" she said. "Twice. You?"

"We read *Alias Grace* in 1st-year. Then later I signed up for a course on Homer—only to find out that the first five weeks would be spent on Atwood's feminist rewrite thing. I ran away at the first break and never looked back."

While Tracy thumped her Ondaatje motherlode onto the front counter, Alex made one last detour to the poetry section. Behind him he heard the cashier whistle in admiration.

Alex didn't read all that many poems, but this section spoke to him even more strongly than the fiction did. Here, every second volume had a massively satisfying title—something like *Works: 1913– 49,* or, better still, *Collected Poems.* Yes, he felt, with that telltale Nabokovian spine tingle, these were the writers who truly *got it.* They understood the lightness that came with indexing absolutely everything in one's desk drawers. These books of poems weren't texts so much as actual lives, shrunken and collated. They dispelled loneliness; they transcended human failure.

Outside, Tracy asked, "So what'd you come up with?"

"Off the list? Virginia Woolf, and this copy of *Master and Margarita,*" Alex said, running his fingers along the cover. "Look at that. It's a beauty."

"Don't you already have that?"

"Not this translation."

"Is that for a class, too?" she said, pointing at the Pym paperback.

Alex shrugged. "No—just for fun, I guess. I heard she's pretty good." He switched his pile between hands, left to right and back again. "But it's worked out pretty well, actually. For once I've got a bunch of novels to read this semester. It'll be a nice note to go out on."

"Right!" Tracy's face brightened for a second. "This'll be your last semester. I'd completely forgotten. How exciting."

"I guess so." Truthfully, Alex felt like his training wheels were coming off, and soon he'd have to back up all that talk about how they were only holding him back to begin with. Soon he'd be held accountable for every wobble.

"So are you done all your pre-reqs?"

"Yep," he said. "I'm even taking an intro film course to celebrate. Figured I'd round out those breadth credits a little."

"I did one of those in 1st-year," Tracy said, nodding. "Is yours a ridiculous, the-history-of-all-movies-in-thirteen-weeks kind of thing?"

Alex said, sheepishly, "It's a bit . . . dumber than that. Apparently we're going to be the pilot program."

"Dumber than *that?* Good luck."

Now they came to that curiously unnamed part of a conversation where the current topic is on the wane, and a decision must be made either to wrap things up and say goodbye, or else broach something brand new—in which case, a change of scenery was also in order. Alex and Tracy had never hung out together outside of school before, and he still wasn't sure if he should assume that this trip had broken down the barrier permanently.

He started to put his scarf back on, beginning his retreat. "Well, this was fun," he said defensively. "If you ever want to—"

Tracy stuck her hip out and her arms went akimbo. "So that's it, huh? You're not even going to ask me about Dave? I was under the impression that this was all about shaking me out of some imagined stupor."

"No, no, it is," Alex said, moving a step closer. "I mean, I really was trying to help. I did need the books, but—I mean, that's obviously not the point." He took a breath and regrouped. "I just don't think this stupor of yours is strictly imaginary. You know? We haven't seen you around the office. You're editing from home so much these days. I didn't see you once during the spoof—and it actually turned out pretty funny, for once. *SFUrks Illustrated*'s swimsuit issue? I still can't believe you let Keith Photoshop the president into that bikini."

"That was a graphic," Tracy reminded him. "Out of my jurisdiction."

"Anyway, we were worried. *I* was worried."

"I see," she said. A bus shot past, kicking up a sheet of dirty mist that fell at their feet. Her expression became a little less strained. "And the books, you say?"

In a split second, Alex decided to go out on a limb, opting for a joke. "Yeah, well. You know how it goes. Two birds, one stone, etc. I'm a busy dude."

After an excruciating pause, Tracy mimicked the ironic gloss in his voice. "Natch."

"So anyway, like I said," Alex repeated, "maybe we can do this again sometime . . ." He took a few exaggerated steps backward. "Now I've gotta run to the hospital . . . Grandma fell into the town beehive again . . ."

She laughed, this time with considerable lightness behind it. "Fuck you."

"Oh, don't you worry," he said. "We're all fucked."

"In that case, you'd better walk me home."

Tracy's house still had a slightly haunted feel to it, where you could see the dust silhouettes of objects recently departed. She was un-usually forthcoming, too. At school Tracy often gave off a vibe that was pleasant but largely inscrutable, iceberg-like; here she insisted on giving Alex a full tour. He realized that this was the first time in weeks he'd been in close proximity to a woman without having to keep his sexual demons in check. It was a much-needed ceasefire. He'd jerked off to the memory of Eleanor's swirling, denim-clad ass three times in the past week alone.

He'd even, once, to his secret shame and puzzlement, hate-masturbated while thinking about Victoria from his old tutorial. But that one felt more like exercise than anything.

Now, however, he was free to wander Tracy's living room and poke at her DVD collection without any hidden agenda to contend with. "Oh, and I got my Shakespeare project back this morning," he said.

"Tell me," said Tracy, sitting cross-legged on her couch. "Tell me, tell me, tell me."

"I actually have a theory about this."

"Great. More theories."

"It's a short one, I promise. Professors and TAs like to talk about the death of the new, right? So why do they keep giving better grades to papers and whatnot that even just *try* to do something crazy and original?"

"I give up."

"Because they have to spend days upon days reading essays that take ten pages to explain that, deep down, Hamlet has an important decision to make. No ideology in the world can stand up to that kind of slow torture. So when you do something even mildly unusual, they're just so grateful for the stimulation that they can't think clearly."

Still, Alex conceded, it was true that all of the really good ideas had been done to death. Formal stunt pilotry (e.g., beginning and ending your essay with ellipses) was totally bush league; comparing a book to its film adaptation, once grounds for automatic expulsion, was now simply called *interdisciplinary*. So you had to aim bigger, flashier. There was a longstanding rumour, whispered throughout the liberal arts, that one frazzled undergrad had actually built a scale model of Bentham's Panopticon out of popsicle sticks for his term paper and left it in front of his TA's office door, alongside a handwritten note that said You Figure It Out.

Which was all to say that when Alex had gone to Eli's office to pick up his screenplay, he was met with the most gushing enthusiasm he'd ever seen from the TA. It caught Alex completely off-guard; nothing, he confided to Tracy, made him more suspicious than unbridled joy, especially when directed at something he'd said or done. But Eli had shaken his hand so strongly, and locked into such a tractor beam of eye contact, that even Alex had to assume the feeling was genuine. Eli had asked him where the hell he'd gotten such a terrific idea. ("He didn't say *terrific*," Tracy objected. "Scout's fucking honour," Alex replied.) The TA spoke so quickly, in fact, slurring entire sentences into long blobs of sound, that sometimes the only discernible word for long stretches of time was *Derridean*.

Alex had only been able to shrug and say, "I just thought it'd be funny if Isabella were a fighter pilot."

To which Eli had thrown his head back and cackled. "Indeed! And having Angelo try and tempt her with that tab of LSD. Ingenious."

The screenplay got an A. "Then again," Alex added, "so did everyone else's project, as it turned out. None of us could figure out how that's even possible. But it is what it is."

While Alex was partly thrilled at receiving such bald-faced, if somewhat qualified, affirmation, he wasn't able to fully enjoy the moment. He knew that it was really garbage, a rudimentary parody, no more clever than those Twisted Tunes cranked out by the local FM stations' cocaine-fueled morning shows. Having it taken so seriously sucked whatever fun it contained right out. It was probably more accomplished than anything else he'd written in recent memory, but *ingenious?* In a better world, he added to Tracy, this kind of idea would've been bathroom graffiti.

"Well," Tracy said as he got up to go, "at least you only have one more semester to get through." She thanked Alex for convincing her to leave the house for a change, and they shared a quick but firm hug at her front door. On his way back to the SkyTrain, Alex ran the numbers in his head: thirteen weeks, four courses, two presentations, six essays, two exams. Then he'd be booted ceremoniously out the door—from cap on head to cap in hand, out to where there were student loans to be repaid and soul-flattening jobs to interview for but never get. If he decided to go the other route, applications for grad school were already on the horizon. *The Peak* might get run out of business even sooner than that. Meanwhile, some C-grade celebrity was about to show up and expose SFU as a literal cultural dumping ground.

One more Editor's Voice, one more feature, a few more Photoshop goofs snuck into the house ads, and that was it. He'd be gone—and all without having had sex in almost two years, while living in the most permissive and socially lubricated environment he would ever know.

As he was boarding the train, he got a text message from Tyson. It read: "Dude. Jsut finished getting my dick slurped in the library by a shelf stocker when wat do I see. Metro guys in big gay aprons in convo mall. The philistines r here."

Merry Christmas, Alex. We're all fucked.

FPA 137: INTRODUCTION TO CINEMA II
Instructor: T. Monahan
Spring 2009

The Cinema of SFU

From 1972's little-seen *The Groundstar Conspiracy* to TV's ongoing sci-fi hit *Battlestar Galactica*, SFU has long been a fiercely sought-after location for filmmakers of all genres and budgets. Who among us hasn't tripped over the odd lighting cable, or had to make a detour around an off-limits catering display? This course—the first of its kind anywhere in Canada—will provide an overview of the many wonderful films and television shows (the latter also a departmental first!) that have called this campus home over the years. We will place a particular emphasis on science fiction and, due to availability of resources, anything involving a high-tech FBI base.

Along the way we will reflect on the role these works play in defining and instructing us about our school and our larger communities. To what extent can we say that we attend class 'at' the ruined Delphi Museum of Colonial History? We will consider the many esteemed actors and directors who have walked the same paths that we do every day. What lessons do they have to teach us?

Also, expect at least a few guest appearances from some of these fine men and women. Most of these remain TBA for the moment, but I can confirm that Duncan Holtz, local golden boy and recently re-enrolled SFU student, has graciously agreed to give a guest lecture about his roles in CBC's *Fang City* and the action blockbuster *Maximum Death 2*, both of which were filmed in part at SFU. You won't want to miss it!

PREREQUISITES:
None.

REQUIRED VIEWING:
The Groundstar Conspiracy (1972) Dir. Lamont Johnson
The 6th Day (2000) Dir. Roger Spottiswoode
Antitrust (2001) Dir. Peter Howitt
Spy Game (2001) Dir. Tony Scott
Agent Cody Banks (2003) Dir. Harald Zwart
My Life Without Me (2003) Dir. Isabel Coixet
Two for the Money (2005) Dir. D.J. Caruso
Maximum Death 2 (2006) Dir. Flex Tannigan
The Day the Earth Stood Still (2008) Dir. Scott Derrickson

We will also consult clips, as required, from TV's *Stargate SG-1* (1997–2007), *Battlestar Galactica* (2004–present), and *jPod* (2008).

COURSE REQUIREMENTS:
20%	Attendance and Tutorial Participation
25%	First Essay (1,250 words)
30%	Second Essay (2,000 words)
25%	Final Examination

13

TRIPLE NOPE

The movie star arrived quietly, with no entourage or pre-emptive press releases. This was intentional. There was no fanfare because he hadn't organized any.

In fact, accounts differed as to when, exactly, Duncan Holtz showed up at SFU for the first time. Everyone agreed that he was in C9001 on that first official morning of the spring semester, sitting there unassumingly in a Yankees cap. The class was 1st-year sociology. Home base for schedule-overloading window shoppers everywhere, as well as those wafflers who had parents demanding a post-secondary education, specifics be damned. But there were earlier rumoured sightings, too: Holtz slipping into the bookstore just before closing, or enjoying a quiet pint of Rickard's on the Pub patio.

By the time he left that first lecture hall, a cluster of students had already gathered in the AQ hallway, waiting to catch a glimpse of celebrity firsthand. To his credit, the star was gracious upon being found out. He signed autographs in the hall and posed for some camera-phone pictures—always remembering to make physical contact with the fan, putting his arm around them or ending their exchange with a high-five. That was how you showed you were sincere. It was one of the first things the media handlers taught you.

Then, with a casual wave, and flashing that permanently boyish grin, Duncan Holtz headed down a staircase and was gone.

A round of giddy texts and status updates went out. The consensus was that he looked even more rugged in person, though surprisingly short.

This turned out to be a typical reaction to his presence anywhere on campus. Students and professors alike would stop him in the halls to shake his hand and say how much they admired his work. For some reason they always named the most obscure film they could think of, as if this were proof of their deeper fandom, and not just that they'd scrolled to the bottom of his IMDb page. The star treatment didn't end with strangers, either—he also got it from his classmates. Even though he attended the same lectures and tutorials every week (by all accounts he was very punctual), sitting alongside the exact same sets of students, hardly a week went by without a collective gasp when he walked into the room.

Mostly Holtz kept to himself. The only visible connection to his past life was his manager, a short, cutthroat-looking man who could be seen whispering sinister nothings into the movie star's ear as he wandered between classes. Still, Holtz kept smiling at passersby, accepting the man's presence the same way a hippo tolerates the chirpy little bird that perches on its back.

The *Peak* staff aimed to reconvene after the holidays with renewed energy, ready to shelve their petty grievances for the time being and put the newspaper's best foot forward. They clomped through the front doors in rapid succession, making a pile of their slushy umbrellas and then setting up shop at their usual posts in the production room. Tracy had rejoined the parade, and was met with polite, golf-like applause as she returned to her desk with a mock curtsy. First on the staff's shit-talking list were the new *Metro* canvassers they'd all had to walk past at the bus loops. These were tall, hunched-over goons, their faces dotted with comic-book stubble, and with all the charm and silhouette of a refrigerator.

A wave of lurching and growly impressions had just broken out when Alex noticed the pink slips.

"*Suze*," he said, his eyes locked on the grid of mailboxes. "What are those?"

The arts editor didn't say anything, and the room went silent around her. When she hesitated again before answering, Alex saw his own fear of conflict reflected back at him, which only made him angrier. By the time she was ready to respond, it was too late—the other editors had already swarmed the cubbyholes, rifling through stacks of neglected mail in search of the unlucky prize.

Just like that, half of *The Peak*'s staff had been fired: Chip (sports), Steve (opinions), and Keith (humour), plus the web editor, photo editor, and associate news rookie. Even though they'd known this was a possibility for months, it still didn't seem real. They looked to Suze and Rachel in bewilderment, grasping for some kind of explanation.

"We didn't have a choice," Suze mumbled. "There was another board meeting, right after Christmas. It came out of nowhere. They cut the page counts in *half.* They wanted positions—whole sections— cut, too. We both voted against it. You guys need to know that. But they outnumbered us." Beside her, Rachel nodded, looking as if it physically hurt her to do so.

"But we . . . we were *elected*," Steve said. "We were voted in. That's got to count for something." In fact *The Peak*'s elections, held every semester, were widely understood to be a formality, since they were always intentionally under-advertised in the paper's musty back pages, and incumbent editors nearly always ran unopposed.

Suze kept her head down; her hair covered most of her face. "What they said was that, essentially, I guess, the section you were elected to edit no longer exists."

"However you want to slice it," Rachel added, "it adds up to the same thing." The news editor, who prided herself on being the smartest person in the room, looked as if she'd had the chip on her shoulder knocked clean off. "No staff," she added, "and no budget. I don't what the hell we're supposed to do now."

Steve hadn't yet taken his eyes off Suze. "And how, may I ask, did the board decide which sections got cut? I can't help but notice arts is left intact—that wouldn't have anything to do with a certain arts editor being *on* the board, would it?"

Suze was almost inaudible. "You don't know what you're talking about," she said. "Don't make this about that."

So Suze and Steve's covert fling was dead in the water, then. Whatever slow-burning lust had built up between them had been totally used up. They'd marathon-fucked on the lounge couches (in Alex's imagination, anyway) for the last time. He felt a little consolation in watching the two of them turn on each other so quickly—at least the people having sex were as unhappy as the people who weren't.

"You think that's what I'm doing?" Steve said. "You think this is about *that?*"

Keith jumped in, mistaking one of the office's great unspoken secrets for another. "Go fuck yourself," he said to Steve. "Suze can carry her own weight around here. You know damn well it's because the board got sick of you making up all your contributors."

"*Excuse* me?" he said.

"Give it a rest, guy. Would you? You barely even cloaked it. We all know what anagrams are, for fuck's sake." Keith stood up. "Is there anyone here who doesn't already know about this? It's about time we said it out loud for once: Steve makes everything up. And he doesn't even have the brains to invent a fake name. He just rearranges the letters in his."

Keith picked up the last fall issue from the racks and flipped to the opinions section. "Let's see here. 'Trent "Whalebone" Sip'? 'Leni "Banshee" Sprowt'? Genius. And what about those online commenters you keep conveniently rounding up?"

"Keith, don't," Alex said.

"Who were they again? 'Absinthe Pelt Owner'? *'Wanton Bleeper Shit'?*"

Now Steve turned on Keith and spat, "You should talk, you fucking Neanderthal. Nobody has cost this place more money than you. Remind me again why we don't have a working scanner? Oh, right: it's because you tried to upload a bowl of spaghetti. They've been trying to fire you for years. You're a walking liability. And you aren't even that funny."

"My god, Suze," Keith said, exasperated. "How did you ever let this guy put his smelly little dick inside you?"

The argument had come stumblingly full circle.

Steve looked at Keith, then Suze, and finally the crowd of editors. "Good luck, assholes," he said, his fists trembling. "If the *Metro* doesn't burn this place to the ground, I'll come back and do it myself." The string of CDs clattered violently against the door as it slammed shut behind him.

For the next hour the other outgoing editors solemnly gathered their things, while the others stared into computer screens, not talking or even clicking on anything. Chip slowly whistled an extra-funereal version of "Taps" while cramming papers into a duffel bag. Rachel came in and announced that the page count for the next issue would be twelve. Twelve whole pages—a massacre.

Alex was one of the few editors who'd truly believed this day was coming, but he felt just as blindsided as the others. There were so many moving parts, and so many things he didn't understand. For want of real answers, he found himself repeating the very worst clichés. Throwing the baby out with the bathwater. Cutting the nose off to spite the face. He was surprised at how easily they rolled off the tongue.

Rachel landed the only laugh of the whole day. "One nice thing about the page cuts," she deadpanned. "Now I don't have to write anything about Duncan Holtz."

The only place Holtz was ever seen buying food on campus was at the White Spot Express in the AQ. It was a local chain, one step above fast food, and distinguished mainly by its secret-recipe Triple "O" sauce and Pirate Pak kids' combos, which came in foldable cardboard galleons that looked like G-rated *Pequod*s. Mostly Holtz ate alone. Once or twice he was joined by his bird-eyed manager. He always sat near the windows overlooking Convo Mall and the library, the latter of which billowed steam out of its futuristic-looking exhaust gills at all hours.

Holtz would sit there for an hour or so, idly flipping through textbooks or listening to music. He ordered sloppy burgers and drank root beer. Other students gawked from afar, marveling at how normal he seemed. Whenever anyone did work up the nerve to approach him—somehow it was harder because he *wasn't* acting all standoffish and celebrity-y—he remained as unflaggingly pleasant as ever. Where, they wondered, was the overwhelming cockiness? Wasn't that what had landed him back at school in the first place?

All of Tracy's classes from the fall semester had been deferred, in essence wiped from her academic record. She'd been in no condition to attend lectures, let alone assemble the usual slew of term papers.

She'd talked it all over with her departmental advisor, and together they had agreed on the course of action—but when the letter finally came, printed on official SFU letterhead, she slumped to the floor of her front foyer, crying and ashamed at how quickly she'd broken to pieces.

What a waste of time, she thought, sniffing mightily. *Even now. Even this. I just keep falling farther and farther behind.*

Tracy began to see everything she'd done at SFU as an exercise in poor time management. And not just Dave. The school had sent a copy of her academic record along with the letter, and here her decisions were laid out as clear as day. Why hadn't she picked a major faster? Why take three linguistics classes? Why hadn't she just gotten *on* with it? Even Alex, who was a full two years her junior, was going to graduate first.

And her job. What on earth had working at *The Peak* ever gotten her? She wasn't going to be a copy editor when she grew up, was she? Tracy didn't even know whether *copy editor* was one word, or two. She'd seen it spelled both ways, but never looked it up.

Christ, she thought. *I could have been halfway through law school by now.*

The *Metro* distribution workers were posted at either end of campus, one to each bus loop. Apparently the usual retirees the daily hired weren't able to struggle up the hill each morning, because in their place was this gigantic pair of goons—six foot six if they were an inch. They also had identically bad, S-shaped posture, as though they'd spent their formative years ducking under one low door frame after another. As passengers spilled out of the overstuffed buses, the goons sprang out right into the thick of the foot traffic, copies of the paper fanned in each hand like novelty playing cards. "Free *Metro*," they bellowed. "Don't be shy, kids. Take a bunch for your friends."

Alex felt like the goons were staring him down personally whenever he walked past—as if they knew he worked for the competition. It was as if he'd been targeted by some shadowy figure high up in the *Metro* bureaucracy; Alex imagined a psoriatic finger pointing to grainy security-camera footage in an ominous, far-off boardroom and a voice wheezing, "Him." Even though he was hidden under scarves, toques, and headphones—not to mention early-morning fog and the other commuters—he could swear the goon's pupils came into sharp focus as he came into view. This one even had mismatched eyes: one dark brown and one icy white. A Bond henchman come to life. The first few times it happened Alex was so spooked he let the goon stuff a paper into his hand.

Their stacks of newspapers gone by lunchtime, the goons silently packed up and disappeared. Meanwhile the nearby *Peak* boxes contained a rain-spattered cube of an issue that was well over a week old.

Great, Alex thought, letting the metal flap slam shut. *Don't tell me they fired the distribution person, too.*

It was shaping up to be a busy semester on all fronts. Through some logistical snafu, there were two competing movie crews on the SFU campus—a big-budget Hollywood epic and a straight-to-DVD sex farce—each scheduled to shoot pretty well every day until exams. Worse, they needed access to the same locations, but for completely different purposes. One was going to use the football field to stage the landing of a massive rectangular alien spaceship; the other for a ragtag group of misfits to beat the varsity football team at their own sport, all with the aim of having sex with the cheerleaders. SFU students were told to expect major delays until further notice.

Elections for the student government took place in the spring, too, the campaign period for which seemed to start earlier and earlier every year.

Alex imagined his self-diagnosed ulcer swelling to the size of a basketball.

"Pay attention," Tracy said. "It's a very precise system. Whatever I'm keeping goes on the coffee table. Everything else—well, everything else gets garbage-bagged."

"But there's only a mug on that," said Anna, surveying the frazzled state of Tracy's living room. "And, what, seven full trash bags?"

"You're right. I might change my mind about that mug."

The two of them were sorting through the junk Dave had left scattered throughout the house. Tracy had woken up that day with the early-morning ambition to take charge and sort things out—starting with all the clothes and bits of paper that were almost invisible on their own, but which quickly added up to a golem of painful memories. The plan was to rediscover a space that was fundamentally *hers*. She'd already taken a few small steps. Moving the toaster from one side of the kitchen to the other that past weekend had made her so happy she'd taken the rest of the day off. But now was the real kick-off point. Tracy wasn't wild about how feng shui the whole project felt, but she couldn't argue with the results: already her mind felt clearer, less blocked up with residual gunk.

She'd called a few people to come and help out, but in the end only Anna had shown up. Tracy's mom was on a work trip; her brother was back at school in Alberta. Most of her other friends sent similar long-distance sympathies, even though they still lived in town. In the end, it took another English major to understand that this whole event was primarily a metaphor. *Dummies,* Tracy wanted to tell the no-shows. *I don't* physically *need help lifting a pile of old records. I just need you to be here while I do it.*

After an hour of clearing brush, the doorbell rang downstairs.

A few seconds later Alex's head appeared above the banister. He held two coffees aloft.

"I only just got your message," he said, coming around the corner. "And check it out—they put the wrong flavour in mine, so I got another one free. You'll like it. It's boring-ass vanilla." When he saw Anna in the room with her, he stopped. "Oh. Hello."

"Hi," she said back. Alex smiled at her, dazed and helpless, as though he couldn't think of another way to organize his face.

"Hooray, you made it," Tracy said, walking over to him. "I didn't think you were coming. This is Anna—she's in my Ondaatje class."

"We call it the Never-Ondaatjing Story," Anna said.

Shit, he thought, *she's funny, too.*

"Alex works with me at the newspaper," Tracy continued. "He's the features editor." Anna pointed at the coffees he was still holding. "And I suppose you couldn't get them to mess up your order twice? Now what am I supposed to drink?"

"I hadn't thought of that," he said. "I guess we could always just add tap water to mine and double it up."

"Funny. And what is your drink that was so complicated to make?"

Tracy realized the direction the conversation was taking, and roughly shook her head. "Don't even ask," she said, wading back into the mess.

"What? It's no big deal," Alex said, taking a big sip for show. "It's called a banana-raspberry latte. My own invention."

Anna wrinkled her nose. "That sounds disgusting."

"So you *don't* want to share."

"I have this policy against drinks that sound like muffins."

"To be fair, the tap water would probably even it out a bit."

Tracy shoved fresh trash bags at them. "Okay, you two," she snapped, "Let's get started. And thanks for your leftovers, Alex—just leave it over there." What were they thinking? They were supposed to be supporting *her* right now, not flirting like teenagers while she stood there like an idiot, knee-deep in Dave's old wool socks. This was supposed to be a pyrrhic victory *over* relationships, not the beginnings of some new tragedy-in-waiting.

Tracy considered pouring her coffee into the trusty old mug that was sitting all alone in her pathetic little salvage pile. What was the point? She picked the mug up and threw it unceremoniously into the shiny new garbage bag at her feet.

Each spring semester, when Burnaby Mountain became overrun with fog and ice wind, Clubs Days was held indoors, the booths squeezed in along the main floor of the AQ. The event's tone was completely different than in the fall. Club reps now had to engage with students walking between classes, who ignored them just as firmly as they did the credit card hawkers and psychology-experiment recruiters who normally trolled the territory. Sign-up rates were abysmal. Camaraderie gave way to full-blown jealousy. Turf wars were declared; undercover agents were sent out to snoop on clubs with similar mandates, each trying to subtly smear the competition.

The Peak's booth, meanwhile, was nowhere to be seen. In the aftermath of the firings, they'd forgotten to reserve a spot. Claude had sent an email to the remaining editors offering to do it himself, but they'd all assumed someone else was going to respond.

Amidst this sour mood, which was only exacerbated by the constant trails of black water left by so many people taking shelter from the rain, Duncan Holtz came wandering through one sleepy afternoon. He paused tentatively in front of several different tables, asked a few questions, and took every one of the pamphlets on offer. Despite the puddles, his sneakers remained immaculately white.

He didn't sign up for anything—signature hounds were quick to verify this—but by all accounts he seemed genuinely interested. It was whispered down the tables that maybe he didn't have many friends at school yet, despite his immense arm's-length popularity. Some found this cute. Said that he was a charity case they wouldn't mind taking on, if you caught their drift. Others thought it sad and vaguely profound. Many snickered. The star of *Maximum Death* was lonely? Take a bath in money, they said. Go fly a diamond-studded kite. Cry me a river of Miley Cyrus's tears.

Alex lay alone on the production room couch, his laptop open and balanced on his chest.

The shortcut to refresh a website is control + R, he thought. *On a Mac, you use the butterfly key instead of control. What's the actual name for that butterfly symbol? That's what they called it back in elementary school. Seems silly to say it out loud now. There's a little apple icon beside it on some versions, so sometimes people call it the apple key. But that doesn't sound right, either. F5 also works. Once you know the shortcut, you can keep on refreshing a given page as often as you like—even before it's had time to reload from last time. It's a muscle that feels good to flex. Like shooting at someone's feet, making them dance around just because you can.*

Refresh, refresh, refresh.

No news to display.

Start again, Facebook. Dance.

So many useless keys on a keyboard, too. What does scroll lock do? Has anyone ever pressed it, except by mistake?

These days most websites have a built-in refresher whenever new content gets added. So, really, butterfly-R has become kind of useless. It's like the close-door button on elevators (which don't work either, by the way). It gives you the illusion of control, when really, someone in a room you'll never see, let alone set foot in, has his own plan, and he's not all that concerned with your precious little input.

No news to display.

"But have you actually *seen* him yet?"

"I told you! We were in the same tutorial, but he had to switch after the first week."

"Probably because you kept taking pictures of him during class."

"Shut up. I was discreet."

"It has a flash!"

"*I could have been texting.* God. He doesn't know anything."

"Uh-huh."

"God! Worst!"

". . ."

"Did you hear the paparazzi were on campus last week?"

"Where?"

"I heard in Convo Mall, outside the Pub. Apparently he was super nice."

"Yeah."

"Like, *super* nice. Like, way nicer than he could've been."

"He is pretty awesome."

"I know! But c'mon: don't you understand what this means for us?"

"What?"

"We could totally get onto *The Superficial* if we play our cards right."

". . ."

"It's simple. We just follow him around and when we see a camera, boom! We jump into the frame and pose."

"Are you kidding? Why would you even want to do that?"

"That's how it happens now! Some designer sees you standing in a photo beside someone famous, and they say, 'Who's that?'"

"You're retarded."

"*It's true!* Look, all I'm saying is that I'd kill someone to get on that website."

"Okay."

"I'm serious. I will switch majors. I'll clear my schedule. I'll bring my lucky green dress into rotation. Don't think I won't do it."

Production, week three, late January.

Two more campus businesses cancelled their advertising accounts, leaving just a half-dozen or so that Rick could even get on the phone anymore. Not only that, word had gotten out about the hidden semesterly fee, as well as the brief window during which students could get their seven dollars refunded. So there was also a constant lineup of disgruntled business and science majors waiting outside Rick's door to contend with.

The *Peak* office had always looked disorganized and endearingly filthy, but now things were downright ruinous. Most of the computers sat abandoned; the accompanying chairs had been sold on craigslist. So, too, had the drawing table, the refrigerator and microwave, one of the couches, and whatever promotional books and CDs Rick had been able to unload at pawn-shop prices. A few lonely cables dangled from the ceiling. The editors had always been encouraged to appropriate pens from other places whenever possible—now Rick was starting to insinuate that they might want to start looking for a photocopier and scanner to use on the sly, too.

So far the remaining editors' approach was to try and maintain, as best they could, *The Peak* as it used to exist. To keep a stone face and carry on with business as usual. They'd had to ditch the humour section, though—nobody was willing to even try to emulate Keith's bizarre vision. Chip's section was also gone. The others had been forced to accept the truth of one of the most enduring stereotypes about student journalists, at least in *The Peak*'s grand tradition: nobody gave a shit about sports. An exception could sometimes be made for the Canucks, but even then only when they were guaranteed a spot in the playoffs.

"Alex!" Tracy called, leaning through the divider window. "What does *Peak* Speak look like? Did you do it yet?"

A few seconds later he appeared at her desk, rubbing his forehead. "It's done. It took forever, but it's done."

The survey had been part of Steve's old jurisdiction, and was initially set for the scrap heap, too, until Alex saw it as an opportunity to put out some feelers, in the hopes of maybe rebranding the paper. The format was simple: you asked five randomly selected students the same question, and then took their picture. It had taken Alex nearly three hours.

He handed Tracy a printout of the page, with the content and graphics half plugged-in. It was far from finished; then again, the sun hadn't even set yet. "'What do you think of *The Peak*?'" she read aloud. "'What would you like to see more of? Or less?'" She frowned. "I don't like that last bit. It's awkward."

Alex shrugged. "That's how I asked it. Nothing we can do about it now, is there?"

She thought about it. "But a real newspaper wouldn't print it like this. So there's the real question: do they just never ask the wrong thing?"

"I always wonder about that. How much are real papers allowed to change quotes, so they make more sense? Who's in charge of deciding that stuff?"

"No idea," Tracy said. "If these rules are so important, you'd think someone would've thought to write them down somewhere."

From the next cubicle over, Rachel was adamant. "You've got to fix the quotes," she shouted. "Take the *ums* out. Polish up their grammar. It's just common courtesy. Plus, if you don't, every quote from an exchange student makes us sound like racists."

"Yeah," Tracy said. "I guess that makes sense. Anyway, look at these *answers*. Three out of the five people said, 'What is *The Peak?*'"

Alex took the page back from her. "Now I don't know whether to pat myself on the back for being such an honest editor, or jump out the goddamn window."

The posters were bland and tiny, printed on regular-sized sheets of paper, but there were dozens of them. Duncan Holtz took a step back from the wall and craned his neck, taking in the checker-patterned rows. Low-level SFSS drones had spent the previous week canvassing as much of the campus as they could physically reach with reminders that elections for the 2009–10 student government were nigh. Nominations had to be in by mid-February. Two weeks of campaigning after that. A debate. Then polls were open from March 16–18, with winners declared by midnight. It was free to run, as the posters emphasized with a double underline, and also low stress; all you needed were ten student signatures. Your friends counted.

Holtz absently scratched his cheek. His lips moved along, subtly ghosting the names, dates, and locations. A small group of the actor's fans stood off to one side, pointing and whispering in wild speculation.

He made a quick glance over each shoulder, then pulled out a pen and started writing notes onto the meat of his palm.

One girl in the fan group let out an involuntary shriek of delight. The outburst startled two students who happened to be walking past, and whose hands fluttered over their chests in shock. They glared at the shrieker, then over to who she was shrieking at.

They rolled their eyes and kept walking.

"Yes, that's the standard line of critique. I suppose it's valid enough. And now, the big one: *Volcano Dreams?*"

"I haven't seen it. I'm familiar with its thesis, but I haven't seen it. Have you? I was under the impression it never made it out of Sundance."

"It didn't. Well, last year I was doing work study for Professor Penrose, and she knows someone on one of the committees there. Somehow she acquired a rough cut. Primitive, but watchable. I made a copy."

"Smart. And?"

"Mm. How can I phrase this? It's as if Eisenstein lived long enough to make *Ivan the Terrible, Part XIX*. It's early Bergman on a steady diet of peyote and lemon Gatorade. It's . . . who's the director who makes those explosion films?"

"No idea, I'm sure."

"*Bay*. It's as if Michael Bay remade one of Ozu's masterworks. It's *Floating Weeds* at three hundred miles per hour—everything's been sped up and edited into trite, barbaric ribbons."

"*Floating Weeds*. Seminal."

"Indeed."

"Which other of Holtz's films have you seen?"

"Nothing lately, of course. The only other film of his I can even think of offhand is *The Last Troubadour,* which was what, 2004? Utter rubbish. What about you?"

"The same, the same."

" . . . "

"You know, I didn't find *Fang City* wholly repulsive when I was younger."

"It did have its charms, didn't it?"

Another advertiser jumped ship.

Alex took a swig of ultra-carbonated lime cream soda and tilted back in his chair. Surrounding him were more than a dozen annual volumes, their spines cracked, their pages crispy and the colour of old mustard. It was amazing, he thought, how even though technology got better and better, the newspaper's content stuck to pretty much the same ten-year loop: a hyper-political editorial staff grew boorish and gave way to a new group of goofballs, who then went too far in the other direction and got usurped by a fresh batch of ideologues, who had no memory of the forefathers in whose footsteps they followed (and with whom they might or might not have even gotten along). Alex had studied these bygone eras for so long that by now he could spot whether an issue from the mid-nineties was helmed by a particular arts editor just by scanning the section for em-dashes. (Apparently she had a zero-tolerance policy that culminated in a rather petulant Editor's Voice in her outgoing issue.) And when he read letters protesting a notorious columnist's trilogy about fucking women of various religions, Alex smiled and flipped ahead to when said columnist followed up with an open letter to Durex condoms, accompanied by a half-page photo of his saggy dick. How amazing was it, he thought, that Keith had no idea this man even existed? They were soulmates, and Alex could find a new one with every decade he skipped backwards. These were the ghosts of *Peak* past.

When he'd first gotten involved with the newspaper, Alex had unwittingly walked into the middle of a backlash against a group of rabble-rousing activists—guys who'd routinely taken aim at local politicians and thumbed their socialist noses at the SFU administration whenever possible. They were one of the first groups on campus to really push the Darfur issue on the general student body; in fact they'd been so solemn and reverential about it that, looking back, there'd been nowhere for the conversation to go but down. And the incoming editors, Alex included, had been all too happy to take it there. Still, it was hard to feel proud of a legacy that included quite so many fart noises and Vin Diesel jokes.

It was strange to think of who he'd forever be associated with in these crusty pages. There was Tracy, obviously. And Steve and Suze he'd worked with for a few years apiece, so that was fine. Yet there were also people like Keith and Chip, pear-shaped oddities whom he never quite figured out, but for whom he felt a kind of accidental, secondhand warmth.

And now the tides were shifting once more. Alex was about to become a relic himself. The disdain for his era and all they stood (or didn't stand) for was getting louder and louder; its rumblings were distant, but unmistakable. He took another swig of the cream soda and put the bottle back down on the desk next to the Barbara Pym paperback, which he'd taken to carrying around in his back pocket like a talisman.

Whenever Alex had talked to his newer contributors lately, he could all but hear them thinking, *Sure, old man. Whatever you say. It's not going to be like this much longer.*

They'd stopped listening to his suggestions for story edits. They'd started pitching him the same feature idea over and over again, until he finally accepted it. And whenever they did come to his office hours, they all smiled like hyenas, looking around at the kingdom they were about to inherit.

Two days after the celebrity was spotted reading the election posters, a small headline appeared in the *Metro*'s entertainment section. From page 14, near the bottom of the page: "Holtz to run for SFU prez." A Mack Holloway exclusive—the official list of candidates wasn't set to be released for days. But his article quoted two sources, both anonymous, who claimed that the actor had handed in his nomination form and was now officially in contention for the SFSS's highest and most visible position. Then, at the end of the piece, a cryptic statement from Holtz's manager: "Duncan just wants to be the best, no matter what he does. Whether it's movies or something like this—which I obviously can't comment on, guys, be serious—you can expect him to give it his all."

At which point Tracy threw the paper across the room. "If the answer was no, he'd have just said no," she said, lighting a cigarette at her desk. "This is getting weirder and weirder."

That day's issue of the *Metro* sold out at SFU in less than an hour. The next day the daily ran a follow-up story, this time at the top of page twelve; the day after that, a half-page profile up front, next to the local news. By the end of the week another campus business had permanently suspended its ad account with *The Peak*.

The week after that, Mack Holloway was reassigned to Burnaby Mountain until further notice.

The Peak, meanwhile, scrambled to stay afloat. Rachel went aggressively after the local beat, sticking to the SFU-centric issues that a paper based off the mountain couldn't compete with: the opening of an all-soup restaurant in Maggie Benston, ongoing concerns about SFU's plagiarism code, and Gung Haggis Fat Choy, the university's annual Robbie Burns Day/Chinese New Year celebration. Suze followed suit in the arts section. Whereas before she'd mostly relegated on-campus performances to the events listings, now she started writing about the sfu theatre and art gallery to a degree that even they found to be a little excessive. Every show, from the twenty-four-hour Aeschylus marathon to the guy who ironically painted a surfboard decal on the side of his car, got a preview and a review.

One thing the remaining staff agreed upon was that Duncan Holtz's name would not appear in the paper's pages. No gossipy letters to the editors, no easy jokes at his expense. He was just another student, and would be treated accordingly.

Let the *Metro* stoop to lowest-common-denominator tabloid journalism. For once in the *Peak* editors' lives, they were going to take the high road.

Another advertiser disappeared.

Tyson looked over at Alex, who was studying with him in a rarely trafficked corner of the library, and said, "We're going to Pub Night."

Alex groaned but didn't look up. "Like hell we are. I think I've had my fill of watching you hit on drunk teenagers."

"You're right."

"Mmm," he said, underlining a passage in his film textbook. "Am I now?"

"Indeed. We're going to watch *you* hit on teenagers."

Now Alex looked up. "We've been over this. Absolutely not."

"Let me ask you this: have you had sex, even once, since the last time we talked about this?"

"I—"

"It was a *rhetorical question,* dick," Tyson said, reaching across the table and slapping Alex clean across one cheek. Someone from a nearby cubicle shushed them. Tyson added in a whisper, "The answer is no and we both know it."

Alex rubbed his face. *"Ow.* And how would you know this?"

"Simple. If you'd gotten even a fiddly little HJ by now, you'd have rubbed it in my face. You're a prude, and self-loathing to boot, but I know you also want to prove me wrong. That's what's really killing you, isn't it?"

Alex wound up to respond, but Tyson was right. It was, he realized, with no small whiff of depression, just like his writing career: Alex wanted the bragging rights that came with being sexually active more than he wanted to actually have sex. Even if just for his own private reassurance. The identities of his sexual partners, like the contents of his unwritten novel, were placeholders, their details TBD. *This can't be healthy,* he thought.

"No fucking way I'm going to Pub Night," Alex whispered back, and waved his hand in dismissal. But his head was already alight with the dozens of covert trysts that no doubt took place there every Thursday night, when drinks other than the rancid mountain ale were on special, and where the social code for sexual attraction was relaxed even further than usual. The truth was, he might not get many more chances like this.

Another.

And another.

Rick went on stress leave.

The enormity of their mistake only gradually dawned on them. But once it did, the editors bailed, and bailed hard.

It was Tracy who first figured out the flaw in their new Holtz-free strategy. She was walking up the AQ's main steps when she was cut off by members of one of the film crews, pushing wheelbarrows of props and equipment across in both directions. As she waited for them to pass, she overheard a group of students breathlessly gossiping next to her about Holtz's run for president. All of them were going to vote for the celebrity, "because wouldn't that be hilarious?"

"Suddenly it all clicked," she told the collective that week. "We've never really been suppressing the story—everyone knew about it already. And now it's a legitimate public *event*."

Alex dropped his head into his hands. Tracy was right. Somewhere along the line, the *Peak* editors had become reactionaries on a whole new scale. And snobs, too: the one thing SFU readers were genuinely interested in was the one thing their newspaper refused to tell them about. Because it was—what? Too obvious? *Oh no,* Alex thought, his imaginary ulcer about to pop. *Our coverage itself has become ironic.*

The rest of the room seemed to be thinking the same thing. Rachel stood up and announced, "I don't know about you guys, but I don't want my section defined by the things I'm *not* writing about."

"You know," Alex added aloud, "the *Metro* is claiming that they broke this whole Holtz story. And that's technically true—we didn't report it. But we could have. We knew about it before anyone else did. It happened down the hall from the room we're sitting in." He was getting excited. It was the kind of riled-up energy he imagined was present all the time during *The Peak*'s political eras, and it felt thrilling to tap into, even just for a few seconds. "Rachel's right, guys. I bet we could still pull it off."

"You mean—" Claude said, perched on the edge of his seat.

"I think it's time to drop the embargo."

Thanks to the *Metro*'s coverage, a wave of other, more respectable media had already started nosing around SFU. First Vancouver's paid dailies and free weeklies, then local TV news and the CBC. By the time *The Peak* decided to dip its toes in the water, the story was getting traction on the national newswires.

But Mack Holloway remained the first reporter on the job. He was also the most visible around campus, chasing students for quotes and scribbling in beat-up, dollar-store notebooks. His was the face you'd recognize: creased but stoic, with a career newspaperman's easy air of exhaustion. He commandeered a table next to the big-budget sci-fi production near the lecture halls; the crew assumed he was some suit from the studio, or more likely the haggard screen-writer. Whatever this shaggy dog was turning into—be it comedy or tragedy—Holloway seemed bent on bearing witness to it.

Another. *The Peak* was a sinking ship, more water than boat.

Alanis Morissette was right, you know.

The truth about irony appeared in the summer of 1996, but nobody recognized it—even though it spent weeks on top of the charts. And nobody talks about it now. They all say, "Isn't it ironic that 'Ironic' isn't actually ironic?"

They're all wrong, the bastards.

A black fly in your chardonnay is ironic. It is. You expect fancy wine to be fancy, and your expectations get thwarted. Boom. A no-smoking sign on your cigarette break is really *ironic—we're talking hearty, old-fashioned, character-building irony here. And ten thousand spoons when all you really need is a knife? Don't get me started.*

You hear the same argument trotted out a million times. In rez hallways late at night, or while lying on the hood of your buddy's car, stoned out of your mind and waiting for airplanes that will never appear. It goes like this: the examples Morissette gives aren't ironic— they're just unhappy coincidences. Sure, I don't want *rain on my wedding day, but that doesn't make me the victim of a fuggin' poetic device* over here.

Alex took a sip of what he called swamp mud—all of West Mall's six drip coffee flavours mixed together. He was clicking around Duncan Holtz's IMDb page, absent-mindedly investigating everything the man had ever appeared in.

Nope. Triple nope. The only reason people accept this kind of asinine logic is because they think different rules apply to irony in real life versus in fiction. If any of this shit happened to Hamlet, they'd have no problem whatsoever. They'd write a term paper about it.

But for some reason, these people are unwilling to treat their lives like a story, and themselves as the writer/director/hero.

Why?

Why do the same people who maintain multiple blogs, soundtrack their every walk to the store (thereby shutting out all competing narratives), cultivate a public list of their top friends, and frame their daily existence as a string of status updates—why can't they recognize the one basic force in their lives that feeds all the others? Why don't they know the name of the most-used tool in their toolbox?

14

IRREGULARITIES ON THE CAMPAIGN TRAIL

In total there were four candidates for the presidency. One was Samantha Gilmartin, a fiery, pathologically focused sociology major who was also the current SFSS university relations officer and, until a few months ago, a shoo-in years in the making. One was Piotr Ivanov, a 3rd-year transfer student who was running on a platform exclusively devoted to getting calamari added to the Pub's menu. One was a mysterious woman known only as Kennedy, who'd filed all of her paperwork through the mail. And one was Duncan Holtz.

These were the faces and statistics running laps through Rachel's head as she swapped tapes in her recorder, last-minute prep before her interview with the head of the Independent Electoral Commission. This was going to be a teaser story, part of her lead-up to the big debate spread later on. The IEC was the official election watchdog, its members charged with the thankless task of refereeing the proceedings and keeping all mud-slinging down to a tolerable level. Inevitably, they were given shit from all directions, and roundly criticized for failures both real and imaginary—even though voter turnout always stalled somewhere around 10 percent.

Rachel took the stairwell two steps at a time. Over the weekend the walls had been stripped of their election notices and replaced with a fresh coat of individual campaign posters. Each candidate was assigned an official colour, meaning that every bare surface on campus was now a pixelated rainbow of lofty promises and almost-catchy slogans. Amidst the chaos, Rachel's eye was drawn to the purple posters of Duncan Holtz, which seemed to outnumber everyone else's 2:1. The guy was clearly making a serious go of it. And you couldn't help but be drawn to the pure Hollywood-ness of his face. Walking across Convo Mall, she passed other candidates shaking hands and handing out even more flyers.

Rachel repeated the names, slogans, and campaign promises until they were committed to memory. Usually she'd have had this stuff mapped out weeks in advance, but this year's temporary Holtz embargo had thrown her off. She cursed herself for walking into an interview so unprepared.

Wanting to appear as neutral and unbiased as possible, the IEC had set up its office this year in the Rotunda, far from the prying eyes of SFSS headquarters. A circular study area that sat directly above the lower bus loop, this was once the epicentre of the entire campus—*The Peak*'s original office had been in there, little more than a typewriter and bucket in a windowless room, way back in '65. Now it housed the women's and LGBTQ centres, CJSF 90.1 FM, and a bunch of other advocacy and research groups. A table on one side of the common area was piled high with old clothes and ragged books, free for the swapping.

The defining feature of the Rotunda, though, was the glass column in the middle, around which all of the desks and tables were organized. That's where Rachel spotted Lana Murphy, this year's IEC head watchdog, standing on a chair and applying a strip of scotch tape to the cardboard walls of her makeshift office. She nodded at Rachel over her shoulder and wearily invited her to take a seat.

Right away Rachel could tell she was a kindred spirit, and an ally in the war against idiocy that was being fought on campus every day. SFU: A Sphincter Says What? Since 1965. The giveaway was Lana's fingernails (polished to within an inch of their lives) as well as the skin around them (ravaged to same). Rachel thought of her own mangled split ends with pride.

"Rachel," Lana said. "Nice to see you. Sorry about this." She stepped off the chair, which wobbled as her weight shifted. Back on the floor, she regained her poise. "It's embarrassing, I know."

"What, specifically, is the embarrassing part?" Rachel put her recorder down on one thigh and got out her notebook.

"Look at me," Lana said. "I'm surrounded by pieces of a refrigerator box. My staff has been wiped out. Our budget this year is less than zero—the SFSS is claiming we owe *them* money." She pointed at Rachel's recorder, whose dusty tape made a faint whirring as it spun. "I guess you guys know a thing or two about cutbacks, too, huh?"

"Actually, that's the same one we've always had," Rachel said. "But yes. Things are rough in our office as well. We just pawned our printer. We're getting lectures about leaving too many lights on.

"You know," she added, the idea just coming to her, "we could put a fiscal spin on this story, if you wanted to. Budget cuts, personnel being stretched thin, that kind of thing. Recession stuff plays really well right now."

Lana shook her head, her smile veering toward the condescending. "No. Thanks, but no. The last thing I need right now is to come off as whiny, or that I came to you guys to vent about my problems."

"Fine by me." Rachel felt a little slighted. Maybe they weren't going to be pals after all. "Let's get started, then. What do you think of this year's crop of candidates?"

"As I'm sure you know, Rachel," she said, slipping into her on-the-record persona, "it's not up to me to say. Obviously it's encouraging to see so many names on the ticket, but I can't speak to the individuals' relative merits. I'm a disinterested third party. The IEC will remain fair and impartial throughout."

"And what do you see as your group's main duties leading up to the election?"

"The IEC's mandate is simple: to ensure that all of the protocols, as laid out in the student society's bylaws, are followed to the word and to the letter. Candidates have strict limits on how much they are allowed to spend and how they are to conduct themselves during campaigning. We've already conducted a thorough inspection of the posters that have been put up, verifying that they fall within set parameters."

Rachel sensed a soft spot. "Have there been any violations so far?"

Success: Lana went briefly marble-mouthed before replying, "Actually, yes."

Rachel was about to keep pressing when another IEC member burst through the Rotunda doors. His face was drained of colour. "We have a problem," he said. "Down at the printer's."

Lana hopped to her feet. "Coming," she said, then looked to Rachel with a sly, relieved smile. "Sorry. Looks like we'll have to wrap up early."

"You know," Rachel said, "I think I'll come along. Just for fun."

The trio hustled along the main drag of the Maggie Benston Centre to Quad Books, the SFSS-owned and -operated copy store from which all elections materials had to be printed. But rather than follow Lana and her IEC cohort inside, where a group of people had already gathered, arms crossed, at the full-service desk, Rachel fell back to chat up the lone guy leaning against one of the grubby old copiers in the hallway.

"Hello," Rachel said to him. "I'm the news editor at *The Peak*." She gestured with her thumb back at the door, as if to say, *Those dummies don't know anything*. "Do you know what's going on?"

The guy looked around for a second. "It's all this election stuff," he said. "Every year it's like this. I've been here for three of these things now, and it never changes."

Rachel's recorder whirred away inside her jacket pocket. "What do you mean?"

"Well, everyone gets fifty dollars to spend on their campaign materials. No matter what. And they have to get their stuff printed from our shop. It's first come, first served. Those are the rules."

"Right. I knew this."

"Yeah," he said, "except you probably *also* noticed that a certain presidential candidate's got his posters in all the best spots around campus." The guy looked around again. "Guess what time Duncan Holtz's posters were supposed to be printed at?"

"Pretty early, I'd have to guess," Rachel said.

"You'd think so." The guy's gaze wandered down to the floor for a few seconds. "Except I'm the one in charge of the wait list. Duncan Holtz was the last person to sign up."

Rachel's eyes lit up. "Which means . . ."

"His posters are still technically in the queue. They shouldn't have even started printing until 4:00 p.m. today."

Oh, blessed dumb luck.

Even Rick was impressed, and he told Rachel as much when he came by the office the next week to pick up his paycheque and—in flagrant violation of his doctor's orders—take a quick look around to see what kind of shape the place was in. Due to budget cutbacks, the board hadn't yet hired his temporary replacement. She held the cover story right up to his face.

"It's good, Rachel," he said. "Real good." He still looked dazed and overtired, as if he ought to have a cartoon bandage wrapped around his head. "Were you able to get any comment from Holtz?"

She shook her head. "I got his manager on the phone, but he said he couldn't comment on the—oh, what was the phrase? The 'efficacy or lack thereof of a business run by the current administration.'"

"Yuck."

"Yep," she said, grinning. "So I just ran that."

"Good girl. Did anyone else up here cover it?"

Alex jumped in from two chairs over. "I heard CBC mentioned it. And the *Metro* got it the day after we did. Just a short thing at the back, though—and Mack Holloway didn't have our source from Quad Books. He was basically cribbing from us."

"Nicely done." Rick started moving toward the door. With his health still fragile, he couldn't afford to be around these kids for more than a few minutes. The way they carried themselves, with an air of independence, but so obviously looking for a parental figure to latch onto and suck approval out of—it put Rick in constant fear of relapse. He was a PhD student, for crying out loud. How had he ended up with a job that was such a terrifying simulacrum of middle age: the equivalent of eleven clingy kids and a mortgage he couldn't afford?

At the door, he turned back and saw, with a wince, the naked expectation on the editors' faces. They had no idea how bad the situation really was. *Well,* he thought, *at least there are some moments you get to relish.* "It's a victory, guys." Then, reaching for the right combination of inspiration and tough-love inflections borrowed from an old soccer coach: "Keep it up. There's lots more work to be done."

Rachel looked down at the cover again in wonder. "*Yeah,* there is," she said.

Lately Alex had been feeling weirdly optimistic. He'd banked a few of the better features from the CUP newswire and so was on easy streak at work, and his classes were as mindless as they'd ever been. The film course was a particularly good wheel-spinner. His professor began every lecture by quoting from that week's film's IMDb page. She had an ongoing pop quiz where students had to identify that particular movie's plot keywords; among the correct answers for *Antitrust,* a 2001 tech-thriller starring Ryan Phillippe, included One Word Title, Racist Comment, and Babe Scientist. One week they'd walked around campus for all three hours, re-enacting scenes from the syllabus and comparing celebrity sightings.

And it turned out that the week of the debate was also the week that Holtz was scheduled to drop by FPA 137 and give his hotly antici-pated guest lecture. Thinking this might be an opportunity to pin the celebrity to the wall about the photocopying scandal, Alex offered to sneak someone else from *The Peak* into the class. There was an allotted time for questions following the lecture. Holtz would have nowhere to hide, and several hundred witnesses would be there in case he said or did anything stupid and tried to lie about it later. Rachel was ecstatic, until she realized she had to give an in-class presenta-tion at that exact time. She groused about having to find a competent replacement, until, to everyone's surprise, Tracy volunteered.

"Copy editors," Rachel muttered. "You people think you can do everyone else's job better than they can."

"'You people'?" asked Tracy.

"Okay. Let's give it a shot. Do you know what you're doing out there?"

"I've been reading your stuff all this time, haven't I?" Tracy replied. "You think I didn't pick up a thing or two? And besides, Alex here will be my co-pilot."

Rachel chewed on a piece of her hair, then nodded. "Take as much space as you need. Just make sure you get a good question in, okay? That pretty boy won't even know what hit him."

15

NERVES

That afternoon Tracy and Alex headed to the lecture together, armed with hidden tape recorders and dummy binders. The class was big enough that Professor Monahan would never notice one new face in the crowd; in fact, other students had already started routinely sneaking in their friends, since it amounted to watching a free movie on a theatre-quality screen in a pleasantly air-conditioned room. But since they had to sit close enough to the front to make sure the *Peak* recorder would pick up Holtz's voice, they weren't taking any chances. It was all part of Alex's plan—he'd even made a photocopy of the course syllabus to stick in the front page of Tracy's fake workbook. When she saw it, she had to laugh.

"So what's this movie we have to watch?" she asked.

"*Maximum Death 2*. You ever seen it? A real thinking-man's killing spree."

"And they filmed part of it here?"

"Yeah. There's this terrorist/computer hacker with a secret mountain lair—located conveniently near Convo Mall."

They stopped for coffee at the foot of the gleaming new FPA wing. Suddenly Alex felt the full weight of his nerves come down on him. He shifted his backpack around and jingled the keys and change in his pocket, too embarrassed to tell Tracy he hadn't even brought his wallet, for fear of being identified. All he had on him was a small wad of bills, in case of emergency. He couldn't remember the last time he'd taken a risk even as slight as the one Tracy was about to—if this was how strongly his body reacted to being an accomplice, how would it feel to be the actual perpetrator?

On the other hand, he was a liberal arts student. Fostering timidity was what the discipline did best. It taught you about Shakespeare and Dostoevsky, and then expected you to venture forth into the world and become a citizen of action? What a joke. Every semester SFU was churning out hundreds of Hamlets, hundreds of men from the underground. The professors made crippling indecision sound like a virtue, those sneaks—and students paid them for the privilege.

Just then Alex saw Tyson strolling down the corridor toward them. "Hiya," he said. "What are you two gaylords up to?"

When they told him, his jaw fell open. "No kidding. I *love* that movie."

"Why am I not surprised?" said Tracy.

"You've got to let me come with," he pleaded. *"Please."*

This was more than Alex had bargained for. Discretion had never been Tyson's strong suit—in a way, it was surprising he'd never applied for a job at *The Peak*. A list of worst-case scenarios presented itself. Would Tyson whoop at every explosion during the screening? Catcall Holtz as he approached the podium? Maybe he'd try to pick up a girl sitting all the way across the hall, just for something to do. And since Alex was the only one actually enrolled in the class, he'd be the one to take blame when the truth inevitably came out.

Relax, he told himself. *Just tell him the room is full. Put your foot down, for once.*

But Tracy was already begrudgingly pointing out the classroom at the top of the stairs. *Never mind.* Alex sprinted a few steps to catch up, scalding his thumb in the process as his coffee splooshed up over the rim.

At the entrance to the class, Alex reeled as he saw Keith and Chip standing there. Neither he nor Tracy had seen either of them since the firing.

"What are *you* guys doing here?" he said.

"We're here for Holtz's thing," Keith said. Chip nodded vigorously in agreement. "And, uh, we figured you might be here, too," he added.

Alex felt sincerely happy to see them. They were from the same generation, after all.

"Not even going to introduce me, huh?" Tyson elbowed his way in front. "I'm Tyson. You assholes must be from *The Peak,* too." They swapped introductions. "Oh! You're the ones who got canned. You must hate my boy Alex right now."

"On the contrary," Chip said. "We all took the same marching orders. As they say, politics stops at the shore."

"You're goddamned right about that, Chippo," Keith said.

Tracy said, "So what's new? Have you guys been—hanging out together?"

Keith and Chip belched at the same time. They both looked a little disheveled, Alex thought. And Keith was sporting what appeared to be the wispy beginnings of his own moustache. "How could you tell?" he said. "Hey, by the way, I have a copy editor question for you."

"Go on, then."

"What's a funnier comeback: stick it in your dick?"

"Well—"

"Or stick it *up* your dick?"

"It's nice to see you, too," Tracy said.

Chip added, "What about, 'Think quick, dick pic'?"

The kid was a quick study.

Christ, Alex realized. *How am I supposed to get all of us in there? I'm gonna get busted for sure.*

He needn't have worried. Inside, the lecture hall was packed to the gills, now more closely resembling an actual movie theatre—right down to the jackets splayed over chairs, placeholders for those yet to arrive, and the kids huddled in circles, staring hypnotically into their phones. The usual pre-class chatter had tripled in volume. *Better still,* thought Alex with relief, *it was crammed full of people who didn't belong there.* He followed Tyson to the middle of the centre section, where his friend kicked three jackets onto the floor and brusquely told another couple to make room. "Go on—*move.*"

Keith whispered to Tracy, "Who is this guy? I like his style."

As for the specific make-up of the crowd, Alex couldn't get a good read. There were some obvious fans—had someone made a *poster* way in the back?—but also plenty of others in full nonchalance mode, not giving an outward fuck about anything. The kind of person who smirked at their every surrounding as if it were quaint enough, passable for now, but so completely outclassed by the places where they usually hung out. Alex found this pose frighteningly convincing, at least until he reminded himself that if such a Mecca of Hip actually existed, wouldn't these people just fuck off there already and leave everyone else alone?

The actual FPA students were easier to pick out. They'd at least bothered to bring books, if not open them. Alex realized the dummy binders he'd rigged up were about a thousand times more elaborate than necessary. A few of these budding cinephiles had removed their glasses and were rubbing the bridges of their respective noses, trying to block out the chorus of idiots surrounding them.

From his pocket, Keith awkwardly pulled out a theatre-sized box of Milk Duds. Tyson leaned across the others to demand a handful; settling back, he said to Alex, "Who is this guy? I like his style."

Alex thought he also saw some of the other SFSS candidates milling around at the back, but he couldn't be sure. This year he'd paid even less attention to the nominations than usual, since whoever won would be sworn in after he'd cleared out his stuff from the *Peak* offices once and for all. They would be the first government of the Post-Alex Era, and he couldn't be bothered to keep up with the new narrative.

"Hey," he said, nudging Tracy. "Am I crazy, or is that Holtz's competition in the back?"

She shrugged. "I have no idea."

"Me neither. Seems weird, though, doesn't it? To spy on a guest lecture about exploding aircraft carriers?"

"Maybe they know something we don't."

"Yeah," Alex said. "Odds are good on that."

After a few minutes, Professor Monahan came in and started anxiously shuffling papers at her podium. Holtz's manager approached from one of the side exits, whispering something in her ear and moving away again. He kept watch at the exit like a bodyguard, hands crossed over his crotch. Professor Monahan looked up, and squinted at the newly tripled size of her audience. The class's hum gradually dwindled, then disappeared.

"Hello, ladies and gentlemen," she began. "I see some of you have brought a friend or two with you today." Alex glanced furtively at Tyson, who was holding his cell phone out in front of him, brazenly filming the whole thing.

Professor Monahan broke out in a girlish grin. "Well, I suppose that's all understandable." She gestured to both sides of the room. "Welcome to FPA 137. This is a course that's 100 percent devoted to filmic media created right here at SFU. It's the first of its kind, I don't mind telling you. We are studying these wonderful films and television series in the hopes of coming to better terms with how our school's representation in the media impacts our own identity as the students, TAs, and faculty who live and work here."

Tyson shouted, "Bring on the Holtz!"

A woollier quiet overtook the room. Alex stared hard at the floor, the guilty ringing in his ears rivaled only by the creak of his tape recorder. Tyson, unfazed, still held his phone aloft; its red recording light blinked on and off, on and off, on and off.

The silence was broken by Keith guffawing, his mouth full of chocolate-caramel goo: *"Fang City!"*

A tidal wave of new chatter rose from the audience, dozens of whispered meta-commentaries from people who all assumed they were speaking much too quietly to be heard. Tyson turned to face the other students, chanting, "Bring on the Holtz! Bring on the Holtz!" A few scattered fans chimed in.

Holtz's bird-eyed manager was whispering to someone hidden in the wings of the lecture hall. He nodded, smoothed his lapels, and coolly walked over to Professor Monahan, who was shouting, "Please, please, class, could you—do you think—?"

The manager gave her the a-okay sign with one hand and neatly shooed her away from the podium with the other. Alex could tell this was how he dealt with a lot of people, the kind of guy whose assistant had her own smaller assistant. The manager gripped both sides of the podium and took a hard look around the room. In a quiet, even tone, he said, "I think that's quite enough."

The volume in the room wavered a little, but too many of the students were once again staring down at their phones, and therefore unreachable. He added, raising his voice only a little, "Mr. Holtz has other places to be, you know."

Dead silence.

The celebrity's name snapped the crowd back to reality like a hypnotist's safe word. Tyson and Keith swallowed their Milk

Duds and sat at attention. Chip folded his hands politely in his lap. Tracy slipped her dummy notebook out of her dummy backpack and uncapped a pen. Even Alex found himself leaning forward in his seat.

The manager looked around the room, then gave a nearly imperceptible nod. "Without further ado, I present to you my client, Duncan Holtz."

16

METHOD ACTING

Duncan Holtz bounded out from behind the curtain, genially waving at the crowd. Tyson and Keith jumped to their feet and hollered with both hands cupped around their Milk Dud–stained mouths. Other whoops echoed around all corners of the lecture hall. This was the true power of celebrity, Alex thought. To incite applause, no matter the occasion. Even the cinephiles and other political candidates were politely clapping. Standing to one side of the stage, Professor Monahan looked serene and lake-surface calm, as if she were in the throes of her favourite recurring daydream.

Holtz let the applause wash over him for a few seconds. He looked almost regal against the polished oak of the podium. Alex checked the tape recorder hidden in his binder. He nudged Tracy and whispered, "You ready?"

"I think so," she whispered back. "Hopefully he goes for it— but it's illegal to actually campaign here. He can't be that dumb."

"You really haven't seen his movies, huh?"

"Thank you all so much for coming," Holtz said. "Okay, okay, settle down, thanks, let's begin—is that all the applause you've got? I'm just messing with you. But really, is that it? I guess the rumours were true: UBC are the real clappers in this city." The man was no amateur. In just a few sentences the crowd had surrendered themselves to his will, cheering themselves into a frenzy. Even some of the luke-warm film students were getting into the act.

Holtz's manager scurried around in the background, doing last-minute checks on the complicated knot of cables running out of a laptop he'd placed on a table. He tucked a remote control in his client's shirt pocket.

"It's so great to be with you today," Holtz continued. "Now, your lovely prof, she brought me in here to talk about some of the movies I've made at SFU. Did you guys know I started out going to school here, way back in, what was it, 2000?" He drummed his fingers on the lectern, squinting at the old memories. "It was great. Really great. But then I got caught up in that big Hollywood machine, and, well, you know how it goes from there. Who has time for midterms when you can hang out with someone as beautiful as Keri Russell all day? This was before she chopped her hair off, mind you. Back when she was still a stone fox. Bookish, like some of the girls here, actually, and with this insane *bone structure*. Cheekbones are real important down in Hollyweird. Speaking of weird? I actually flew down there for the first time on September 10. Just before the attacks. Now doesn't that just put it all in perspective . . ."

Alex glanced at Tyson and Keith, who were both utterly en-thralled. Chip kept looking to Keith, a little confused, then back to the podium. Tracy was scribbling furiously in her notebook.

"Don't tell me you're using any of this garbage," Alex hissed.

"Context," she said.

Holtz was spinning every moment of his time in Los Angeles into the stuff of beer commercials and tabloid escapism: Hollywood as one long, impossibly sunny boulevard, where famous people stood shoulder to shoulder with one another, and where even the guy run-ning the taco truck used to be in the Shins.

Then he sighed wistfully (a little *too* wistfully, Alex thought—

this whole thing reeked of schtick) and pulled a small deck of flash cards out of his pocket, bound with a rubber band.

"Now, seriously, folks, let's get down to business." Holtz slid the band off and kept the cards in his line of sight. "The first time I ever came to SFU was for *Fang City,* back in the summer of '98. I was heading into grade twelve, and I didn't get to see much of the sights around here, what with being a werewolf and all." Everyone chuckled obediently. "Night shoots, am I right? I spent five hours in that make-up chair every day. But the funny thing is that even then I could tell this school was something special. It had that *pop,* you know? It was different. Unique. I remember thinking, 'How is it that this place isn't world-famous? It's got so much character.' And I still think that. What SFU needs—what it *deserves*—is a motivated group of people who are willing to make that leap. To bridge that gap. It deserves a government that cares. A government that recognizes and embraces our uniqueness. Right now I simply don't think we have that."

Tracy stopped writing notes and looked up. The cluster of people at the back, the people Alex had pegged as other SFSS hope-fuls, started muttering amongst themselves and glaring daggers at Holtz. It looked as if they knew this was coming.

"Anyway, 1998, we shoot the pilot for *Fang City,*" Holtz con-tinued, returning with a wink to the cue cards. "My character, Vince Mountains, was stuck in the evil doctor's medical lab, along with all the other hybrid prototypes. So I didn't have much in the way of actual lines. I was hardly onscreen at all, actually, but they still needed me around to do some vocal stuff. Meanwhile I'd fallen in love—or what I *thought* was love, at the time—with the lady who did my make-up. So let's just say I was keeping myself busy."

The class chuckled again, faux-knowingly. But Tyson started looking bored and restless. The politicians at the back kept grum-bling. It was a strange moment. Who'd have thought that this was the place where the Venn diagrams of *student politics* and *Tyson* overlapped?

Holtz shuffled to the next index card. "Over the next two years we did some more shooting on campus, and every time we did I thought, 'You know what? I *like* it here.' Sounds corny, I know. But it's true. The air was so clean, and the buildings were so . . . different, y'know? It felt like I was entering someplace special.

"Then, as you know, we got cancelled." Holtz paused for boos; the crowd was happy to oblige. Keith wound up and, in solidarity, hurled the rest of his Milk Duds toward the podium, where they scattered in a shower at Holtz's feet. The manager shot him a withering look. "And yeah, it wasn't fun. It was my first real gig, and I was sorry to see that whole universe get packed away. And the crew, you guys. What great people. Seriously, the little people never get their due.

"But it wasn't all bad—I mean, we were one of the first shows to get out there on DVD. I think it was *Babylon 5,* then us. So we were second. Or maybe . . . *X-Files* was in there somewhere, too." He flipped through the cards in search of this phantom piece of data. "And sales were, just, *real* strong. I got to go to a few conventions and meet a bunch of fans." Pause. "Just a second. I'm wondering what our exact sales were on that first season. Mitch?" He looked to his manager, who doled out his second severe look in as many minutes. Holtz got the message. "Anyway. It was something just *crazy.*

"Then I was off in Hollywood for the next couple of years, just trying to make a living, you know what I mean? It's a real grind out there. I got my first real break with *Maximum Death.* Yes. Yes. Thank you, sir. You're too kind. Alright, really. That's enough. No: please stop."

Tyson grinned and put the air horn back in his pocket.

"I'm guessing most of you have seen this little flick," he continued, and the room roared. The cinephiles, meanwhile, visibly cringed at the word *flick*—and said in the hallowed halls of their film department, no less! Professor Monahan nodded along with Holtz so intently that when she went to rest an elbow on the overhead projector, she missed completely and nearly swatted her head against it.

"Grossed six hundred million dollars worldwide—but who's counting." It didn't come out like a question. Holtz winked again. "For the three of you out there who haven't seen it yet, I'll give you a quick recap. I play Blair Williams, badass without a cause."

"'Without a cause'?" Alex whispered. "He was a government agent. He had a *million* causes."

"Shh," said Tracy.

"And so I'm up against, just, the most diabolical group of terrorists you've ever seen. A nasty syndicate that calls itself the Blue Cutlass. Their headquarters are in this Aztec-y fortress, on top of some remote mountaintop. Those are the parts we shot at SFU. Come to think of it . . ." He trailed off, apparently lost in thought. "You know, I was just thinking, it's not unlike the political situation here today. You've got a group of fat cats who'll do anything to hold onto power, and an edgy outsider willing to call it how he sees it." He nodded to the politicians at the back. "That's so funny," he called to them. "I can't believe I never saw the parallel until now—hey, guys?"

The politicians paced back and forth in a pack, furiously whispering to one another.

Alex felt the nausea of impending conflict. He fumbled with his recorder, double-checking he had enough tape, then looked at Tracy. "Is this—"

"*Shh*," she said, pulling the top of her own recorder out of the binder. "Backup," she added.

One of the politicians, his face brick red, burst from the group and shouted, "You're going to get run up the flagpole for this, you bastard. Just wait 'til the IEC gets wind—"

"*Excuse me*," interrupted Professor Monahan, her loose, swaying posture now turning rigid. "This is a classroom, young man. I will not tolerate these kinds of disruptions."

"Are you kidding me?" he shouted back. "Are you *fucking*—" A female politician grabbed the guy by the shoulders and yanked him back to the relative anonymity of the alcove.

"That's Samantha Gilmartin," Tracy whispered to Alex. "I'm sure of it."

"I am so sorry about that," the professor said, re-surrendering the podium to Holtz. "Please. Go ahead."

If Holtz was thrown, he didn't show it. "Oh, it's fine," he said casually. "This just goes to show the kind of entitlement this administration has. They think the laws don't apply to them. And yes, I know, I know, they don't want me talking about that kind of thing here—but then they *wouldn't*, would they? They're the ones who made the rules in the first place. Luckily, a stacked deck doesn't mean anything to a guy with an ace up his sleeve."

While Alex groaned at the gridlock of clichés, the rest of the crowd broke out in applause. But could he blame his fellow students for being so easily courted? Odds were they couldn't pick the current SFSS board out of a lineup, but pop culture had expertly trained them to recognize a few key storylines: (a) The Establishment Is Corrupt; (b) The Hero, Humbled and Returning from Exile, Makes a Comeback; (c) Famous People Know Things the Rest of Us Don't; (d) Rules Are Dumb, Made to Be Broken. With this speech, Holtz had tapped into all four at once.

It didn't take a genius to figure out that this kind of steamrolling charisma was going to be dangerous for campus politics.

But what did it mean for *The Peak?*

"Listen. You don't have to just take my word for it," Holtz continued. "I decided to bring in a friend of mine—a guy I go way back with, all the way to that first day on the *Maximum Death* set. You've probably already seen his wardrobe and make-up people running around campus." A burst of electricity shot through the room. "Ladies and gentlemen, straight from his lunch break on *YO2: The Awakening,* your friend and mine—"

The mystery actor poked his head out from behind the side curtain, and if the crowd had been enthusiastic about seeing Holtz in the flesh, this time they acted as if the rapture itself was upon them and they'd all made the shortlist. The raw noise from the yahoos, plus screeches from Tyson's air horn, drowned out the end of Holtz's introduction. This was the kind of Hollywood encounter every single person in attendance could go home and tell mom about. The man was a household name, and a committed Method actor, too, though this fact was hotly disputed on his Wikipedia page.

As the mystery actor made his way to the podium, someone yelled, "His outfit!" The crowd gasped: he was wearing a T-shirt that read, across the chest in huge purple block letters, "PRESIDENT HOLTZ." In one hand, he carried a kind of plastic-tubed cannon, which connected to an oversized backpack. In the other, a mesh bag full of strange little fabric bundles.

They were T-shirts.

He was holding a T-shirt gun.

Alex froze in his seat. He could feel confrontation bearing down on the room. This was no longer potential; it was going to happen. The only thing he couldn't figure out was whether this, too, was part of Holtz's plan. A splashy, ethically dubious endorsement was one thing, but a soccer riot in a film class?

Holtz's friend patted him warmly on the back, gave the manager a quick finger-gun salute, and took his place at the podium—but as he opened his mouth to speak, the politician with the brick-red face sprinted down the auditorium steps, his fists swinging like a third-string gladiator. The rest weren't far behind, and included in their ranks a positively homicidal-looking Samantha Gilmartin. Stumbling backward, the household name accidentally set off his T-shirt gun. A purple bundle clocked the red-faced politician right in the nose; he lost his footing and tumbled down the stairs. The rest of the politicians threw themselves toward the podium. Holtz's manager yelped and tried to pull his client out the side door to safety, but when Holtz brushed him off, instead taking cover with his friend behind an overturned table, the manager didn't hesitate in fleeing the scene on his own. The crowd jumped to its feet. Some looked about ready to enter the fray, but decided to hang back, standing on tiptoe to get the best view of the action. Dozens of camera phones made their little synthetic clicks.

Tracy grabbed Alex by the sleeve and pulled him to the ground, where they both took refuge behind the seats in front of them. He, in turn, reached for Tyson, but too late: the air horn's honks preceded him in his mad, whooping rush toward the front of the room, pulling some of the crowd along with him. Where were Keith and Chip? Alex couldn't see them anywhere.

He turned to Tracy, who was peeking between seats and trying to scribble notes as quickly as she could. A wave of adrenaline turned Alex's limbs loose and warm, bringing an unfamiliar but welcome clarity of mind. "Where's your cell phone?" he shouted to Tracy. "We need photos."

"No good," she yelled back. "It doesn't have a camera. Where's yours?"

"At the office." At the time he'd been afraid it could be traced back to him. How could he have been so stupid? For nearly four years he'd been calling himself a journalist. Where were his *instincts*?

He'd have to start building them now. "Okay," he yelled. "Here's what we're going to do. Get down there, as close as you can, and record everything." Two fire extinguishers erupted spontaneously, sending jets of foam spraying across the auditorium in tall, sloppy arcs. Professor Monahan had pulled a whistle from god knew where, and was blowing it as hard as she could.

"What are you going to do?" Tracy said.

Alex held out his hand. "Give me your phone. I'm going to get us some backup."

She handed it over, then grabbed her recorder. "Damn," she said, holding it up to her ear and shaking it. "Dead. After all these years. Well, looks like it's all on you now—let's just hope your tape doesn't run out." She threw the busted recorder over her shoulder, then crept out into the aisle, and was gone.

Holtz and the mystery actor were still hunkered down, near the projector screen. They managed to fend off a few of the more feral attackers with a barrage of chalk brushes and dry-erase markers; Alex noted how easily Holtz slipped back into his *Maximum Death* persona, delivering his character's trademark "Believe it!" whenever a missile hit its target. Gilmartin stayed crouched behind the first row of lecture seats, and directed her troops with a flurry of quick nods and arm movements. They charged forward, using discarded film textbooks as shields.

From out of nowhere, Keith and Tyson appeared together in front of Holtz's overturned table. They tackled two of the closest politicians while Chip yelled out a series of football plays and World War II–era attack codes from a few feet back.

Jostled by the crowd around him, Alex scrolled through Tracy's phone for any *Peak* contacts. Steve. Suze. Rick. All either off the payroll or on bed rest. *Shit,* he thought, reciting another law of the internet. *Pics or it didn't happen.*

Chip. Keith. *Shit shit shit.* Then he spotted it: Claude. Of course. *Time to prove yourself, kid.* Alex fired off a text, in all caps to prove he meant it, then surveyed the scene to plan his next move.

A second, reorganized group of politicians—combined with a few of the brawnier cinephiles—made a new attack on Holtz's group on its weak side. Meanwhile, three or four others, each wielding a stray plastic chair, rushed from the opposite flank. A pincer attack.

But just as the two groups converged on the desk, Holtz's celebrity friend burst out from behind the table, channeling his inner dystopian soldier, desperate and bug-eyed. Holding the T-shirt gun straight out in front of him, he took aim and pumped a dozen rounds of hot, purple cotton-polyester blend into the faces, chests, and kneecaps of his attackers. Alex was impressed. "Looks like he's Method after all," he said into the recorder.

Somewhere in the fracas Holtz's laptop was hit by a stray arm or marker, and a PowerPoint presentation sparked to life on the lecture hall's theatre-sized screen. It started with a clip from the climactic scene of *Maximum Death 2,* a kinetic shoot-out that obliterated a pristine snowy mountainside in slow motion. The flashing, ultra-realistic digital images bathed the real-life combatants, at times making the real Holtz look like no more than a pixie-sized sidekick to his gigantic, begoggled counterpart. Just off-screen, Tracy was tucked away behind the auditorium curtain, taking rapid-fire notes from the best seat in the house.

Alex looked back just in time to see the first wave of campus security pour into the room. Waving their batons around, they looked confused and shell-shocked. Behind them—Alex punched the air and actually whooped—burst a triumphant Claude, holding a high-end DSLR above his head and snapping away at anything he could get a shot of. And behind him, trying to shove his way through, was the *Metro*'s own Mack Holloway. He didn't even have a notebook with him. Another fire extinguisher went off in the background. The air bristled with *thunk*s from the T-shirt cannon, wails from Tyson's air horn, and panicked blasts from Professor Monahan's emergency whistle. From the dozen or so speakers circling the classroom, in state-of-the-art Dolby surround sound, Special Agent Blair Williams yelled, "Believe it!"

Alex grinned up at Mack and wiggled his tape recorder, which now shuddered to a halt as the tape side finally ran out.

17

ONE HUNDRED BEERS

Outside the lecture hall, Alex was jittery with adrenaline. "I can't believe what just happened," he said. "Will we have to give a police statement? I've never given a police statement before." He turned to Tracy, who was still writing notes as fast as she could. "How'd we do? Is there enough for a story?"

"Oh yeah," she said, shaking her hand to fend off the cramping. "All I need is to get one of those SFSS guys on the record while he's still nice and pissed off. They're probably back at the office by now."

He tossed her his recorder. "I think it's safe to say Rachel will make this a priority."

"She better," Tracy said, shoving it and the notebook into her dummy backpack. "Okay. I've gotta get to work on this. I'll probably have a draft ready by the time you get in tomorrow."

"Don't forget the debate," he said.

"Jesus. This is going to be a miniseries by the time it's all settled."

"Oh, who cares," said Tyson. He was panting and nursing a bruise on his cheek. His air horn had been confiscated. "The real scoop would be figuring out why Holtz treats his sex life like it's god-damned classified information."

"What?" Alex asked. "You mean—that make-up lady? *That's* what you're taking away from all this?"

Keith and Chip sat on a nearby bench, eating fistfuls of Sour Patch Kids. Claude stood a few tentative steps away, cradling his camera with both hands.

"It's not like he's campaigning on his virginity, is it? It's like, *c'mon* dude. Spill the beans already."

"I don't know," Alex said, watching Mack scurry through the crowd in the distance, trying to get some kind of coherent quote from anyone who would talk to him. Holtz, his manager, and the other celebrity were all nowhere to be seen. "Isn't that kind of private?"

"Fuck *no, it is not,*" Tyson hollered. "I learned more about that guy in five minutes of googling than from anything he's done since coming back here. The internet already showed me pictures of him filming at SFU. I saw his signed contract for *Maximum Death 2,* page by page, on *The Smoking Gun.* I even saw a picture of that make-up artist's tits. It was decent, but kind of blurry. You could barely make out how big her nipples were." Tyson sighed, then winced as his cheek muscles twitched involuntarily. "*That's* the kind of knowledge I want dropped on me. Not all this political bullshit."

Tracy looked up from closing her backpack. "You're not a very likable person, are you?"

"I'm a pragmatist. If they're not embarrassing themselves for my benefit, what are celebrities good for?"

She turned to Alex. "Thanks for your help back there. I hope I didn't give you too much of a panic attack."

"You wish," he said.

Alex felt a little light-headed, and, in his endorphin binge, something that could easily be mistaken for powerful. He'd just been part of a legitimate *event.* Forget a piddly little police statement. Right now he could alter reality itself with a nod. Or maybe even just by showing up.

But first he needed a drink.

"Hey, Tyson," he said. "When does Pub Night start?"

"I dunno. An hour. Why?"

Alex put his arm around his friend's shoulder and playfully slapped the bruise on his cheek. "Let's go drink a hundred beers." He looked to the bench. "Keith, you're in on this, too."

"Actually," Keith said, "I'll have to pass. Sorry, dude. I promised Chip I'd go to his place and watch some DVD about Vimy Ridge if he came here with me."

"DVD *set*," corrected Chip.

"Yeah. But I don't know. It actually sounds kind of cool?"

"Suit yourself," Alex said. "Claude?"

"Me?" Claude said, fidgeting with his lens cap. "Really?"

"You better believe it," Alex said. The three of them walked off toward the Pub. "One hundred beers. It's happening."

Elaine

Hey. Sorry for the late notice, but can't hang out tonight after all. Rain cheque? Sorry.

What? Why? I just got back from the video store.

Something's come up.

Don't understand. What is it? Are you mad?

Lainey. THEY ASKED ME TO HANG OUT.

Really????? That's great!! I'm so proud of you!! Go have fun.

Are you sure?

Omigod yes. You've been waiting how long for this? Go.

K. Thanks. Love you.

Love you too. And be safe.

18

ALL THOSE SAD LITTLE JUMP KICKS

Sure, there were the rumours about suicide rates, supposedly brought on by residence kids looking out into nothing but fog and concrete for months at a time. Not to mention the hazy symbolism of the AQ Garden. But perhaps SFU's greatest mystery was how the Pub—the only place where you could legally obtain alcohol on the entire mountaintop campus—consistently failed to turn a profit. Alex, Tyson, and Claude scurried into seats at the last empty table, only to realize that thanks to the Pub's most recent round of budget cuts, there wasn't a single server in sight. And the place was packed.

Alex got back to his feet. "Wait here," he told them.

Behind the bar, Saul, the latest in a series of short-lived general managers, was rushing from side to side like a grocery-store crab. Alex liked Saul—and not just because he shared a first name with Alex's literary hero. He carried himself like a gruff teamster, the kind of guy who liked nothing more than taking cheap shots at the establishment. As such, he'd always had a soft spot for *The Peak,* whose editorial cartoons, he'd told Alex more than once, if not exactly sophisticated, were at least unrelenting in their snippy disapproval.

Alex muscled through a handful of patrons who were already stationed there, snapping and waving their credit cards like cloudy Polaroids.

"If it isn't the newspaper guy," Saul said, lining up a string of glasses on the counter. "What can I do for you, buddy?"

"This is a big one, Saul. I need a hundred beers. It's premature celebration time."

He chuckled. "That's good. Real good. You might have noticed that I'm a little fucked up here right now. A pint or two, I could maybe sneak you to the front of the line. But something like that? That's gonna have to wait a minute."

Under ordinary circumstances, Alex would've slunk away and accepted his fate. The fact that he'd even gotten a bartender's attention would, on any other day, have been a miracle in and of itself. But now, thanks to the energy he'd siphoned from the Holtz fiasco, there was no stopping him. He was Wile E. Coyote, barreling over a cliff at full speed. As long as you kept your eyes on the horizon, nobody could touch you.

"Hey, what's going on here?" the other guys at the bar complained. "We've been waiting for ten minutes."

"I've got an idea," Alex said to Saul, and he took the wad of emergency money out of his pocket. Combined with his loose change, a total of $93 spilled out onto the counter. "How about you hold onto this, Saul, and write me up a cash tab." He pointed. "In the meantime, pass me those pitchers. For the next few minutes, this bar is self-serve."

With a bemused look, Saul pocketed the cash and stepped aside. Alex leaned over the counter and poured himself two frothy pitchers of Sleeman's Honey Brown. Let those other guys—business majors, Alex figured—look on in awe. They thought bravado was supposed to be their domain, not some faggy book reader's? Guess again.

Back at the table, even Tyson was impressed. "Shit, son," he said, plucking some unused pint glasses from a nearby table. "Real nice work." They each poured a glassful and pounded it back. With a little nudging, so did Claude. Then Tyson wiped his mouth and started gathering his things. "One problem. I maybe forgot to mention it earlier. I have an exam in ten minutes."

"Seriously?" Alex said.

"For really real. Thanks for the drink. Dare I even ask if you'll be here later?" Alex could almost see the porn-lair scenarios reflecting off Tyson's pupils. "Or will you be fucked out and unconscious in some 2nd-year's townhouse?"

"I'm just here to soak up some of this energy," Alex said, leaning back in his chair. "Watch the booze and hormones smash into each other. Maybe breathe the fumes a little."

"Whatever," Tyson said. "When I come back I'm getting my balls chomped. Bet on it."

Claude stood up next to him. "I actually have to go, too."

"No," Alex said in disbelief. "Not you, too."

"Yeah. Just for a bit." Claude patted his camera. "I have to get these photos uploaded and over to Rachel. Plus I promised Suze another CD review for tomorrow. And I need to have a clear head while I write." Alex thought he already looked a little tipsy, but didn't want to jinx him by saying so. "But I'll come back soon, okay? An hour or two, tops."

"Claude, you know CD reviews are only a hundred and fifty words, right?"

He nodded vigorously. "It's just, I want them to be really good. It takes me a little longer than most people, I guess. I'll be back as soon as I can, okay? Don't leave."

Once they were gone, Alex poured himself a second glass of beer. There was still a good pitcher and a third left on the table—and Saul was holding onto the rest of his money up at the bar. He couldn't go back and get it now. The whole performance would be shattered. And he couldn't leave *beer* unattended, especially on the cusp of Pub Night. He'd have to wait it out.

In search of something to do in the meantime, Alex hoisted his backpack onto the seat next to him and dug through the pile of decoy equipment he'd brought for the Holtz lecture. Nothing. No laptop, no iPod, no phone. He'd been so afraid of getting caught that he hadn't even brought his real school binders, packed as they were with telltale course information and handwriting samples. The decoy binders held only packages of lined paper dumped in for effect. So he could write something, maybe—but his notebook, maybe a quarter full of ideas, was also safely stashed away in the *Peak* offices downstairs.

Then, stuffed at the very bottom, he found the Barbara Pym book he'd bought back in the fall. Alex took a sip of beer and studied the jacket copy again. This woman, whose fall to obscurity had so terrified and intrigued him, whose legacy would be defined more by her accidental proximity to a genius than anything within her control— she'd come to represent all of Alex's insecurities about becoming a writer. So far he hadn't been able to crack so much as the opening paragraph. He was actually afraid of solving the mystery of Pym's talent. Hell, she might be bad—or, worse, boring. Where would *that* leave him? Could he live with being middlebrow, second-rate, a guy with more hustle than skill? Could he settle for anything less than being a timeless genius? And what right did he even have to hold himself to those kinds of standards?

He looked up and glanced around the bar again. So much was happening around him these days; it was all he could do to keep the different options straight in his head, let alone take charge and commit to one of them. He tried to feel that giddy, mountain-thin air of optimism again. What would a *man of action* do?

The answer came to him surprisingly quickly. Alex took a deep breath, bent the paperback's spine hard in his hands, and started to read.

It turned out Tyson had the time wrong—Pub Night didn't start until nearly two hours later than he'd thought. But it didn't matter to Alex. He barely looked up from his book, pausing only to refill his glass and make the occasional sprint to the bathroom. The crowd in the bar grew steadily larger as new clusters of undergrads spilled in. They were even more jovial than usual, either celebrating the completion of some essay or drinking to forget those deadlines that still lay ahead.

By the time Alex registered just how much time had passed, he'd made it well over two-thirds of the way through the Pym book. In the meantime the sun had set, and social vultures were starting to circle his table, looking to snatch up the extra chairs. A DJ had set up shop on the little stage above the dance floor. He was playing a woozy, swirling, vaguely anthemic track from the new Animal Collective record.

Both of Alex's pitchers were empty. Pub Night had begun.

With the beer sloshing through his head like a carpenter's level, Alex felt the great magnetic pull of being drunk, non-threatening, and anonymous. He'd never lived in residence, and while he'd kept something like a public profile via *The Peak,* nobody had ever recognized his face from the little picture that ran alongside his byline (in which he was basically unrecognizable anyway, thanks to the novelty coffee mug obscuring the bottom half of his face). Here he could wander through and pinball off the rest of the crowd, basking in their exuberance.

The beer and the book had put him in such a convivial mood that the first thing he did, after jumping to his feet and feeling the added punch of a head rush, was march back over to Saul behind the bar and loudly order two more pitchers of Sleeman's "for the room." Everyone within earshot spun around, incredulous, and whooped.

Alex grabbed the pitchers and put them on the tables closest to him. He was met with a round of shoulder punches from cheery strangers, who all suddenly wanted to pull him into their respective groups' conversations. Within seconds he was a hot commodity: this enigmatic, charmingly tipsy philanthropist who would huddle up to someone long enough to laugh gamely at their jokes, then float off to the next empty chair.

Alex revised his earlier philosophy. *Mystery is everything,* he decided. Thanks to this newly self-willed charisma, he didn't even feel awkward anymore. Everything was perfect. What was that *song,* anyway? Fuck, man. So familiar, but just out of reach. He felt like air drumming along with it.

Mostly what he was thinking was: *These girls are all so beautiful. Where did they all come from?* The weather had been unusually warm for March, which meant there were artfully cut sundresses and bare legs as far as the eye could see.

Once Alex's initial peace offerings ran empty, new rounds of drinks started to appear in front of him. Pints of hefeweizen, then whiskey gingers and a few medicinal-tasting shots of Jägermeister. The Pub was at capacity. Alex was talking to someone he was pretty sure hadn't been at the table an hour earlier. Mini-expeditions were taken to the dance floor, but Alex made a lightly ironic broken-toe joke and was let off the hook. The first wave of beautiful girls was slowly replaced by a second, nearly identical one from a parallel dimension—one where the bangs were a bit longer, the lipstick a little more prominent, and where legs had to be covered up but shoulders most certainly did not.

For a while Alex could simply turn his head, find someone new sitting there, and off their conversation would go. He was willing to jump into any subject offered up to him: federal politics, gardening tips, whatever.

Some time later he found himself in the middle of a freewheeling argument about concert movies with two skinny guys in plaid and one of the parallel-universe hot girls, who looked weirdly familiar. She wore circles of eye shadow that made her eyes look attractively raccoon-like, and took greedy sips from a Long Island iced tea as big as her head.

"Come *on*, man," one of the guys yelled to the other. "Van Morrison is the best *part* of *The Last Waltz!* All those sad little jump kicks he has to do? And so fat. God, he's so fat."

"You ever hear about the giant chunk of cocaine sticking out of Neil Young's nose?" Alex said. "They had to completely chop it out during post-production—and this was the seventies. CGI wasn't a thing yet. It cost four million dollars to remove it, it was so big."

"Van Morrison had to do eight million jump kicks to pay it off."

Alex turned to the girl. "What about you? Actually, no, let me guess: you're more of a *Stop Making Sense* kind of lady."

"Oh, I love that movie! How'd you guess?" she said.

"It's a theory of mine, actually."

"Really? What is it?"

"Well, girls today are into skinny, nervous, David Byrne types, right? And guys might act that way on the surface, but deep down, we all want to pretend we're in The Band. We're all just repressed lumberjacks, and *The Last Waltz* is our Bible. I think it comes from the fact that none of my friends even owns a toolbox."

The iced tea swished around the cup as the girl laughed. "That's funny," she said. "I thought you were going to say something way weirder. Pub Night tends to bring out the plastic-bag lady in a lot of people."

"Oh?" Alex leaned in conspiratorially, arms crossed, and she laughed again. "You're speaking from experience. Give me an example of the mega-crazy."

"Yeah?"

"Yep. C'mon. Let's hear it."

"Okay. Um . . ." The girl bit her lip in thought, her eyes darting off up and to the side, and Alex instantly gained half an erection. If this girl were to walk away right now, without even finishing her sentence, she'd be the one he would imagine in soft focus before going to sleep that night. It was something about that eye make-up. He pictured her putting it on in front of her bedroom mirror, so sublimely aware of how good it looked.

"Well," she said, "there was this one guy who kept telling me about how every essay he'd ever written was about *The Tiger Who Came to Tea.*"

"Wait—the kids' book?"

"Yeah. Weird, huh?"

The riff appeared in Alex's mind fully formed, as if by magic. He was really on a roll now. Everything he said was hilarious, his every look perfectly calculated. Just for tonight, he was physically and socially invincible.

"Makes perfect sense to me," he said. "I can see it now: 'Tiger Stripes and Cardigans: Sartorial Politics in *The Tiger Who Came to Tea.*'"

She giggled and drank.

"How about '"It Can't Be Daddy, He's Got His Key": Patriarchy and Domestic Trauma in the Literature of Post-War Britain'?"

"*Riiiiight . . .*"

The ideas wouldn't stop coming. "'Tiger as Chaos Grenade: A Marxist'—wait. You don't find any of this funny, do you?" *Shit,* he thought with a twinge. Keith would've loved that one. Or what about Anna, Tracy's knockout Scandinavian pal? He'd have to remember it for later. No sense in letting such a good joke go to waste.

"No, no, I do," the girl insisted. "I just can't think of them that fast." She took another gulp of iced tea. "To tell you the truth—I don't even know why I'm telling you this, but there you go—I actually think he might have been for real."

"What do you mean?"

"I like to pretend he was, anyway. For some reason people tell me these ridiculous stories. I don't know why. But I always want to believe they're telling the truth."

That's stupid, Alex thought. But what he said was, "Aren't you worried they're just fucking with you?"

"I guess," she said. "I am pretty gullible. But there are worse things to be. And besides, there's so much crazy stuff out there that *is* real, you know? Why not go with it, just in case?"

The cynic in Alex's head had about a dozen answers for her, all of them witty, and all of them cruel. But this time he decided to keep them to himself. He'd spent years cutting people down for the slightest inconsistency, logical or ideological. What had it ever gotten him? A hair-trigger temper and a library full of angry scribblings in the margins. That was the problem with airtight philosophies: you had to spend the rest of your life failing to live up to them. At that moment, looking into those beautiful raccoon eyes, Alex thought a margin of error sounded pretty good.

Out of the corner of his eye he saw Claude stumble his way, waving and smiling. Alex had completely forgotten about the kid. *Is he even drunker than I am?* Alex thought.

"Hi!" Claude cried. "I finally found you!"

"Hey, Claude," Alex said, shouting over the music. "I didn't even know you came back! Where've you been?"

Claude's beer spilled a little as he shifted his weight to the other foot. "I was just sitting at our table, waiting for you. And drinking." He snorted. "But who cares? Listen. I was in the office. Suze was down there, doing early layout or something." Claude's grin stretched to twice its previous size. "She's running all of my CD reviews on a full page together, man. She showed me my byline and everything. I convinced her and Rachel to come meet me up here later, to celebrate. I just—I fucking love this newspaper. You guys are *so awesome*."

Alex scrutinized Claude more closely, and for the first time recognized a bit of himself in there, back when his face, too, had been soft and line-free. Before he'd seen behind the curtain and become permanently jaded. Alex realized there were still people out there who had faith. Maybe that was how you really got the good work done. Maybe he should've packed it in a long time ago.

"Congratulations," Alex told him. "Really. We're all proud of you. It's about time we had some fresh talent come in and leave a mark on the paper. Lord knows we could use some new ideas right about now."

"Yeah?"

"Oh yeah. The crazier, the better. It just takes a little initiative, you know? Break a rule or two. It's good for you." Claude nodded slowly and seriously, repeating Alex's advice to himself. "And, hey, listen," Alex added. "Have you ever thought about running for an editorship? It's not that hard—Suze could even show you where the forms are." Claude was sprinting back down the stairs before he could even finish the thought.

Alex turned back to the girl. "Sorry about that," he said. The DJ put on the same Animal Collective song again, as anthemic as ever, and this time the entire Pub cheered with recognition. He felt himself click into the next stage of drunkenness, and knew his charisma wasn't going to stick around forever. "What's your name?"

She smiled. "Maggie. You?"

"I'm Alex."

"Nice to meet you, Alex," Maggie said, slowly blinking her thick black lashes.

"So," he said, "do you live on campus?"

"As a matter of fact, I do."

They held eye contact for a second, each taking a last sip of liquid courage.

Maggie broke the silence first. "You want to come see my room?"

He was immediately back inside his head. Weren't you supposed to lose yourself in the moment at times like this? But from the second he and Maggie slipped out the front door together, down the stairs and past the coat check, he was aware of each second as it passed, and trying desperately not to fuck it all up. They were going to have sex. Weren't they? Oh man. She probably looked so good naked. And did he have a condom? Shit. He most definitely did not. Wouldn't it be weirder if he did? Yeah, that's what he'll say. Who was going to instigate things? That was the guy's job, usually—then again, Alex considered himself a feminist. He was 99 percent sure they were at least going to make out. But he didn't want to get maced if she turned out not to be into it. Maybe he'd wait, hang back, look suave. Or maybe he should just enjoy this blissful walk down the corridor, their footsteps softly echoing off the concrete.

Oh dear sweet lord, she took his arm.

They talked about nothing in particular. Alex restrained himself to short, clipped jokes. Maggie laughed a lot; she was now making a point of touching him whenever she could. Alex shivered a little, goosebumped and walking at a slightly awkward angle to fight off the hard-on. A smattering of other voices filled the space around them, groups of kids moving in the opposite direction. The girls looked at Maggie, jealous that she was so far ahead of schedule. The guys catcalled.

Inside Shell House, Maggie led Alex by the hand down a hall-way and around a few corners, before coming to a door that looked exactly like all the others. Hers had a couple of photos pinned to it, some concert ticket stubs, all orbiting the same standard-issue mini white board in the centre. Alex marveled at it. If *this* was about to happen here, what was going on behind all the other doors?

Hey, he thought with a start. *This is it. It's really happening.*

"You coming in?" Maggie asked from inside. The lights were off, and it took Alex's drunk eyes a few seconds to locate her in the darkness. The top four buttons on her shirt were already undone, and he could see the traces of a heavenly plaid bra underneath.

He took a few steps in, and closed the door without looking back. Then their lips were connected. Tongues were involved. The air felt warm and sweet. He was so close that he could hear her eyelashes flutter shut.

Then her hand was on his crotch, and suddenly he wasn't thinking about anything.

19

ARTS / CRAFTS

Midnight, Maggie Benston Centre.

The only active lights were the ones high up, the second string-ers, indented into ceilings and just a little too dim. You never saw these lights, never even thought to look for them in the daytime, but now, without any competition, they happily buzzed their insect song.

A team of janitors glided across the hallway floors, mopping and sweeping and making less noise combined than any one of the lights overhead. Their job was to clean the nooks and crannies that students barely even noticed: forgotten spots behind photocopiers and fuzzy juice stains underneath the few remaining pay phones. The offices behind them were all dark and empty, except for one.

Duncan Holtz sat bow-legged on the floor inside the SFSS head-quarters. He rubbed his nose and continued gluing dollar-store stars to a big slab of purple poster paper. Tomorrow was the big debate. Mitch had said he ought to have a new poster ready. The campaign is entering its second phase, he'd said. *So make sure the new ad is handmade, or at least looks it. These university types are all about authenticity.*

He put the glue stick down and held up his night's work, thinking that this wasn't what he'd imagined when Mitch first pitched him the idea of going back to school. Barely a year ago he'd been coming off the success of a romantic comedy set at a ski resort that had a one hundred and twenty-four million–dollar domestic take. (*Domestic* here meaning the U.S., of course.) It was no *Gone with the Wind,* but the studio was pleased. His next project, a more cerebral kind of think-piece that he'd also written and directed, had gotten the opening night slot at Sundance and what had sounded at the time like Oscar buzz.

He was in the tabloids. He had a growing reputation for punching the paparazzi. He was bankable. How, Duncan wondered, had everything fallen apart so quickly?

He compared this updated poster to the ones he'd used in phase one. On the new one was a cut-out photo of him holding a basketball above his head, wearing a white mesh jersey over a T-shirt. He'd stood a bit too close to the camera, and had cut the photo a bit too close to his head, making his hair look all weird and blocky. The text read, in seventy-two-point all caps, "ON MARCH 17, SLAM DUNCAN!!!"

No, this didn't feel right at all.

Acting hadn't always been the plan. His original dream job, conceived in the split second when he'd overheard his first-grade teacher telling his parents that little Duncan had a talent for memorizing the names of dinosaurs and the order of the planets, was a mix between palaeontology and rocket science—what he'd dubbed *astronauting.* As a rakish prepubescent on family vacations in Tofino, he became convinced that life was best lived in a wetsuit, tied to a neon surfboard. And if the perfect wave turned out to be too shy to reveal itself, there was a sandy beach right there on which to nap the day away. A few years later he gave up the sport but held onto the attitude, so laid back it was practically horizontal. He still hung out at the beach, only now he spent all day blowing spasmodically into a harmonica and kicking his feet out to the side after a cute girl in a green sarong burned him a Blues Traveler CD. These were memories he didn't bring up in interviews.

He uncapped a Sharpie and started tracing over the bubble letters that spelled out his name at the top of the page. Two janitors on the other side of the floor-to-ceiling window struck up a conversation in a language that didn't sound like any he'd ever heard before. Mitch had used pencil for the rough draft in case Duncan misjudged the width of the paper and ended up trying to cram the last few letters against the right margin instead.

Once the acting gigs had started coming in, the summer of his fifteenth birthday, Duncan hadn't much looked back. His first jobs were small but respectable. The sullen teen in prime-time ads for divorce lawyers. Breakfast cereal commercials where he had to look awestruck while a cartoon logo (which was really an empty spot marked with tape—the actual logo was added in post) came to life in his kitchen. Soccer player #2. Truth be told, when he thought of those early years, Duncan could barely recall the work itself. Instead, he saw a series of increasingly attractive women coming over to introduce themselves. He slept with more of them than he probably should have.

Duncan sat in near darkness because technically, he wasn't allowed to be in this office. Students were welcome during business hours, obviously, but a non-sitting candidate in there by himself, at this time of night, using it for campaign purposes? Explicitly forbidden. If the IEC saw him here, they'd freak. But Mitch promised he'd "take care of it," just like he'd taken care of everything else so far. Jumping the line at the printer's, setting up that so-called guest lecture—and probably a bunch of other stuff that Duncan didn't even know about yet.

The janitors' conversation started speeding up. They were getting excited about something, and finishing each others' sentences. Duncan couldn't help but imagine they were looking at him. His back was to the window, though, and it would've been gauche to turn around and check.

His career had skyrocketed so quickly and effortlessly that he'd taken success a little for granted. The TV jobs segued into movies; the make-up and wardrobe women segued into co-stars, then models, and then lawyers at the very top. They were still his favourites. He was helpless before their thousand-dollar suits and the way their apartments gleamed spartanly, as if he were the first man ever to set foot inside. There was money, but more importantly there was the constant promise of more work. With *Maximum Death* he signed a seven-picture deal within minutes of walking into the room. He'd gotten cocky. He admitted that. But at least he'd kept his work ethic.

Things started going wrong when *Variety* published its pan of *Volcano Dreams* two hours after the Sundance premiere. It was all over the internet within seconds. His credibility was called into question, as well as, once again, his heterosexuality. Somehow the reviewer from the *Times-Picayune,* notorious prick that he was, snuck his BlackBerry inside the next screening—which was a fundraiser! For *diabetes!*—and liveblogged the whole thing, heckling it moment by moment. Then CNN picked up the juiciest phrases and used them in its scrolling newsticker across the bottom of the screen.

Suddenly what had seemed like an easy sell was dead on its feet. Momentum ground to a halt, and a week's worth of lunches were mysteriously cleared from his schedule. Most of the major studios read *Variety;* they all followed the blogs. Walking back to the hotel on the festival's closing night, he'd noticed people on the street were already looking at him as if his face were one giant birthmark.

Mitch called him in his suite later that same night, even though he was staying in the next room over. He asked Duncan what the fuck they planned on doing now.

In the dim SFSS office, Duncan thought about how this whole reinvention, the heartwarming story of a performer given a second chance to make good, felt like yet another role. He was investing time and energy into creating a character who was a minor variation of himself but not quite the real thing, and he still had no control over the finished product. It was in the hands of another director, whose goal was to get Duncan back into Hollywood. But this was real life, not *Maximum Death III*. That still seemed to Duncan like an important distinction, even if it no longer bothered anyone else.

He'd already seen some election polling data. (Apparently Mitch knew someone who owed him a favour over at Harris/Decima.) The numbers looked good, too—but it was hard to be sure. A big chunk of those polled admitted they would vote for whoever seemed the funniest. After all, said one respondent, there wasn't a joke party this year. Or were they just getting subtler?

On the whole, Duncan thought everyone at SFU was extremely nice. That was the real tragedy. His professors, the people who stopped for high-fives, even that terribly focused girl from the student paper who'd tried to interview him. They seemed like real fans, or at least real people. And they'd all been far more pleasant to him than anyone in California had for the past year—far more than was necessary. Manipulating them like this, especially when he had no particular feelings for government, or university, or even plans for sticking around Vancouver longer than a couple of months, felt more ethically grey than he'd first thought.

That last night at Sundance, after getting reamed out by Mitch over the phone, Duncan left the hotel to try to calm down and clear his mind. But outside the lobby, he was ambushed by a paparazzo aiming a huge camera at him. *A-ha!* he thought. Here was a chance for some easy press. Time to take PR back into his own hands. As the photographer came right up close to him, Duncan wound up and hit the man square in the temple. He fell to the ground with an awful thump. Duncan tried to channel the rage and exasperation of a decent guy who was simply at the end of his rope, dealing with the vultures of New Hollywood. It was the very same expression that the internet had found so endearing the month before, back at the Houston airport, when he wasn't faking. The punch felt terrific.

Unfortunately, the man wasn't a paparazzo. And what the bloggers reported minutes later was not that Canadian indie-heartthrob Duncan Holtz was in fact still on top, critic-proof and feistier than ever. The man was a fan. He was looking for a picture, and maybe one of those legendarily firm handshakes.

Duncan Holtz had punched out the president of his own fan club.

Just as quickly as it had started, the janitors' conversation in the hallway ended, replaced by the automated hum of their vacuums as they split up and quietly got back to work.

Duncan finished underlining his name and held the new poster up again. It was still too dark to see it very clearly, and his eyes were tired and strained from being awake for so long. He recapped the Sharpie. Finished. He still wasn't sure the pun worked in his favour, but Mitch told him not to overthink it.

Duncan Holtz

Photos (see all 147 | slideshow)

Overview

Date of Birth: 9 July 1981, Vancouver, BC, Canada **more▸**

Contact: View agent, manager and publicist contact info on IMDbPro.

Mini Biography: Duncan Holtz was born and raised on the west coast of Canada in... **more▸**

Trivia: Built a frisbee golf course in his backyard. **more▸**

STARmeter: Down 41% in popularity this week. See rank & trends on IMDbPro.

Awards: 1 nomination **more▸**

NewsDesk: "Holtz for prez?"

(4 articles)   (From The Vancouver Sun, 2 February 2009, 8:36 AM, PST)

"'Back to school' for troubled Holtz"

(From Metro News Services, 20 November 2008, 4:33 PM, PST)

Filmography

Actor:

1. Volcano Dreams (2008) .... The Wanderer
2. Two If By Ski (2007) .... Martin Finn
3. Rodrigo (2006) .... Rodrigo
4. Maximum Death 2 (2006) .... Agent Blair Williams
   ... aka Maximum Death 2:Jagged Edges (Australia) (Hong Kong: English title) (International: English title) (Malaysia: English title) (UK)
   ... aka Maximum Death^2: Jagged Edges (Singapore: English title)
   ... aka Blair Williams In... Jagged Edge (Philippines: English title: review title)
   ... aka Maximal Deaths 2 Sequel Film (Philippines: English title)
5. Has Anyone Seen My Girlfriend? (2005) .... Marcus Eagleton
6. Migraine Season (2005) .... Ed
7. The Last Troubadour (2005) .... Young Ezra Pound
8. Maximum Death (2004) .... Agent Blair Williams
9. Avengers: Ultron Rising (2004) (V) (voice) .... Hawkeye

10. Kissing Booth (2003) .... Steve Booth
11. Tomorrow (2002) .... Allan
12. The Baby Shower (2002) .... Ricky S.
13. "Felicity" .... Ted Zybrowsky (2 episodes, 2001-2002)
    - Spin the Bottle (2002) tv episode .... Ted Zybrowsky
    - The Last Summer Ever (2001) tv episode .... Ted Zybrowsky
14. Against All Odds (2001) .... Chuck Flanagan
15. A/S/L (2000) .... Hot Guy on Escalator
16. "Fang City" .... Vince Mountains (18 episodes, 1998-2000)
    - Fang You Very Much, Part II (2000) tv episode .... Vince Mountains
    - Fang You Very Much, Part I (2000) tv episode .... Vince Mountains
    - The Talisman (2000) tv episode .... Vince Mountains
    - A Werewolf Betrayed (1999) tv episode .... Vince Mountains
    - Nice Trenchcoat (1999) tv episode .... Vince Mountains
    (13 more)

Director:

1. Volcano Dreams (2008)

Writer:

1. Volcano Dreams (2008) (written by)

Thanks:

1. We Heart Duncan (2007) (very special thanks)

Self:

1. "Canada A.M." .... Himself (1 episode, 2008)
   ... aka "Canada A.M. Weekend" (Canada: English title: weekend title)
   - Episode dated 22 January 2008 (2008) tv episode .... Himself
2. "Total Request Live" .... Himself (2 episodes, 2006-2008)
   ... aka "TRL Weekend" (USA: informal alternative title)
   ... aka "TRL" (USA: promotional abbreviation)
   ... aka "Total Request with Carson Daly" (USA: alternative title)
   - Episode dated 18 January 2008 (2008) tv episode .... Himself
   - Episode dated 9 September 2006 (2006) tv episode .... Himself
3. "Today" .... Himself (1 episode, 2006)
   ... aka "NBC News Today" (USA: promotional title)
   ... aka "The Today Show" (USA)
   - Episode dated 8 June 2006 (2006) tv episode .... Himself
4. "Maximum Death 2: Behind the Death" (2006) (TV) .... Himself

Additional Details

Other Works: Appeared in Gap print ads for fall 2005 collection **more▸**

Publicity Listings: 5 Interviews / 9 Articles / 2 Magazine Cover Photos **more▸**

Genres: Drama / Crime / Action / **more▸**

Plot Keywords: Character Name In Title / Hairspray / Vampire Driving Car / Fall From Height

Message Boards

Discuss this person with other users on IMDb message board for Duncan Holtz

Recent Posts (updated daily)	User
Where did dude go	HarryOru
Captain America?	Djcraig987
Gay?	violetsky_
No Felicity	picsamscotgirl
Long hair or short hair	benjifish

more▸

20

KONW

Tracy started work at the *Peak* office nice and early—dangerously close to sunrise, in fact. She needed a big head start before production day set in around her. There were the usual dregs of first copy to attend to, but nothing serious. Mostly she was worried about her own story. She leaned over Suze's temporarily commandeered keyboard and cursed at the screen every couple of minutes. Then she started pacing the hall.

It's just such a different muscle, she thought. *I can edit this stuff in my sleep. So why can't I do the first part?*

Rachel had saved the front page of the news section, as well as the cover, for Tracy's story. She'd also reminded her to keep the focus tight: stick to the illegal campaigning angle, the SFSS's response, and the potential consequences. Keep descriptions of the actual melee to a minimum. In a perverse way, Tracy was actually compromised by having been there in person—she was now implicated in the story, and, as a result, subject to all kinds of bias. Right now they couldn't afford the slightest whiff of conflict of interest. But there was nobody else with clean enough fingers to write the thing. Rachel was already covering the debate later that day—which would also be the place to follow up with Holtz and finally get him on the record about this whole mess.

After a few laps through the office, Tracy sat down again. She commanded her brain to focus. The fact that this was the most important thing she'd ever done at the paper loomed overhead like a nagging rain cloud. She'd intended the story to be an act of reclamation, a kind of validation for all the time she'd spent here, but she was discovering that having good intentions wasn't enough. Sentences needed to be written. You could only type one word—one letter—at a time.

And yet the panic and nail biting were accompanied by an unexpectedly pleasant tingling feeling. The negative side effects of the writing process were familiar from the dozens of essays she'd cranked out as an English student. But what was this new sensation? Maybe knowing that this was a piece of writing that students might *choose* to read was releasing some hidden stockpile of endorphins. Tracy had heard countless fellow editors whine and moan about having to serve their readership. Plenty of her classmates had a similar attitude toward academic writing—as if it were just so much fuel for an anonymous, unthinking fire. But that never rang true for her. The way Tracy saw it, all writing was seduction. And readers didn't owe her anything. It was her job to rein them in, and her job to keep them glued to the page. She was grateful they showed up at all.

Of course, they'd be showing up to the lowest page count in *Peak* history: eight pages, covers included. Tracy would be providing 25 percent of the entire week's content all by herself. *Stop thinking about it,* she told herself, and got up to pace around some more.

The office looked like it had been looted by an angry mob and then left to decompose. Writers no longer dropped by to say hello. No one even bothered to come yell at them anymore. Chairs, tables, computers, cutlery: all sold. Some of the old *Peak* covers on the wall, formerly a proud reminder of the paper's glory days, had come unstuck and flopped over in surrender.

One of the few remaining centres of activity was Rachel's news bunker, where she'd assembled a big poster outlining each of the four presidential candidates' campaign promises, as well as some basic biography and a photo. Tracy paused her pacing to consider Holtz's jawline, the tragic scope of Samantha Gilmartin's resumé, and Piotr's fractured English and unfortunate official photo—he'd been caught in mid-sneeze, and afterward had insisted, without so much as looking at the first take, that it was good enough. The space left for Kennedy was almost completely blank. The only information she'd supplied was a single sentence that listed Emma Peel and Eddie Izzard as influences. In lieu of a picture, Rachel had swapped in a clip art question mark.

Joke candidates, Tracy thought. *They only get weirder every year.*

Time for a smoke. Tracy headed outside, and without quite realizing it, ended up walking halfway across campus, turning her story over and over in her head. She trotted up the AQ steps, still cracked and deformed from the time Arnold Schwarzenegger had driven a tank down them, nearly a decade earlier, in pursuit of his evil clone. Nobody knew if they'd ever be fully repaired. Then it was up through the gardens and past the statue of Terry Fox. Tracy tapped a knuckle against his artificial leg—a neat, albeit accidental, complement to the school's reputation in the world of sci-fi. Maybe some of his luck would rub off on her, talismanically. True, a twenty-two-year-old kid diagnosed with fatal bone cancer probably wasn't the best personification of luck. What he really offered, as every SFU student well knew, was hope.

At the edge of campus, Tracy took a seat in the courtyard next to the Higher Grounds where she'd spilled her guts to Anna about the breakup. Thoughts of Dave still occasionally flickered through her head, and every once in a while she'd come across a memory as raw as a canker sore, the kind so deep-seated that your entire mouth had to reorganize itself around the pain.

But these moments were rare, and getting rarer all the time.

On the other side of campus, Alex wandered back from Shell House, fuzzily hungover and replaying the previous night's events on a mental loop. The light rain on his head and shoulders felt like splashback from the world's biggest waterfall.

A handjob isn't nothing.

He said it to himself again and again, like a mantra.

A handjob isn't nothing. A handjob isn't nothing.

They didn't have sex. But it wasn't a failure—no matter what Tyson might say later. He came. She came. It was undeniably sexy. Romantic, even. Afterward they cuddled on her mini-couch and watched old *Arrested Development* episodes on her laptop, touching each other's fingertips until Maggie, at least, was up for another round. Alex grinned and ducked his head under the covers.

Then they'd both slept for ten hours, legs entwined. When he eventually woke up, Alex spent a full minute taking in the bristly white moustache staring down at him from the wall. It belonged to NDP leader Jack Layton, and his head was offset by the flare of party orange around him; in the picture he looked just about ready to tackle someone.

Maggie rolled over and propped herself up on one elbow. "Looks good, right? I mean, it's no Norman Rockwell, but I like it."

Alex turned to look at her. He put his face right up close to hers and scrutinized each feature in turn. She laughed, then clamped a hand over her mouth to cover the morning breath. It was the eye make-up—he'd been so distracted by it last night that he hadn't processed why the rest of her had looked so familiar, and why his attraction felt oddly like déjà vu.

"The poster sale," he said.

"Bingo."

"That is so unfair. My god! Why didn't you say anything last night?"

"Me?" she giggled. "Why didn't *you?*"

Alex slowly pieced the details of their first meeting back together. "You were with your friend," he said. "The one Tyson said he did all that crazy stuff with." He faltered, embarrassed to say it out loud.

Maggie said, "You mean coming, like, all over her?"

"Uh, yes. Exactly."

"Yeah," Maggie said, rolling her eyes. "He probably did. I wouldn't get jealous, though. Christine lets all the guys do that to her. It's kind of her thing."

Am I really having this conversation right now? Alex thought. "Really? Well, then—what's your thing?"

She jabbed a finger into his ribs. "Don't tell me you've forgotten already."

As Alex walked into the Mini-Mart, he replayed the whole exchange over again in his head. He said hello to the owner en route to the drink coolers. She got an impish look on her face and replied, "Someone's in a good mood today."

"Me?"

"Oh, yes," she said. "Usually you are—how to put it?" She made an exaggerated frowny face.

"Grumpy," Alex suggested.

"Yes. Exactly right. But today, it is different."

Alex placed a bottle of water—plain, unflavoured, caffeine- and mascot-free water—on the counter. "I'm just hungover," he said. "My mouth is made of sand right now. But thank you."

Outside, he gulped down half the bottle in one go. In the distance a crowd was forming, near the cafeteria where the debate was due to start any minute. It looked like some media people were there, too—plus two security guards he could have sworn were the *Metro* goons. But they weren't handing out newspapers now. They weren't even wearing green. They were just standing there.

Alex made his way up the ramp to the office to go assemble the troops.

The cafeteria was filled with the usual piles of grubby old newspapers (the *Metro*s outnumbering the *Peak*s at least 3:1) and hard plastic chairs, though today the former had been haphazardly swept to one corner and the latter organized into a grid. It was as packed as the film class had been the day before. The irritable politicians who'd stormed Holtz at the lectern so valiantly now looked simply run down, rubbing their puffy faces and continent-shaped bruises. Overall the shift in the crowd was mostly along departmental lines. The film kids had been replaced by bemused-looking political science majors. Mack Holloway sat in the third row, holding a fresh notebook. Alex, Tracy, and the other *Peak* editors slipped past the unblinking security guards and set up shop against the back wall. The debate was already under way.

Four podiums had been placed near the floor-to-ceiling windows. Behind them stood Piotr Ivanov, Samantha Gilmartin, and, sporting heels, a wobbly head of black hair, and massive fuck-off sunglasses, the enigmatic Kennedy, who was apparently not a figment of the imagination after all. They were all screaming at one another. Standing at one side was the IEC's Lana Murphy, looking very tired indeed.

"Candidates, *please*," she pleaded. "That's enough."

The fourth podium was empty. Holtz hadn't shown up yet. His manager wasn't in sight, either.

"Now, as I was saying," Lana continued, "I'd like to welcome everyone to this, the presidential debate for the 2009–10 SFSS elections—Piotr, please. Enough."

"It is all irrelevant!" Piotr boomed. "Let us get down to the brass tax, yes? Calamari on Pub menu. Yes/no vote. It is simple."

"That's easy for you to say," Samantha hissed. Her meticulously cultivated image as the SFSS's heir apparent had, in the twenty-four hours since she'd helped instigate the riot, cracked to the point of near-uselessness. "You're running on a squid-based platform. Your entire career is an *Onion* headline, you moron. The rest of us have important things to discuss here."

Kennedy leaned forward over her podium. "I agree with Ms. Gilmartin. Calamari is gross."

"That is *not* what I said."

"Do you provoke me wilfully?" asked Piotr. "This will not stand." He pointed at the scattered cameramen and photographers in the front row. "Reporters! Document this statement. It is sitting on the record."

Alex whispered to Rachel, "You getting all this?"

"Unfortunately, I am," she said. "Your breath is terrible, by the way."

"Enough," Lana said. "Let's just get through this." She turned to the crowd. "First, let me say that our office has received several complaints about each one of these candidates over the past few weeks, and more than one investigation is underway. Rest assured that we will get to the bottom of every one of them. But, since these allegations are as yet unproven, I will not be addressing them in my questioning today." The noise started to grow again. "Of course, you all are under no such obligation. So have at it. We're moving alphabetically—first opening remarks go to Ms. Gilmartin."

Samantha cleared her throat and flashed a rehearsed, if somewhat desperate smile. "My fellow students, we are living through strange times, and at SFU those times have been stranger than usual lately. But times of uncertainty call for a rock to lean on. Not some flash in the pan, but a known quantity. Someone who knows the course, and more importantly . . . who knows how to return to it, when we've lost our way. And to stick to it. That's also important." She heaved a heavy sigh, and her smile wobbled. "A vote for me, Samantha Gilmartin, as your student society president is a vote for quality. I have three years' experience in student politics. The other three candidates, combined, have zero. I mean"—an even heavier sigh—"seriously, just do the fucking math."

Polite applause. "Thank you," said Lana. "Next would be Duncan Holtz, but he still hasn't arrived. So we'll move on to Piotr Ivanov."

Piotr gripped the podium with both hands. "Calamari on Pub menu. I say yes. Are you an asshole? Also say yes."

More polite applause, and a few scattered coughs.

"Well, then." Lana drummed her fingers. "Is that all, Ivan?"

He squinted. "Only assholes say no to calamari."

"Oh, give it a rest," Samantha said. "This is a serious election. *I am a serious politician.* Does everyone here know that you got kicked out of the Pub because of this calamari bullshit? You're *banned*. For life. I mean, really."

"That's enough," Lana said.

"Who's going to vote for a head case who can't even attend his own victory party?"

"We're moving on," Lana said. "Kennedy, please. Your opening remarks."

Alex tried to pay attention as the enigmatic presidential hopeful adjusted her huge sunglasses and cleared her throat. But he couldn't stop thinking about Maggie, and his graduation, and this whole bizarre world that had snowballed into what could now be called his university career. It was difficult to wrap his head around. He'd spent four years in the thick of something that he'd always assumed was a relatively normal experience. *The Peak*, he'd figured, was as good a front-row seat for university life as you could ask for. But now that he felt himself drifting away from it, an astronaut untethered from his space station, it was becoming more and more obvious that this would be the part of his life he'd spend the rest of it reminiscing about. For all his complaining, he was gradually accepting that he'd never know anything like it again.

No wonder he didn't care about these people onstage. They were already part of a generation of students he couldn't relate to. Alex already had *his* peer group sorted out—he had no interest in acquiring a new one so late in the game. He wanted to reminisce about a shared experience of the recent past, when Facebook was only for university students. He wanted to make sly references to old Swollen Members songs. He wanted to find a way to make the culture sit still, even for a minute, so he could find a way to enjoy it for a little while longer.

Alex was so caught up in his thoughts that he almost didn't feel his phone buzzing in his pocket. He'd left it in the *Peak* offices overnight and hadn't even had time to check his messages yet. He flipped the phone open to a new text message from Maggie: "had fun last nite. this is my number. use it sometime, k? and u konw, ive never actually seen the last waltz. . . . just an idea. :)".

Konw, Alex thought. *And* emoticons? *Jesus Christ.* But already his heart was betraying him, doing a few reckless somersaults in his chest. Clearly, it knew nothing of grammar.

A crash from the front of the cafeteria brought him out of his reverie. Kennedy had tripped on the dangling fringe of her dress, and was keeled over next to her podium. Around her were scattered cue cards, her glasses, which she was straining to reach, and a chunky tape recorder, humming obliviously. Strangest of all, her hair had done a full ninety-degree pivot, revealing the buzz cut underneath.

It was a wig.

It was Claude wearing a wig.

The crowd froze, unsure how to react. Tracy and Alex turned on Rachel as the implications started to dawn on them. "Did you know about this?" Tracy demanded.

"No!" she said, as stunned as they were. "No, I never—why would I do something so—" She turned to the front of the room. "Claude, what the *fuck?*"

From the ground, he said weakly, "I thought it would help." He covered his face with his dress. "Oh god."

Lana was kneeling at the front of the room, trying to convince Claude back to his feet. But when he rolled away from her, in complete and next-level embarrassment, she stormed over and aimed a shaky, accusatory finger at the editors. "If this is what I think it is," she said, "I will bring the full force of my office down on your heads. *The Peak* will pay for this. Honestly, is there a single person in this place who can do their job without committing a felony?"

She barked something over her shoulder and the security guards appeared. The first thing Alex saw was their shadows as they blocked out the overhead lights. "Looks like you guys really stepped in it this time," one said with a chuckle.

"Time to call it a day," the other added.

"Get these guys the *fuck* out of here," Lana said to them, then left to try to bring what remained of the debates to a close. Claude remained on the floor in the fetal position, dress over his head. Samantha and Piotr were yelling into cell phones at opposite ends of the room. Cameras were flashing non-stop. Mack Holloway was hunched over his tape recorder, dictating into it with a huge smile on his face.

As the editors were being escorted out of the cafeteria, Alex stared into the eyes of the guard next to him: one was icy white, and one dark brown. "Hey, wait," he said. "You *are* the *Metro* goo—I mean, the *Metro,* uh, distribution guys. Right?"

The one with the mismatched eyes nodded.

"Then—what are you doing here at the debates?"

"Our regular line of work is security," the second guard said, shrugging. "All over town. Most afternoons we work at banks. You know the strip mall at Hastings and Willingdon? But after that dustup yesterday, we got called in to do this gig."

The first guard added, "Handing out newspapers in general is pretty bush league, if you ask me. But times are tough. We both got kids to feed."

Alex took this in for a minute. "So it's a 'fuck you, pay me' type situation," he said.

The guard looked down at him warily. Alex noticed for the first time the deep lines creasing his face; in this light, the guy could've been pushing fifty. "Yeah. I guess you could call it that."

21

ONE HUNDRED AND ONE BEERS

"I mean, what the fuck was he thinking?"

"Yeah. Yeah."

"This is pretty bad."

"How did he even think this was going to go? What was his best-case scenario?"

"Mind-boggling."

"But, I mean, it's not *that* bad—is it?"

"Hello? We're finished!"

"There are things you just *do not do.*"

"Did you see the look on Holloway's face? It'll be all over the *Metro* tomorrow."

"Clear out your desks, people. Sneak out the back door."

"Would you guys relax already?"

"Is anyone else a tiny bit proud of him?"

"Fuck him. That fucking fuck wrecked everything."

"If you break the rules, there are consequences. That's how rules work."

The CD string on the office door clattered, and a familiar-looking cross-dresser entered the room.

"Speak of the devil," Tracy said. "Why don't you have a seat for a minute, Claude?"

Rachel stormed over and yanked him by his ears into the closest computer chair. "What do you have to say for yourself?" she said, pointing a finger in his face. "Do you even realize what this means, you idiot?"

Claude nervously fidgeted with the hem of his dress. "It's just— last night—Alex said we needed some new, crazy ideas."

The others turned to look at Alex. "What?" he said. "I was drunk. *He* was drunk! And we *do* need new ideas. But Jesus, Claude. This is not what I had in mind."

Rachel went on, "So you've been Kennedy this whole time?"

"No, no," Claude said. "She was just this fake, joke candidate. Some guys in my department thought it up—I overheard them talking about it. Back in January."

"Well, *that* could've been a great story!" Rachel said, exasperated. "Instead you had to pull this shit. Claude, there are rules in journalism. Have you ever heard of conflict of interest? Our whole credibility is shot."

Suze added, "They're going to shut us down!"

Claude's face went white. "Really?"

"Okay, why don't we all take a deep breath?" Alex said. "Listen. Nobody's getting shut down. You think this is the first time someone at the *Peak* has embarrassed the paper in public?"

"Isn't it?"

"Jesus. Not by a long shot. And we're still standing here, aren't we?"

"Well—what do we do, then?" asked Rachel.

Alex thought for a second. "We do our jobs. Which means the two of you"—pointing at Rachel and Tracy—"have to figure out the new angle, and then write your asses off for the rest of the day." They exchanged a nod. "Suze, if you're still going to run Claude's CD reviews next week, you might want to put a pseudonym on them. Keep a little distance from the problem, you know?"

"And you," he added, pointing to an expectant Claude. "You do absolutely nothing. I will duct tape you to this chair if I have to, so help me god."

Tracy said, "Can we at least get a drink first?"

"I could really use something," Claude said. His hands were shaking.

Alex sighed. "Fine. But ditch the dress, would you? And as soon as we get back downstairs, it's duct tape time."

They headed upstairs and found a circle of seats near the pool tables. To everyone's surprise, a chipper server appeared with menus, and nervously laughed while taking a drink order big enough to fill an entire page in her little notebook. The Pub must've been hiring again.

During the first lull in conversation, Alex snuck away to the bar, where Saul was wiping down pint glasses in anticipation of the dinner rush. "Buddy!" the manager called. "How're we feeling today?"

"You tell me," Alex said. "Listen: you didn't happen to find a backpack around last night, did you?"

Saul pointed over Alex's shoulder. "You mean that one?" And there it sat, in the same exact place, pinned against the wall by a chair. "It's been there all day," he said. "I just haven't had time to go pick it up yet."

"Perfect." Alex turned to leave, then hesitated. "Actually, there's something else."

"Your tab."

He nodded sheepishly. "I don't suppose—"

"I can't refund the leftover part," Saul said. "It's already on the books. Sorry, man."

"Actually, I was thinking . . . how much is left over?"

Saul consulted a piece of scrap paper taped to the register. "About forty bucks. Just under."

Alex pointed to the *Peak* table below. "It's been a rough day. Can you just turn the rest into beer and send it down to them?"

"Sure thing. Coming right up."

"Thanks, Saul. Also?"

"I won't tell them where it came from."

Alex nodded. "Thank you."

He went over and picked up the backpack, its black sheen now muddy with liquor stains. The Pym novel was still inside. It was a little warped from the chair, but otherwise intact—his bookmark was even in the right place. Alex pulled the book out, then stuffed the backpack and all of its fake supplies into the nearest garbage can. He was about to head back to the *Peak* table when a low voice called out to him.

"Hey, kid."

Mack Holloway beckoned Alex over to his table and motioned for him to sit down. Alex looked back—none of the other editors had even noticed he'd left. He carefully edged into the chair across from the journalist.

"I'm glad I caught you here," Mack said. He had a pile of note-books next to him. Each was thoroughly pummelled with use. There were probably a dozen of them, stacked precariously. "Listen. I just want to apologize for how a lot of this nonsense has played itself out. Fact is, we're all in a tough spot right now. The whole industry's a mess—hence my current gig, chasing around teenagers." He laughed a dry, salty laugh and took a sip of his beer. "Of course, you sure don't help yourselves with that stunt your guy pulled today. Man, that was something."

Alex couldn't think to do anything but keep nodding. He had so much to ask a guy like Holloway, he didn't know where to start. And it was already starting to feel like a wasted opportunity.

A confused cheer erupted from the *Peak* table as a couple of mystery pitchers arrived.

"So what's your story?" Mack said. "Do you want to do this for a living?"

"I don't know," he said. "Maybe. Why? What do you think?"

"Honestly? I think some of you guys have talent. That story you broke about Holtz's queue-jumping was nice." Alex's eyes lit up. "Don't get me wrong: you're all lazy as hell. And my God, you can *taste* how much you guys despise your audience. You can't keep a straight face about it, either. Every story has to have some little meta-commentary on how ridiculous it is that you're even writing a story. That stuff might be fun to write, but it is absolute torture to read." Mack paused. "Tell me if I'm way off."

"No, no, not at all. I've actually been thinking the same thing lately."

"You know, the last thing the world needs is more writing. We're full up as it is, and most of it is useless. So if you're not in it to really connect with someone, then do us all a favour and pack it in. Let the rest of us have a go at it instead. I know my paper doesn't exactly have a lot of credibility around here, but at least we're trying. *I'm* trying. Are you?"

There was a long pause. Alex's head was swimming, trying to absorb all of it. Then he remembered he still hadn't said anything. He blurted out, "What do you guys call house ads?"

"What?"

"You know, those little ads that advertise other parts of the newspaper. I heard somewhere you call them fills. Is that true?"

"Yeah," Mack said slowly. "That's what they're called."

Alex tapped his fist against the edge of the table. "Oh. Cool. I always wondered."

"I don't want to keep you from your friends," Mack said. "I just wanted to tell you that, you know, none of this is personal. So good luck to you—I got my start at university, too, actually. I'd never have written my book were it not for a couple of people I met there."

That's right, Alex thought. Mack had published a novel a few years back. It was one of those polite, small-town Saskatchewan things, with lots of flowery descriptions of gravel roads. Part of it took place in a post office full of gently eccentric customers. Alex hadn't read it, only a few of the equally polite reviews.

"Let me ask you something," he said to Mack. "When they stocked your book in stores, weren't you worried about who you'd be sitting next to on the shelf? I mean, who would pick you over a guy like Hemingway? No offense."

Mack considered it. "Was I *worried?*" he asked. "No. Not at all. What a strange thing to think about. And besides." He smiled. "My book wasn't anywhere near Hemingway. There's a little section called 'Canadian fiction.' Trust me, nobody gets too riled up about anything over there."

Alex shook his hand and got up. He tried to gather his thoughts and shape them into something coherent. Then it came to him.

Again, he thanked Mack for the advice.

"Sure, sure," he said. "And hey." He pointed at the Pym paperback, stuffed under Alex's armpit. "How's the book? I heard she's pretty good."

"Yeah," Alex said. "She's pretty good."

He slunk along the wall, trying to get past the *Peak* table. The editors had poured most of their free beer and were locked in a heated argument about whether the sofa on *The Big Comfy Couch* could talk, or if it just wiggled its eyebrows. Tracy had an arm around Claude's shoulder, and was telling him to lie low for the summer. Then, when everyone had time to forget all about his stunt, he could come back and apply for an editorship. Alex chuckled quietly as he slipped past.

He skipped down the concrete stairwell and pushed through the front door of the office (left unlocked, as usual), walking straight past the remaining computers and stacks of election flyers and silhouettes of all the stuff that had been stripped for parts, way back into the archive room—where he pulled out the volume marked 2005. He sat down and leafed through the pages, eventually coming to the first story he ever wrote for *The Peak,* back as a bright-eyed, eighteen-year-old volunteer.

It wasn't anything flashy: four hundred words on a new effort to clean the scum from the AQ pond. There was a typo in the headline (*initative*). Alex remembered how his recorder hadn't worked properly during his interview. He hadn't known how to adjust the volume, either, and so had to press the machine to his ear while transcribing later on, a few garbled words at a time.

But after the news editor had read it, peering over Alex's shoulder at his computer screen, he'd clapped Alex on the back and said, "Not bad."

Edmonton, 2008–2011

ACKNOWLEDGEMENTS

Thank you to the professionals: Kelsey Attard, Meghan Macdonald, JoAnn McCaig, Natalie Olsen, Barbara Scott, and J.C. Sutcliffe.

To the early readers: Delia Byrnes, Laura Drake, Warren Haas, Mark Little, Cameron Maitland, Paul Matwychuk, Stephanie Orford, Matt Smith, and Rob Taylor. (I did bribe you with spots on this page, after all—the least I can do is follow through.)

To the insiders: Derrick Harder and Larry Van Kampen.

To the professors: Susan Brook (for Amis), Michael Everton (for Melville), and Paulo Horta (for the rest of the world).

And to my family: Bridget, Finn, and especially Kate.